"Max is harmless."

"That's not what you were saying last night."

"Come on, Kevin. It's a beautiful June day. The flowers are blooming. The sky is blue. I'm sure you can think of something better to do than worry about your grown-up cousin and whatever passing fancy she's taken up with Max."

He'd been staring after Helen and Max, but he turned then and stared into her eyes. "Something more interesting to do, huh?" he said softly. "Only one thing I can think of that might distract me."

Gracie's breath caught in her throat. "What's that?"

He reached out and skimmed a finger along her cheek, then dragged it oh-so-slowly across her lips until they parted in a gasp. She swallowed hard as his head descended and his mouth met hers.

Oh, yes, she thought as a sweet thrill reverberated through her. From her perspective, this was definitely better than worrying about Max and Helen. She opened her eyes and met Kevin's gaze. He smiled.

"Feeling better?" she asked.

"Not just yet," he said. "But I'm definitely getting there."

BOOK YOUR PLACE ON OUR WEBSITE AND MAKE THE READING CONNECTION!

We've created a customized website just for our very special readers, where you can get the inside scoop on everything that's going on with Zebra, Pinnacle and Kensington books.

When you come online, you'll have the exciting opportunity to:

- View covers of upcoming books
- Read sample chapters
- Learn about our future publishing schedule (listed by publication month *and author*)
- Find out when your favorite authors will be visiting a city near you
- Search for and order backlist books from our online catalog
- Check out author bios and background information
- Send e-mail to your favorite authors
- Meet the Kensington staff online
- Join us in weekly chats with authors, readers and other guests
- Get writing guidelines
- AND MUCH MORE!

Visit our website at
http://www.zebrabooks.com

Amazing Gracie

Sherryl Woods

Zebra Books
Kensington Publishing Corp.
http://www.zebrabooks.com

ZEBRA BOOKS are published by

Kensington Publishing Corp.
850 Third Avenue
New York, NY 10022

Zebra and the Z logo Reg. U.S. Pat. & TM Off.

First Printing: June, 1998
10 9 8 7 6 5 4 3 2 1

Printed in the United States of America

One

Walking briskly through the small, elegant lobby of the Maison de Sol in Cannes, Gracie MacDougal noted every tiny detail, from the single wilted daffodil in the lavish arrangement of spring flowers to the fingerprints on the beveled glass in the double mahogany doors. She plucked the offending flower from the arrangement, then beckoned to the young man working behind the reception desk. André was one of her best, most dutiful employees. They'd become friends. Someday, she was sure, he'd replace her.

"André, call housekeeping at once, *s'il vous plaît*. Take care of that window."

"Of course, madame," he said dutifully, then discreetly studied the glass to figure out what was wrong with it.

"Fingerprints," Gracie said, grinning at him.

He peered more closely at the decorative windowpane. "Ah," he said when he discovered them.

"You'll learn, André. You'll learn. Our guests expect perfection down to the tiniest detail."

"Our guests, madame, or you?"

"Perhaps you're right," she conceded. "If I'm doing my job, then the guests will take it for granted. I only wish . . ."

"What?" André asked, regarding her intently. "What is it that you wish?"

"I only wish our new boss cared more about the details than the bottom line."

"Monsieur Devereaux is a bit of a . . . What is it they say in America, a suit?"

Gracie fought a chuckle and lost. "That he is, André. He is a bit of a suit."

Handsome, distinguished, and annoying, Maximillian Devereaux was, in Gracie's opinion, more of an accountant than a hotelier. If the books balanced, he wouldn't care if there was a layer of dust an inch thick on the gleaming antique tabletops in the lobby. His attitude and the battles it engendered were beginning to take a toll.

He was the third CEO of Worldwide Hotels in the last five years. He'd been brought in to improve the bottom line after Worldwide was acquired by a larger chain to add some class to its image. Though Worldwide continued to operate as a separate division with its own corporate identity, in Gracie's view the small chain of exclusive, luxury inns was in serious danger of losing its reputation and its clientele. The wilted daffodil in her hand was symptomatic of the problem.

Less than an hour later, after inspecting every nook and cranny of the hotel, she dropped the flower on Max's desk and said just that. He peered down his long, aristocratic nose at her, glanced at the broken petals, then sighed with evident exasperation.

"What is it now, Ms. MacDougal?" he asked, as always reverting to formality to indicate his own annoyance with her.

"The flowers weren't changed this morning as they should have been," she said.

"There is no need to change them daily. We've discussed that. Every three days will be sufficient and will cut the flower budget by two-thirds."

"And our guests will find wilted flowers in the lobby and assume that if we no longer care about appearances in such a public area, we will be even more careless in places they don't see, such as the kitchen. Details like this make a lasting impression. If you doubt it, check the reservation book."

"We're booked solid for the next month."

"And this time last year we were booked solid for six months in advance," she countered. "At this rate, we'll have rooms available for every Tom, Dick, and Harry who forgot to book a reservation before leaving the States."

"Don't exaggerate, Gracie."

"It's true." She studied Max intently. "You really don't see it, do you? You don't see what you're doing to this hotel, to this entire chain."

"Have dinner with me tonight and explain it," he suggested.

This time she was the one who sighed in exasperation. The man was relentless, when it came down to something he wanted, namely *her*. On paper, she and Max Devereaux were a perfect match. They were both tall—even at five eight, she barely reached his chin. Max had dashing, Cary Grant looks. Gracie prided herself on her polished, classic appearance. Max's intelligence, his quick rise in the international hotel industry paralleled hers.

But the man had no real passion for it. It was all numbers to him. Gracie cared about the guests and their comfort, the lasting impression they would take home with them. Max worried only about the size of their bill.

No, she concluded. It would never have worked. He was certainly bright enough to have figured that out for himself, but his masculine ego kept him in the game. With another man, the unwanted attention might have bordered on harassment, but there'd never once, in any way, been a hint that Gracie's job hinged on whether she said yes or no. Asking was just something Max did, pretty much like breathing.

"Max, I will not have dinner with you," she told him for the umpteenth time. "Not tonight, not ever. How many times do I have to say it?"

"Not even to save your precious flower budget?"

"No, Max. It's a very bad idea. You're my boss. Socializing

would only complicate things. Besides, you and I don't see eye to eye on anything. We'd just ruin our digestion."

He shrugged as he always did after she'd rejected one of his invitations. "Suit yourself." He returned his attention to the paperwork in front of him, dismissing Gracie as clearly as if he'd gestured toward the door.

Maybe it was because she was tired or frustrated or angry or all three, but Gracie stared at Max's down-turned head for several minutes, then reached a decision that had been several weeks in the making.

"I quit," she said softly but firmly.

That brought his head up. "What?" For an instant, shock registered in his usually cool gray eyes.

"You heard me. I quit."

"Now, Gracie—"

"Don't you *now-Gracie* me," she snapped back. "You won't listen to a thing I say. You're determined to run this chain as if it were a string of economy hotels. Obviously, I am no longer of any value to Worldwide, so I might as well take my expertise to another hotel chain where they care about appearances and service and comfort."

There was the faintest hint of worry in Max's expression, but once again he shrugged and said, "Suit yourself."

Stunned by his indifference, Gracie paused long enough to sweep that blasted daffodil up and drop it into the trash can before leaving. Tempted as she was to slam the door, she didn't want to disturb the guests by creating a scene. Even now, old habits died hard.

Back in her small suite of rooms off the hotel lobby, fighting tears, she began methodically packing. Because she moved frequently from hotel to hotel to troubleshoot problems, there was very little to pack, nothing personal needing to be shipped. She could be on a plane back to the States tonight . . . if only she had someplace to go.

Realizing that there was not one single destination in the

entire world where someone would be waiting for her hit her like a blow. She sank to the edge of the bed.

"What now, Gracie?" she whispered.

Though her decision to quit had been far from impulsive, never once had she considered the next step. Now she had just abandoned the most exciting, rewarding, wonderful job she'd ever had, one she'd worked very hard to get. She was twenty-nine-going-on-thirty. Her last three relationships had been total disasters. All three men had ended up married to someone else—someone who stayed, put—within days of breaking up with her.

The relationships weren't worth talking about, but her career, well, that was not something she was quite so willing to walk away from without a fight. She had loved the hotel business from the day she first discovered room service. In Monopoly, hotels were always her primary objective. In her mind's eye, they were always small, elegant, and discreet.

Worldwide had always exemplified that image. At least until recently. Shifting gears to accommodate all of the executive changes had turned a dream job into a nightmare. She'd been right to quit, she consoled herself. It was a smart decision.

So why did she feel so lost and empty?

A knock on her door prevented her from having to come up with an answer for the inexplicable "Yes?"

"Gracie, it's Max."

"Go away."

"I think we should talk."

"I disagree."

"Would you open the blasted door and let me in, please. Or do you want the entire hotel to hear our conversation?"

That caught her attention as nothing else might have. She opened the door. She did not move aside to let him in. Max was much too forceful a presence to allow herself to be alone with him while she was in such a vulnerable state. He'd tried too many times to turn business conversations into something personal for her to trust him—or herself, at the moment—in such intimate surroundings. She might not much like the man at the moment, but he had a very attractive shoulder she could cry on.

"Yes?" she said.

He peered past her to the row of suitcases. "You're determined to leave, I see."

"I told you I was going."

"Where?"

Ah, she thought, that was the million-dollar question. Money wasn't a problem. Her heart was the problem. The only place she wanted to be was at the center of a thriving hotel. Her parents were dead. There had been no brothers or sisters, not even an extended family of aunts and uncles she'd been close to. She'd made a few close friends in college, but over the years, thanks to so much job-related traveling, she'd lost touch with all of them.

"That's none of your business," she said, hedging.

"No place to go, huh?"

"Of course I have a place to go," she snapped. "I'm going to . . . Virginia." She seized the destination out of thin air, based solely on some distant, idyllic memory of a family vacation in a small beach town there twenty years before.

"Virginia?"

Max said it as if he weren't quite familiar with the state or even the country it was in. He'd obviously been in Europe way too long. Maybe she had been, too.

"Yes," she said, warming to the idea. "It's lovely there this time of year."

"How in hell do you know that?"

"It's spring," she said. "It's lovely everywhere in spring."

"Of course," he said wryly. The worried frown was back between his brows. "You'll stay in touch?"

"Why?"

"In case you decide you want to come back, of course."

"I won't," she said with certainty. Whatever happened,

whatever she decided to do with her life, she would not come back to Worldwide as long as it was in the hands of Maximillian Devereaux.

"You'll always have a job with us," he said anyway. "Remember that when you tire of watching the dogwood and the cherry blossoms bloom."

"I'd keep the flower references out of the conversation, if I were you. Flowers are what brought us to this impasse, remember?"

"You'll be back," he said with arrogant confidence. "You and I have unfinished business." His gaze settled on her and lingered. "Professional and personal."

She refused to be shaken by the intensity of his gaze, but only because there was no responding, wild leap of her pulse. She stared straight into his eyes and slowly shook her head. "Don't bet the wine cellar on it, Max."

And then she slammed the door in his face. Forever after, she thought she would remember with a great deal of satisfaction his thoroughly stunned expression. She doubted Max could recall the last time a mere mortal, especially a woman, had ever said no to him and not left the door open for a yes.

Gracie checked her bank balance and gave herself five months—the rest of spring and the entire summer—to pull herself together. She made that decision on the plane. Then, exhausted and emotionally drained, she slept the rest of the way to Washington.

At Dulles Airport, she bought a map, rented a car and started driving east on the Beltway, turning south on I-95 to Fredericksburg then heading east again. Seagull Point was a tiny speck on the map, tucked between Colonial Beach and Montross, right in the heart of history as the guidebooks liked to say.

Passing gently lolling farmland along the Rappahannock River, she began to have her doubts. Would she be able to survive for long in the middle of nowhere? True, the dog-woods were blooming in profusion, their white and pink blossoms standing out against the budding green of giant oaks. Tulips and the last of the daffodils bobbed in the lilac-scented breeze. The scenery was idyllic, but the only town she passed through, King George, was hardly a metropolis. There wasn't even a traffic light in the middle of town. She barely had to slow down until she hit the intersection with Route 205 and made the turn toward Colonial Beach.

Pausing at the next red light at Route 301, she considered turning left and heading north, across the Potomac River Bridge, back to D.C. or maybe Baltimore. Instead, though, she kept going, determined to follow the plan she'd set for herself. Making plans, seeing to details, was something at which she excelled. It was why, until recently, she'd been such a valued Worldwide employee. She was organized to a fault.

By three in the afternoon she'd found a small hotel on the Potomac River. No one would ever confuse it with a World-wide property, but it was clean and the mattress was firm, just the way she liked it. It would do until she could find a rental property for the summer, she concluded.

By five she'd finished a take-out carton of Kung Po chicken, showered and watched the early news out of Wash-ington. Though she'd intended to shift her body onto local time by staying awake until nine at least, by five-thirty she was sound asleep. Naturally, because of that, she was wide awake before dawn.

Years of starting the day while others slept made the early hour seem almost normal. Except there were no lists to make, no calendar to check for meetings, no details to see to. There was absolutely nothing demanding her attention and no rea-son at all to get out of bed.

"Go back to sleep," she coached herself, forcing her eyes shut and trying to stay perfectly still. She willed herself to relax. After fifteen increasingly restless minutes, she realized she didn't know how.

"Tomorrow will be better," she promised herself as she dressed and headed out to find someplace serving breakfast.

Over scrambled eggs and toast at the Beachside Cafe, she read the *Washington Post*. As she lingered over coffee, she dug in her purse for paper and made a list of things to do, starting with contacting a real estate agent about available rentals. She wanted something small, facing the river so she could sit on the porch and drink her morning coffee or her evening tea and watch the play of colors on the water.

"More coffee, miss?"

Gracie glanced up at the waitress and smiled, noting that her name was Jessie and that she had the reddest hair Gracie had ever seen, especially on a woman who had to be in her sixties. "Yes, please. Any idea what time I'll be able to find a real estate office open around here?"

"Oh, it's catch as catch can until nine or so, though Johnny Payne usually stops in here around eight. If he doesn't have what you're looking for, he can find it for you."

Gracie glanced at the clock behind the counter. "Maybe I'll just stick around then. Do you mind?"

"Be my guest. We're never full on a weekday till after the season starts. I'll send Johnny over when he comes in. Having breakfast with a pretty woman for a change will make his day. Those old coots he's usually with ain't nothing to look at."

Gracie grinned. "Thanks."

"You need anything else, just holler. I'll check on your coffee now and again."

It was three cups of coffee later, just as Gracie was beginning to get a worrisome caffeine buzz, when the man who turned out to be Johnny Payne ambled in. He headed for the counter, only to be waylaid by the waitress and directed toward Gracie. He was tall and raw-boned with a flushed complexion, liberal gray in his once brown hair and a twinkle in his hazel eyes.

"Mr. Payne?" Gracie guessed when he stood beside her table, his hands shoved in the pockets of his chinos. Christmas-red suspenders held them up.

"Yes, ma'am, that would be me. What can I do for you?"

"Sit down, if you have a minute. I don't want to keep you from your breakfast."

"Not me," he said, and pulled out a chair. "I had breakfast at home an hour ago. I come in here to fuel up on coffee and gossip."

"Well, I certainly won't keep you from having your coffee. As for the gossip, I'll try not to keep you from that for too long, either."

He grinned at her. "Not to worry. Nothing much happens around here anyway, leastways nothing that's more exciting than a pretty stranger asking about property. That is what you wanted to see me about, isn't it?"

"It is. I'm looking for a summer rental."

"On the river?"

"Absolutely."

"Big or small?"

"Small will do."

He looked her over, his expression thoughtful. "You mind investing a little elbow grease?"

"Not at all." It would keep her mind off of the decisions that had to be made.

He gave a brief nod of satisfaction, as if she'd just passed some sort of test. "I've got just the place. Owner died a few years back and his kids don't give a hoot about the house. Can't seem to agree about selling it, either. In the meantime, it's for rent. Won't suit just anybody because of its size. Two bedrooms, a big kitchen, and a living room. Most folks want the Taj Majal in the summer, so they can fill the place with everyone from back home they were trying to get away from. You know what I mean?"

Actually, she had no idea. She'd taken only one real vacation in her entire life—to this town, as a matter of fact. She nodded just the same.

"Anyway, the price is negotiable depending on how long you want it for and how much work you're willing to put in yourself to clean it up and save me calling in a maid service." At Gracie's surprised look, he chuckled. "That would be my wife. She'd be mighty happy to let someone else chase the mice away for a change."

Gracie swallowed hard and reminded herself she wasn't at Worldwide anymore. "There are mice?"

"Not so many now that the weather's warming up. Once you sweep away the dust bunnies and get to stirring around inside, the last of 'em will go."

"I certainly hope so," she muttered. "When can you show it to me?"

"Now's as good a time as any, I suppose. You have a car with you?"

"I left it at the hotel."

"Then you can ride with me. I'll stop by the office and pick up the keys."

Gracie wasn't sure what she'd expected, someplace ramshackle and neglected, probably. At any rate, it wasn't the tidy little white cottage with the Wedgwood-blue shutters and sprawling porch across the front. A pair of white rockers had been upended on the porch. That was all she needed.

"I'll take it," she said at once.

"You haven't even been inside yet," Johnny Payne protested.

"Okay, maybe you're right. Maybe I was being impulsive, but this is exactly what I was looking for."

"Miss, if you don't mind me saying so, you must not do much negotiating."

If only he knew, Gracie thought. She'd handled more tough negotiations in recent years that Johnny Payne probably had in his lifetime. "I've done my share," she said modestly. "I just don't believe in playing games once I've made up my mind about something."

"And you want this house?"

"I do."

He shrugged. "Then let's see how many mice took up residence this winter before we settle on the details."

The details were a snap. The asking price was so reasonable, Gracie saw no reason to argue about it, though Johnny Payne looked a little disappointed when she didn't.

By nightfall, Gracie had swept and vacuumed and dusted away cobwebs. She'd left the windows open to the cool April breeze off the water. More than once she'd slipped outside to sit on the porch for just a minute and take in the view of the wide, wide Potomac with the Maryland shore in the distance and a peek at the banks of Robert E. Lee's birthplace, Stratford Hall, off to one side.

After dinner, her muscles aching and her clothes and hair an untidy wreck, she took her cup of herbal tea onto the porch for one last time. An unfamiliar feeling stole over her as she sat there with the sky darkening and the waves lapping on the narrow patch of beach across the street. She felt at peace. Worldwide Hotels and Maximillian Devereaux were very far away. She could almost imagine a time when neither would so much as enter her thoughts.

That moment couldn't possibly come soon enough to suit her.

Two

By the end of the week Gracie had established a routine. Still up at the crack of dawn, she went for a walk along the river, always winding up at the Beachside Cafe for breakfast.

On her second visit, Jessie and everyone else in the place already seemed to know that she had just rented the Taylor place on the waterfront. They knew she wasn't from the area and that she planned to stay at least through summer.

"I'm surprised they haven't nailed down my credit rating," she commented to Jessie, laughing at the accuracy and thoroughness of the waitress's report.

"Oh, Johnny has that, too, I'm sure, but there are some things he manages to keep to himself." She eyed Gracie with curiosity. "Why here? You look like a big-city girl to me. I'll bet you don't even own a pair of jeans."

That was true enough, but Gracie decided not to confirm it. "Maybe I've just had a little too much of big-city living," she said, which was the truth as far as it went.

"The fast pace'll kill you, that's for sure," Jessie agreed, then peered at her thoughtfully. "Or was it a man?"

She nodded sagely, though Gracie hadn't said a word. "It usually is, if you ask me. At the heart of any woman's troubles there is guaranteed to be a man."

"Not this time," Gracie replied, even as an image of Max popped into her head. Max wasn't a problem, not for her heart, anyway. He was just a simple pain in the neck, professionally speaking.

Unfortunately, her conversation with Jessie had stirred up the very memories she had been trying so hard to forget. Thanks to Max she was in a strange place, completely at loose ends. Listening to Jessie's curious speculation reminded Gracie that this little sabbatical of hers would end sooner or later. What then?

Maybe thinking about the sorry state of her life and the dim prospects for her future explained why she noticed the house, the huge Victorian with its dilapidated, sagging porch and its intricate gingerbread trim. It was hidden away behind an overgrown hedge and a heavy wrought-iron gate.

Gracie figured she must have passed it half a dozen times before as she strolled along lost in thought, but this morning with the sun glistening on its fading white paint and grimy windows, it caught her eye.

Three stories tall, with a widow's walk on the top, it was like something out of a book, albeit a Gothic horror novel at the moment. It was the kind of place kids would assume was haunted.

But despite its state of disrepair, Gracie could envision it all primped up with fresh paint and shining windows. In her mind's eye, pots filled with bright flowers decorated the front porch and the lawn was tended, the hedge neatly trimmed. She could also imagine a simple, discreet sign hanging by the gate, declaring it a bed and breakfast.

"Ridiculous," she muttered the minute the idea struck. She hurried her step as if to escape her own thoughts. Though the house was clearly unoccupied and ignored, there was no For Sale sign out front. Even if there had been, she wasn't interested in staying in Seagull Point for more than a few months.

Was she?

Of course not, she insisted, again picking up speed after a last backward glance over her shoulder. Coming here in the first place had been impulsive. Staying would be, what?

Lunacy? Jessie had pegged it. She was a big-city girl. The more exotic the city, the better. Seagull Point was a far cry from Cannes, France.

Still, she found herself strolling past the house again that afternoon and pausing in front of it on her way to breakfast the following morning to study it with a critical, experienced eye.

"It wouldn't take much," she murmured, ignoring the little voice inside that suggested boredom, not good sense, was behind the notion of buying the place. Once again, she dismissed the idea.

Unfortunately, it kept coming back. When she stopped at the hardware store to pick up a new broom and some nails to fix a loose board on the porch of the rental, she couldn't help looking at the paint chips. Before she knew it, she had a whole handful.

"Johnny hasn't talked you into painting the Taylor place while you're here, has he?" the man behind the counter asked when he saw the collection of paint chips.

Gracie grinned. "No way. I have another project I've been thinking about, that's all. It probably won't come to anything. Is it okay if I take all these samples?"

"That's what they're there for. Let us know if there's anything you need. I've got a fellow working for me who takes on odd jobs painting. Needs the extra money. He does good work, too, as long as you don't mind him doing it evenings and on his days off from here."

"Thanks. I'll keep that in mind."

On her way home, she stopped in front of the old Victorian once again. This time, though, she opened the rusty gate and stepped through. The grounds were far more expansive than she'd envisioned from the street, though at the moment they were a tangle of weeds. There was room enough for a badminton net and a croquet course in the back, plus an area with a brick fireplace that would be perfect for family-style barbeques for guests. The concept had an old-fashioned charm to it that appealed to her. Surely there were still people in the world who longed for the days when video games weren't the entertainment of choice. Surely there were families that sought out low-key vacations far from the crowds at Disney World.

She tested the steps and found them solid enough, but to her regret the windows were too filthy to permit a halfway decent view of the interior.

"It doesn't matter," she told herself sternly. It was only a pipedream, after all. It wasn't as if she were going to buy the place and settle down here to run it. She had a job waiting for her in France . . . if she wanted to go back. She could land another position with another hotel chain at the drop of a hat . . . if she chose. The sleepy town of Seagull Point, Virginia, was not what she needed, not in the long run. It was a temporary balm for her soul, no more.

Even so, she found herself spreading the paint chips out on the kitchen table when she got home, playing with combinations of color until she had two that she liked, a third that was a possibility. When the phone rang, she guiltily shoved them all back into a pile as she answered it.

"Hello, Max," she said, anticipating who would be on the other end of the line. Max was the only person she'd told where she was going. Even though she'd given him the entire state to choose from, Max was apparently every bit as good at narrowing down possibilities as he was at spotting a discrepancy of a few francs in the Worldwide books. It had taken him less than a week to find her.

"Bored yet?" he inquired.

"Of course not."

"What are you doing with yourself?"

"Nothing, Max. That's the whole point of a vacation."

"A vacation?" His voice brightened perceptibly. "Then that is all that this is? You will be back?"

"No, Max. I will not be back."

"The staff misses you," he said, trying a different tack.

"I miss them," she said. She had felt vaguely guilty about abandoning them to Max's puritanical fiscal whims. André in particular would not fare so well without her as a buffer between him and Max.

"Guests have asked about you."

She did brighten at that. "Really?" She'd hoped that the regulars would notice her absence, but hadn't really expected Max to tell her.

"Actually, they have mentioned missing the floral arrangements you put in the lobby."

A twinge of panic fluttered in her stomach. "Where are the flowers, Max?"

"The florist and I had a slight disagreement," he admitted. "He prefers dealing only with you."

Gracie laughed as she thought of gentle Paul Chevalier standing up to Max and refusing to deliver flowers to the hotel. He must have been incredibly insulted to have taken such a stance.

"Would you like me to call him?" she offered. "I can smooth things over."

"Would you?" he asked, sounding relieved, perhaps a bit too smug.

"Of course. But Max, you're going to have to start dealing with these little crises yourself or else bring in a new manager."

"I can't do that, not when I'm holding the job for you. In the meantime, the rest of us will do the best we can. The hotel will not fall apart overnight."

"Overnight? Max, I've told you not to hold the job."

"Allow me my fantasies, *ma chérie*."

"Max!"

"Au revoir."

Gracie sighed as she hung up. A moment later she placed the international call to the florist. Even though it would be evening in France, she knew she would find Paul Chevalier in his shop, tidying up after a hectic day, checking his orders, planning his trip to the flower market at the crack of dawn. Sure enough, he answered on the first ring, sounding distracted and rushed as he always did.

"Bon soir, Paul."

"Ah, mademoiselle, *bon soir,"* he said, his voice brightening. *"Comment allez-vous?"*

"Très bien. And you, Paul? How are you? I understand Monsieur Devereaux has upset you."

"The man is an imbecile," he declared.

"What has he done?"

"He has asked me to pluck out only the dead flowers and replace them. He does not seem to understand that each arrangement is a piece of art, unique, magnificent in its own right."

"Definitely an imbecile," Gracie agreed. "But, Paul, think of the guests. They appreciate your arrangements. They have told Monsieur Devereaux that they miss them. *S'il vous plaît,* Paul, for me. Will you try to work with him?"

"You are coming back soon?"

"No, I'm afraid not."

"You have abandoned us, then, left us to this imbecile?"

"Max is okay. Just be patient with him. He will learn."

Paul sighed dramatically. "For you, mademoiselle, but only for you."

"Thank you, Paul. You are a treasure."

"You are sure you will not be back?"

"Very sure. Not to the hotel, anyway. But I will come back to visit, Paul. I promise."

"Very good, mademoiselle. *Au revoir."*

Dealing with that one little detail reminded her that she was only postponing the inevitable. She loved handling the day-in day-out crises that went with running a hotel. If Paul's ego required careful handling, it was nothing compared to those of the chefs. More than once she had walked into a hotel kitchen to find the chef and the sous-chef squared off in a battle that shook the pots and pans. One terrible night she had ended up putting the final touches on elaborate desserts under the watchful gaze of the artistic, temperamental pastry chef after his own assistant had quit in a huff.

In truth, there was very little she hadn't pitched in and done at one time or another to keep the hotel operating smoothly. Which meant, she concluded thoughtfully, that surely she could run a small little bed and breakfast in Virginia on her own. It would be an investment in her future, to say nothing of a home, something she hadn't had since she'd sold off her family's property, such as it was, in a long-dead Pennsylvania coal mining town.

There had been nothing charming or quaint about the place where she'd grown up. It had fallen to ruin years before, leaving behind citizens who were every bit as depressed as the local economy. She had been all too eager to see the last of it. She had known when she left after her mother's funeral, less than six months after her father's, that she would never go back there.

Seagull Point, Virginia, however, had promise. In only a few days she had seen that. There was hope in the burgeoning business district and in the freshly painted and recently renovated homes along the river. The people were friendly and upbeat. They were rooted, not in misery as her old neighbors had been, but in life. Gracie had seen evidence of prosperity in the packed seafood restaurants and actual traffic jams at the town's main intersections on weekends.

There weren't enough hotel rooms, either. She'd stayed in the only national chain hotel in the entire area. The others were all small, family-owned motels with a very limited number of rooms. A bed and breakfast, especially one in a house with historic charm and architecture, would fit right in. She didn't have to make one of her notorious lists to add up the pluses and minuses. Fiscally the decision was sound. Emotionally, well, in the last couple of days she had developed a surprising longing for roots, sparked by that surprising and devastating discovery back in Cannes that she had no real ties in the world.

It wouldn't hurt to ask a few questions, check on the property's availability. Gathering facts wasn't the same as making an impulsive offer. It was testing the waters, not jumping off a bridge. She would make a few casual inquiries, assess the possibilities. She would approach the whole thing in a slow, logical manner.

Famous last words.

"Not available," Johnny Payne told her succinctly when, Gracie asked him about the old Victorian.

Naturally that stirred her competitive spirit. Overcoming, obstacles was her specialty. She thrived on it. "Why?" she asked.

He regarded her as if she had a screw loose for asking such an obvious question. "Because the owner don't want to sell," he explained patiently.

"How do you know? Have you asked?"

"It'd be on the market if they wanted to sell, now wouldn't it?"

Gracie decided on another tack. "Johnny, what would that house be worth in today's market? Can you give me a ball-park figure?"

"Don't know," he insisted. "Never thought about it."

"You're in real estate. It's your business to know property values in the area. Surely you have some idea."

He shook his head. "You ask me about a cottage on the riverfront, I could tell you in a heartbeat. That old Victorian's one of a kind. It's been in the same family since it was built as their summer home way back at the turn of the century or before, when this place was bustling with tourists running away from D.C. Haven't been inside it myself in a dozen years or more. Can't say what condition it's in now, though from the looks of it, it can't be good."

He peered at her curiously. "Why are you asking so many questions? You thinking of sticking around, after all? If that's it, I could probably get you a deal on that place you're in. It's more your size, anyway. You'd just be rattling around in that big old Victorian. Must be ten, fifteen rooms in there, altogether. The place sprawls all to hell and gone."

Gracie wasn't prepared to show her hand. If the owner thought there was an anxious buyer out there with plans for the house, the price could escalate beyond her reach. Assuming this mysterious owner could be located in the first place. Johnny was as tight-lipped as a clam about the owner's identity. Maybe he feared he'd be cut out of a deal if she decided to contact the man directly.

"Could you at least look into it for me," she pleaded, partly to reassure him that the deal would be his, if one were struck. "What would it hurt?"

"I don't go around begging folks to sell their property," he retorted. "It's not polite."

"Isn't that carrying southern courtesy to an extreme?" Gracie asked. "Maybe they just haven't thought of selling. Given the look of the place, maybe they've forgotten all about its existence. Or maybe they figure they'd have to pour too much into repairs to put it on the market. Coming to them with a prospective buyer and a firm offer could be an easy commission for you."

"Sorry."

"Johnny, for heaven's sakes, tell her the truth," Jessie prodded. "You haven't said one word to Kevin Patrick Daniels since he beat out your boy for all-state in basketball their senior year."

Gracie stared from Jessie to Johnny's suddenly beet-red complexion. "This reluctance of yours is due to some old feud over basketball?"

"Around here, folks take their high school basketball seriously," Jessie explained. "Don't they, Johnny?"

He scowled at her. "You've got a big mouth, missy."

Jessie gave him an impertinent grin. "Truth's truth. You wouldn't talk to Kevin Patrick if there was a million-dollar commission in it for you."

"The man stole that title from my boy," he muttered. "Ruined his scholarship chances, and for what? Not a damn thing. He didn't need a scholarship. He was already headed for the University of Virginia, just like his daddy before him and his daddy before that."

Jessie shook her head. "Kevin Patrick could hardly help the fact that he was named to that all-state team. He'd been high scorer here for his entire high school career. Derek was second best and that's no reflection on him. It's just that Kevin Patrick had a gift. He had one of those exceptional, once-in-a-lifetime records. It was too bad they went through school at the same time. Any other season, Derek would have been the superstar."

"Damn right," Johnny said.

"Let me get this straight," Gracie said, trying to grasp the conflict between the two men. "You're refusing to even check on this house for me because it would mean dealing with a man you blame for cheating your son out of a college basketball scholarship?"

"In a nutshell," Johnny confirmed without embarrassment.

"How many years ago was this?"

"Eighteen. Right, Johnny?" Jessie said.

"That'd be about right," he agreed.

"Eighteen years? You've carried on this feud for eighteen years?" Gracie was incredulous. "Why not put the screws to him, then? Make him sell me the house for a fourth of what it's worth. Think what a laugh you could have over that."

"Can't do it," Johnny said with finality. "I refuse to be in the same room with the arrogant, no-good son of a gun. You want to deal with him you're on your own, but don't say I didn't warn you. The man's a cheat and a scoundrel. He's been managing that property for the past few years and you've seen it. He's let it go to seed."

Cheats and scoundrels were among Gracie's favorite people. Negotiating with them and winning thrilled her almost as much as terrific sex. Not that she'd had much experience with either lately.

She studied the real estate man carefully. "You're sure about this, Johnny? Selling real estate's how you make your living. You don't mind if I track down this Kevin Patrick Daniels and deal with him directly?"

"Suit yourself," he said with an indifference that rivaled Max at his worst.

"Where can I find him?"

When Johnny remained stubbornly, steadfastly silent, it was Jessie who gave her directions. "Believe me, you won't be able to miss it. There's not another place like it on that road. Think of Tara and then exaggerate."

The man lived on a blasted plantation and he allowed that beautiful old Victorian to fall to ruin? Gracie decided she might come to dislike Kevin Patrick Daniels almost as passionately as Johnny did. That would make buying the house for a pittance of its worth all the more satisfying.

If, of course, she decided she really wanted it.

Which she didn't, she insisted. This was purely an exercise, a gathering of facts. Nothing more.

Two hours later she was searching a country road for the lane that would take her to Kevin Patrick Daniels, current manager of the property. If that run-down state was his idea of management, he ought to be a quick sell.

She knew the type. Never spend a dime unless the roof is actually falling down. Which it was. No doubt he'd rather accept her offer than put a new coat of paint or a new roof on the place. Her adrenaline pumped just thinking about the negotiations. She felt more alive than she had in months. Hopeful.

And that was before she glimpsed the Daniels estate. Jessie hadn't exaggerated a bit. It was Tara on steroids. Every bush was tidily trimmed, every blade of grass on the rolling hillside had been neatly shorn to the precise same length. The house and the columns across the front were pristine white, which probably required regular touch-ups. The windows, tall and stately, glistened.

Oh, yes, indeed, Gracie thought, staring at it with a mixture of awe and disgust. Stealing that neglected Victorian from Kevin Patrick Daniels was going to make her day.

Three

The discussion had gone on for an hour, about fifty-nine minutes longer than it had needed to, Kevin thought. Most of it had covered the same ground over and over. It was time to put an end to it.

"Absolutely not," he said with finality, leveling a look straight into his cousin's eyes. "I will not finance another one of your ridiculous, get-rich-quick schemes, Bobby Ray. It's time you grew up and got a job, like the rest of us."

"When did you ever hold down an actual job?" his cousin retorted. "All you do is play around with your inheritance—and ours, I might add—like it's Monopoly money."

"That Monopoly money has kept you and Sara Lynn afloat for the past five years," he reminded Bobby Ray. "That's about four years longer than the marriage would have lasted without it."

Bobby Ray didn't even flinch at the shot. Kevin's opinion of his marriage was clearly old news to him by now. Kevin had repeated it often enough. He'd seen Sara Lynn for the little gold-digger she was from the minute she took up with Bobby Ray. His cousin, reeling from his second divorce and unable to handle life as a bachelor, had jumped straight from the frying pan into the fire.

"If I'd had that money, I could have been a rich man by now instead of living off what you dole out," Bobby Ray complained bitterly. "I feel like a damn beggar."

They had been over this turf again and again. Kevin actually felt a certain amount of sympathy for the position his uncle had left Bobby Ray in, but Uncle Steven had known what he was doing. Bobby Ray might be the same age as Kevin, thirty-six, but he had the attention span of a five-year-old. He was on his third wife, even though it was Kevin's opinion that his heart remained with the first one. Kevin had lost count of the number of jobs he'd had and the number of failed business ventures he'd tried, then lost interest in.

"Unfortunately, you gave your father proof-positive that you lack a certain financial savvy," he said, wishing there were a kinder way to state the obvious. There wasn't, so he hammered home his point . . . again. "Be grateful your father had the foresight to put your trust fund into my hands so you couldn't blow all of it. Maybe if you'd shown the slightest evidence of responsibility, he wouldn't have done that. Instead, you took thirty thousand dollars from him and sank it into a taco stand."

"It was a fried chicken franchise," Bobby Ray protested, his expression sullen.

"Oh, yes, that's right. Next door to a Kentucky Fried Chicken," Kevin reminded him.

"This chicken was better. It was Ella Mae's recipe. Everybody in the Northern Neck of Virginia loves Ella Mae's chicken."

"Maybe so, especially when she cooked at your mama's house and served it up free. But you don't take on a national franchise with a thirty-thousand-dollar investment and an advertising budget of zilch. The only people who ever ate there were related to you, and as big as our clan is we couldn't support an ice cream stand on the boardwalk in summer, much less an entire restaurant year round. This latest scheme of yours is every bit as ill conceived. Get a job, Bobby Ray. It'll do you good."

"Go to hell."

"No doubt about it," Kevin said. Bobby Ray Daniels wasn't the first member of his family to wish him a speedy end and a fiery destination.

The Daniels family wealth, accumulated over generations, thanks to wise investments and savvy handling, had never once been endangered until the current crop of cousins had landed on earth. Thanks to some very unfortunate marriages, the genetic pool had spawned—with one or two notable exceptions—an entire generation of irresponsible males and throwback southern belle females, who wouldn't deign to lift a finger if the house was burning down around them.

Entrusted with what was left of the family fortune, Kevin had his work cut out for him. He wasn't sure which his cousins resented most, the fact that he held the purse strings or the fact that he didn't give a damn about the money they craved. He'd have given them each their fair share and been done with it if he hadn't known they'd be back on his doorstep within a year, desperate for more.

What every single one of them needed, far more than they needed cash, was self-respect. Kevin didn't have a clue how to go about giving them that, except by forcing them to actually work for a living. He'd opened door after door, only to have them blow the chances. He was running out of friends who'd hire them. There was a chance that Dick Flint in Richmond would find something for Bobby Ray. Dick had half a dozen used car dealerships and a penchant for losing at poker. He owed Kevin bigtime.

"I'll call Dick Flint, if you'd like," he offered.

Bobby Ray stared at him as if he'd suggested he take up sky-diving. "You want me to be a used car salesman?" he asked, as he straightened the monogrammed cuffs on his two-hundred-dollar shirt.

"I want you to do something that would excite you, something at which you'll succeed." Something that would justify those expensive, imported shirts and pay for the fashionable lifestyle to which Bobby Ray and Sara Lynn aspired.

"Well, it sure as hell won't be selling those broken-down heaps Dick Flint passes off on an unsuspecting public," Bobby Ray snapped. "One of these days you're going to push me too far, Kevin. Me or one of the others."

Kevin was tiring of Bobby Ray's idle threats. One of these days he was simply going to pummel some sense into the overgrown jerk, just as he'd tried to do on more than one occasion when they were kids. Come to think of it, it hadn't worked then, either. Instead, he leveled a look straight into his cousin's eyes.

"Meaning?" he asked, his tone icy.

Not even Bobby Ray was able to mistake the fact that he'd gone too far. "Forget it," he grumbled. "Just forget I stopped by. Forget I exist."

As if I could, Kevin thought as his cousin stormed out of the house. The wills of various and sundry uncles had made sure of that.

As it always did, talking to Bobby Ray had worked up a mighty big thirst. Kevin wandered into the kitchen of his ridiculously huge house and found a pitcher of lemonade in the refrigerator. Molly, the housekeeper as far back as he could remember, made sure they were never out, just as she'd always kept the cookie jar crammed with ginger snaps, once she'd discovered he was partial to them.

Kevin filled a tall glass with ice cubes, then poured the lemonade right to the brim. He took a sip and felt his lips, pucker. Perfect. Just enough sugar to take the edge off but not enough to ruin the sour taste of lemons. There was nothing better on a hot summer day.

Not that it was summer yet, but it sure felt like it. The temperature had hit eighty by noon and was still climbing The humidity was every bit as thick as it was in mid-August. It struck him that was a sure-fire indication that he ought to spend the afternoon doing just what he always did in the middle of a sultry summer heat wave . . . absolutely nothing.

Carrying his lemonade and a handful of cookies, he

headed outside and settled into a hammock spread between two massive oaks. Why work up a sweat—mental or physical—when he didn't have to. He'd dealt with just about as much family business as he could in one day without throwing up.

First, Cousin Carolanne had dropped by hoping for a handout to pay off her charge cards. Then Tommy had called from North Carolina needing money for a lawyer to get out of his latest jam. Bobby Ray had been the final straw. A nice nap seemed called for.

He was just drifting off when he heard the roar of a distant engine. Since Greystone was not exactly on a superhighway, the sound was enough to disturb his rest and cause speculation about who was coming calling unannounced. With any luck at all, it wouldn't be another of his devilish cousins. Of course, he'd had enough practice saying no today to be getting really good at it. He supposed uttering it a few more times wouldn't he a strain. He probably wouldn't even have to sit up and glower at them fiercely to make his point.

He took a long, slow sip of lemonade and watched the lane leading up to the house until he spotted a flashy red convertible zipping along the cedar-lined drive. Since he hadn't seen any bills from auto dealerships on his desk that morning, he had to assume it didn't belong to anyone in the family. He relaxed again and closed his eyes.

He didn't intend to budge one inch from his current comfortable position in order to greet the uninvited guest. Aunt Delia would probably accuse him of being deliberately rude if she was observing the scene from her suite just above him. He glanced up and grinned at the sight of the shadow behind her curtains. Yep, he'd get a lecture over supper, all right. Aunt Delia was very big on manners and she told him repeatedly that his were atrocious. He'd promised to change . . . sooner or later.

At the moment, though, it seemed to him that his uninvited guest had probably hightailed it out here on some mission or another and it wouldn't do at all to show so much as a hint of retreat. Normally he was as keen as the next man to do business across a desk or over a fine lunch, but certain circumstances required a different tactic. Pure instinct told him this was one of those times.

It was several minutes, during which he was aware of the car getting closer and the engine cutting off, before he sensed a presence and bothered opening his eyes again. The sight before him was enough to cause his pulse to skip a beat or two, but he tried real hard not to let his reaction show.

The woman was a knockout. Tall and curvy and classy, all at the same time. The demure outfit she wore did absolutely nothing to mute her sex appeal, and it was definitely at odds with that fire engine red convertible. Kevin had always been fascinated with contradictions and this woman radiated them. Amazing, absolutely amazing.

"Mr. Daniels?"

"Yo," he said without moving.

"Kevin Patrick Daniels?"

He hid a grin as he heard the impatience in her tone. "Yep, that's me. You a process server, darlin'?"

"No, though I have to wonder why that would be your first guess. Do you spend a lot of time in trouble, Mr. Daniels?"

"Not half as much as I'd like to."

"Perhaps if you would haul yourself out of that hammock occasionally you'd have more success at it."

He marveled at her tart tone. Ms. Whoever-she-was seemed to have taken an instant dislike to him. That was promising. Nothing got his adrenaline flowing better than a real challenge.

"Southern hospitality precludes me from pointing out that you've just arrived at my home uninvited and now you're insulting me. Must be a Yankee."

"I suppose, if you go strictly by geographical birthplace, that I am," she conceded. "And I'm sorry if I appear rude, but I find it very difficult to do business with a man who's half asleep."

"Darlin', let me assure you, I am wide awake. Have been ever since you walked up. I could prove it, if you'd like to snuggle down here next to me."

He could practically hear her swallowing hard as she absorbed the implications of that. He'd lay odds that if he checked her complexion it would be one shade shy of the color of her car.

"Why don't you tell me who you are and what you want?" he suggested.

"I'm Gracie MacDougal," she said, and waited as if to see if the name meant anything to him.

"Ah," he said. Suddenly he understood all the reports he'd heard about the city girl who'd just moved to town and started asking questions about Aunt Delia's property on the Potomac. He'd figured she'd come calling sooner or later.

"Pretty as a picture," several of his friends had told him. Even with his eyes half closed, he could see that they hadn't done her justice.

"One of them globetrotters come home again," said an old-timer with the derision of one who couldn't imagine any legitimate need to leave the South in general and Virginia in particular.

Kevin thought that one was probably mistaken. If Gracie MacDougal had ever lived in these parts, he would have remembered. She wasn't coming home. In fact, from the determined jut of her cute little chin, he guessed she was invading new territory, sort of like the Yankees did a hundred and some years earlier.

"You talk to her, watch your privates," another acquaintance had warned. "She's the kind who'll chop 'em off."

That, of course, remained to be seen. No matter who was right, obviously it was going to be a fascinating encounter, he concluded, observing her surreptitiously from hooded eyes.

"What can I do for you, Gracie MacDougal?"

"Actually, I have a business matter to discuss, but I find that rather difficult when I can't even sit down and look you in the eye."

Kevin patted the edge of the hammock. "There's plenty of room right here next to me."

She sighed heavily, her exasperation plain. "Mr. Daniels . . ."

"Don't worry, darlin', I don't bite. Not on the first date, anyway, unless you ask nicely."

"Mr. Daniels!"

Kevin concluded from her tone that she wasn't going to get on with her business or give up until he sat up and took notice. He doubted that directing her to a chair a few feet away was going to satisfy her. If she wanted formality, he'd give her hundred-year-old formality.

"Ms. MacDougal, you surely do know how to spoil a man's relaxation," he said, rising. "Let's go on inside and get this over with."

He led the way to his office and noted the surprise on her face when she saw the book-lined shelves with volume after volume of leather-bound classics, the state-of-the-art computer system on his desk, the fax machine, and all the other accoutrements of running a business on the cusp of the millennium. Her gaze returned to him, and this time she seemed to be assessing him a little more carefully. He gestured toward one of the leather chairs left over from his father's reign over the family fortune, then seated himself behind the desk.

"Talk to me," he said.

"I understand you manage a property on the riverfront."

Actually, he owned half a dozen of them, but since he knew which one she was interested in, he saw no reason to belabor the point. "I do."

"I was wondering if the owner might be interested in selling?"

"No," he said, relieved that he'd had all day to practice

saying the word. Otherwise, seeing Gracie MacDougal's crestfallen expression might have had him waffling.

"Absolutely not," he added for good measure.

"But . . ." Clearly taken aback, she peered at him intently. "Are you sure?"

"Very sure."

"Couldn't you at least ask?"

"No need to," he insisted.

"Aren't you doing the owner a disservice by not taking my offer to them? In fact, isn't that illegal?"

He shrugged. "I don't think so."

"You don't even know what I'm willing to pay."

"Trust me, it won't be enough."

"The place is a shambles."

That was true enough. Kevin had been meaning to get over there and make a few repairs, cut the grass, maybe even trim the hedge. Had he done so, though, Aunt Delia—actually, his great-aunt on his mother's side—would have wanted to go along for a nostalgic visit to her home and the next thing he knew she'd be demanding that he let her move back there. He couldn't allow it.

The sad truth was, Aunt Delia had no business being on her own anymore. She forgot to take her medication. She left the stove on. She wandered off and left the front door standing wide open. It was a wonder she hadn't been robbed blind. Kevin had never known what to expect when he'd driven over to visit. Most of the time he hadn't liked what he'd found.

Finally, eighteen months ago he'd insisted Aunt Delia move in with him. He'd actually managed to make it sound as if she were the one doing him a favor. By now, she'd probably figured out that he'd bamboozled her, but they'd both grown comfortable with the new arrangement. That didn't mean she wouldn't love to be back in that drafty old house again. Nope, he couldn't risk going near the place and she wouldn't allow him to hire a stranger to do the work, not without being there to supervise. It was a Catch-22 of the first magnitude.

"There's nothing wrong with the place that a little spit and polish cleaning wouldn't fix right up," he insisted.

"Then why don't you take care of it? It's a crime to allow it to go to ruin. It's probably riddled with termites and over-run with mice."

He grinned at her unconscious shudder. "Then I'm surprised you'd want to buy it,"

"I would fix it up," she said,

She made the declaration in that haughty little way that made him want to scoop her up and kiss her until she went weak in the knees. He settled for an indifferent shrug.

"Sorry, it's not for sale."

"I've been checking into real estate prices in the area and I've come up with a ballpark figure that I think is reasonable," she went on as if she hadn't heard him. She snatched a piece of paper off of his desk and scribbled a figure on it, then shoved it in front of him.

"Nice ballpark, if I were playing, which I'm not."

Scowling at him, she scratched out the amount and wrote another. Kevin stared at the paper and managed to hide his admiration. She'd pretty much nailed down the current market value and tacked on an extra ten thousand. She'd been one very busy woman since hitting town. Most people undervalued the property around here because the town had been slow in grasping its own potential. This outsider had apparently seen it right off. Since she was playing fair with the money, he wondered if she'd be honest about a few other things.

"Tell me, Gracie MacDougal, why are you so hot to buy that particular house? Do you have a husband and half a dozen kids stashed away somewhere?"

"I don't see how that's relevant."

"It would give me a clue about why you're interested in such a huge old house. Doesn't seem like the logical choice for a woman all alone."

"Sometimes logic doesn't have a thing to do with wanting a piece of property. Sometimes you just fall in love."

He'd never met a woman less inclined toward indulging a whim. Hot as it was, she was dressed in a suit, hose, and high heels that would have knocked the socks off a New York businessman. For his own purely masculine reasons, he'd have preferred she come calling in a sundress. Be that as it may, Gracie struck him as an exceptionally practical, businesslike lady, which meant she had plans for that house. It didn't take a genius to figure out what they might be.

"Or sometimes you decide you'd like to start a little bed and breakfast maybe," he suggested quietly and watched the telltale color bloom in her cheeks.

He was glad he'd done a little checking when he'd first heard about Gracie MacDougal and her fascination with Aunt Delia's house. He knew all about her career with Worldwide Hotels. It hadn't required a huge leap to figure out what she had in mind for the old Victorian. Without saying a word, she'd just confirmed his guesswork.

"If you think I'll raise my offer, you can think again," she said.

"Wouldn't matter if you did," he said. "It's not for sale."

"Then I suppose I might as well be going," she said, then met his gaze evenly. "For now."

"Then you'll be back?"

"Oh, you can count on it, Mr. Daniels."

Kevin couldn't explain the odd sense of relief that stirred in him. He'd intended to rid himself of her, once and for all. He'd been as adamant as he'd known how to be about Aunt Delia's house. And still, some part of him had obviously relished the first skirmish in what now promised to be all-out warfare. He couldn't help wondering what wiles Gracie MacDougal had up her sleeve.

Not that it mattered. His cousins were masters of every form of sneaky manipulation in the book. Not a one of them had put anything over on him yet. He doubted Gracie Mac-Dougal would, either.

It would be downright entertaining, though, to have her try.

Gracie had negotiated for supplies and equipment for entire hotel chains with more success than she had in that first meeting with Kevin Patrick Daniels. The man obviously had no idea of the actual worth of that rundown property. Didn't seem to care, either. Otherwise, he would have recognized her bid for the preemptive strike it was and snapped it up.

All in all, the meeting had been a frustrating waste of her time. She had left his house feeling disgruntled, off kilter, and thoroughly frustrated.

Of course, that might have had something to do with the fact that the man had been half nude, with his shirt undone and jeans so old they were practically threadbare in some very revealing places. She had tried not to look, she really had, but it had been impossible not to notice the curling, dark chest hair and the very impressive bulge beneath the zipper of his jeans. Unless she'd been very much mistaken, the man had been turned on by taunting her.

Whatever, she had left Greystone Manor more determined than ever to get her hands on that house . . . or around Mr. Daniels's neck.

She had grown very tired of hearing him declare the property wasn't for sale. Of course it was. Everything in the world was for sale, for the right price. She just had to figure out what would be persuasive enough to get his attention.

No, check that. She'd had his attention, all right. There was hard evidence of that, so to speak. Plus, she had caught the speculative, masculine gleam in his eyes, once he'd bothered to open them all the way. She supposed there was a way to use that to her advantage if she were that sort of woman. But, alas, she wasn't.

No, what she needed to do was to get him focused on business, caught up in the deal, challenged by the negotiations.

Unfortunately, she had a feeling one of those day-long motivational seminars couldn't stir up Kevin Patrick Daniels. One thing she had to say for Mr. Daniels, he was no Max. Obviously, he had about as much ambition as a slug. Lying around in a hammock in the middle of a workday said a whole lot about the man, none of it good.

Of course, some would say that maybe she ought to take a few lessons in relaxation from him. She'd been on vacation less than a week and already she was caught up in a business deal when *she* should have been following his example and sipping lemonade and lolling around in a hammock. What was it about her that drove her to succeed? If she could figure that out, maybe she could bottle it and slip a little into Mr. Daniels's lemonade.

A good shrink would probably tell her that she spent so much time on her career, because she was better at it than she was at relationships. In fact, she'd grown so leery of men in recent years that she'd worked very hard to attain the kind of independence that made a male protector unnecessary. She could count on her career in ways she'd never been able to count on another human being. At least she'd been able to until Max had come along and thrown a monkeywrench into that side of her life, too.

Maybe that was why she had seized on the notion of getting that Victorian and turning it into a bed and breakfast. It was just one more way to solidify her independence, to make sure that she alone was in control of her future.

Right now, though, Kevin Patrick Daniels stood between her and the control over her own life that she craved. That put him in a very dangerous position. A woman scorned in love was nothing compared to the ire of Gracie MacDougal when she'd been scorned in business.

Yes, indeed, win or lose, the next few months were going to be very interesting.

Four

"Why on earth didn't you sell it to her?" Aunt Delia demanded of Kevin, after Gracie MacDougal had stalked out of the house, her spine rigid and her cute little behind swaying provocatively despite her annoyance.

"You been listening at keyholes again?" Kevin asked, regarding his eighty-seven-year-old aunt with amusement. She was wearing bright red sneakers, a purple skirt, and a blouse with most of the colors of the rainbow in it. Compared to Gracie, she was a fashion nightmare.

Aunt Delia also had the hearing and curiosity of a kid. Nothing much got past her, as he had learned to his everlasting chagrin when he'd tried to sneak Marge Taylor up to his room late one night right after his aunt had moved in. Even though their rooms were in opposite wings of the house, Aunt Delia had apparently heard every creak of the stairs and enough of their whispered exchange to tell her they were up to no good.

Aunt Delia's disapproving frown over breakfast the next morning—when Marge was long gone—had had a chilling effect on his lovelife. Of course, that scowl might have had something to do with the fact that Aunt Delia regarded that particular branch of the Taylor line as little better than trailer trash. Nothing he could say about Marge's superb wit, high IQ, and college degree was likely to change her opinion.

"You keep snooping like that, you'll get a crick in your back," Kevin told her now.

"Didn't have to put my ear to the keyhole this time," his aunt replied, clearly unfazed by the accusation. "You two had the volume up so loud it interrupted my favorite show. It was a lot better than listening to some cross-dressing weirdo on a talk show."

Kevin shuddered, appalled and thoroughly baffled by her addiction to tabloid TV. "Why do you watch that stuff anyway?"

"A woman my age has to keep on top of what's going on in the world."

"Then you must have a mighty peculiar view of the state of affairs," Kevin said. "You need to get out more. See some normal folks."

"You took away my car keys," she reminded him.

"After you mowed down six mailboxes in a row."

She shrugged. "Accidents happen."

"A few too many times in your case. I'll take you anyplace you want to go."

"So you say."

"I will."

She gave him a sly look. "Including that off-track betting parlor on the river?" she inquired a bit too eagerly.

Kevin saw too late the trap he had set for himself and resigned himself to an afternoon of keno and horse racing. "Tomorrow," he agreed.

Aunt Delia seemed surprised by the easy capitulation. "Must mean you're hoping to run across that woman again. What did you say her name was?"

"I didn't. It's Gracie," he said, rather liking the way it sounded. Old-fashioned. Prim and proper. Yep, that was Gracie, all right. Getting her to loosen up was going to improve his summer considerably.

"She's right pretty, if you like the type," Aunt Delia said slyly.

"I didn't notice."

"Hogwash! The day you don't notice a woman will be the day they put you in the ground, Kevin Patrick. It amazes me still that one of them hasn't caught you by fair means or foul. Goodness knows, half the female population of the Northern Neck has tried hard enough."

Her expression turned thoughtful. "Of course, that's the problem, isn't it? They're all trying too hard. What's the challenge in that? You need a woman who won't go all weak-kneed just looking at you. Struck me that this Gracie of yours has spunk."

"I just met the woman. She is not *my* Gracie."

"Whatever. She looks as if she could keep you on your toes. Probably too much woman for you, now that I think about it."

Kevin fought a surge of indignation and lost. "The woman hasn't been born who'd be too much for me," he grumbled.

"So you say."

"Do you have a license for all this analysis you're doing?"

"I have something better. I have years of experience. You'd do well to listen to me once in awhile."

"I listen to every word you say."

"And then pick and choose which half of them to ignore."

He couldn't deny that at least half of it fell on deaf ears. "Okay, Aunt Delia, let's leave me out of this for a minute," he suggested on a more somber note. "Bottom line. Do you really want me to sell your house to Gracie MacDougal so she can turn it into a bed and breakfast?"

For a second, she looked nonplussed by the direct question. Then she squared her shoulders and looked him in the eye, challenging him right back. "Might's well," she said. "You won't let me near the place. It's a shame to let it sit there, when it could be filled with laughter again."

His gaze narrowed. He was missing something here. She had fought tooth and nail every suggestion he'd made about putting the house on the market. She'd insisted, in fact, on putting it in his name, though as far as he was concerned it was still hers to do with as she liked.

"Do you mean that?" he asked. "I thought you loved that old house."

"I do. I spent my entire life in that house. Not a minute goes by that I don't miss it, but I'm not a fool, Kevin. I know it was getting to be too much for me. I'm better off here with you, though why you'd rather be out here in this mausoleum instead of in town is beyond me."

She surveyed him, then shrugged. "Besides, you need somebody around who can stand up to you. None of those pitiful Daniels relatives of yours has the gumption to put you in your place when you deserve it. And Molly's been catering to your every whim since the day you were born. I've never seen a housekeeper who's so taken in by a smile and an occasional kind word. That leaves me to see you don't get too big for your britches."

Her eyes sparkled mischievously. "Something tells me that MacDougal girl could hold her own with you, though. I wouldn't mind watching the negotiations for the house, just to see the sparks fly."

"Maybe," he conceded cautiously. He knew what she was up to. She was laying the groundwork for throwing him into more frequent contact with Gracie. He had a hunch, though, that any actual deal would be a very long time coming. Aunt Delia was especially fond of fireworks, especially of the human variety.

"She didn't back down when you said no, did she?" his aunt pointed out.

"True. She said she'd be back."

"Good. Next time, I want to meet her."

The very thought of such a meeting sent a chill through him. He shook his head. "I don't think so."

"Why on earth not? It is my house she wants to buy, isn't it?"

"And we both know you'd give it away if you took a shine

to the potential buyer. I won't have you being cheated. If the time comes when you've given the matter some thought and you decide you want to sell, I'll handle the negotiations."

"Then keep the lines of communication open with Gracie MacDougal. Something tells me she'll pay top dollar," she said, regarding him with a canny look. "If that's all you're interested in."

"We'll talk about it when you've thought it over," he repeated. "In the meantime, you stay the heck away from Ms. MacDougal."

She shook her head. "I don't know, getting to know a stranger might relieve some of the boredom around here."

His aunt went to more luncheons and tea parties than the Queen of England, but Kevin played along.

"I already told you I'd take you to the off-track betting place tomorrow," he reminded her. "We'll have lunch, watch a few races. You can throw some of your savings down the tube."

"Yes, and that will be real nice, but there's a movie I've been wanting to see, too," she mentioned oh-so-casually. "It's playing in Fredericksburg."

For pure sneakiness, Aunt Delia could put the Daniels side of the family to shame. "And you think these two outings will relieve the tedium?" he asked.

"It'll be a start."

"Okay. What movie?" Kevin asked suspiciously. "Not another of those violent, blood and gore things. The last one had no plot."

"Of course it had a plot. It also had that hunky Jean-Claude van Damme in it. That alone was worth the price of admission."

Kevin sighed at the thought of his aunt having fantasies about an action-movie superstar. "I worry about you, you know that."

"Why? Just because I can appreciate a hunk when I see one?" She regarded him with another of those sly looks.

"Bet that Gracie MacDougal can, too. I saw her looking at you, you know. Little wonder, given the way you dress."

Since they'd had the discussion about the way he dressed about a hundred times, he seized on her revelation about Gracie MacDougal.

"She was checking me out?"

"Ogling you, in fact. You let her catch another glimpse or two, you can probably drive up her offer on that house by another fifty thousand."

Kevin stared at her, astounded by her suggestion. "Why don't I just sleep with her?" he grumbled. "Maybe then she'd fork over another hundred thousand."

Despite his facetious tone, Aunt Delia took him seriously. "Nope, I think building anticipation is a better approach. You'll have her so muddle-headed, she won't know what she's doing. Once you've gone to bed with a person, nothing much is left to the imagination."

Kevin thought of Gracie MacDougal's singleminded negotiations earlier. "I think you may be underestimating her, Aunt Delia. I doubt she's distracted easily. She's a tough cookie."

She feigned shock. "Don't tell me you're scared of her."

"Scared? Who said anything about being scared?"

"Well, then, don't let any grass grow under your feet. Get busy and reel her in, boy."

Kevin had a feeling they weren't talking entirely about a real estate transaction now. "I'll see Gracie MacDougal again in my own good time. In the meantime, you do some serious thinking about whether you're really ready to sell that house to her or anybody else. We've had other offers in the past and you haven't been interested. In fact, you chased that last man off with threats of bodily harm a lady shouldn't even know about. Made my blood run cold."

"Times change. People change."

"Not overnight they don't."

"Okay, okay, if it'll make you happy, I'll think about it.

You set up an appointment with that MacDougal gal for to-morrow. Invite her to have lunch with us at the races."

"Not on your life."

"Coward."

"Bossy old lady."

She chuckled. "You'll call."

"Will not."

But he did. He told himself he didn't do it because he wanted to. He swore to himself he did it only to satisfy his aunt. He was more relieved than he could say when he got an answering machine. The sound of Gracie's voice, all prim and prissy, did astonishing things to his pulse, which just proved beyond a shadow of a doubt why he needed to conduct this negotiation—if there was to be one—very, very carefully. Otherwise he, not Aunt Delia, would be the one giving the house away.

In the end, he didn't leave a message and he didn't call again. Might have been stubbornness. Aunt Delia certainly would have called it that. More likely, it was just plain good sense kicking in in the nick of time.

Aunt Delia looked around the smoke-filled Riverboat with its banks of TV screens with absolute delight.

"Get me a *Racing Form,*" she ordered Kevin. "And hurry up. I don't want to miss the first race."

Aunt Delia had been spry as a young chicken ever since she'd hatched this plot to get him and Gracie MacDougal together, Kevin noticed. She was bossier than usual, too.

The truth was, though, he enjoyed matching wits with her. Nobody had ever put anything over on his aunt. She'd remained unmarried by choice, claiming that there wasn't a man around who could tolerate the fact that she was smarter than he was. Kevin had the distinct impression, though, that that hadn't stopped her from having a few serious male friends over the years. She was too darned savvy about relationships not to have been through a few herself. Not that she'd ever admit it. She'd go to her grave implying that she was as innocent as a newborn babe. But the twinkle in her eyes when Kevin suggested otherwise proved his point.

"Five races, that's it," he said, as he handed her the *Racing Form*. "I'm not letting you wager your life savings today."

"What if I win? Do we stay longer?"

"We'll discuss that when—*no, if*—it happens."

"Then keep quiet and let me do my handicapping in peace," she said, snapping open the paper to the day's races in New York.

Kevin sat back and sipped his beer. For a weekday, the Riverboat had a modest crowd, including a few locals and quite a few unfamiliar faces in town just for the chance to bet on races at tracks across the country. Some of them would be here until the last race ran in California hours from now.

He wondered how Gracie would react to this simple place out over the water with its basic menu, plain tables, and noisy patrons. He'd lay odds if she'd ever placed a wager it had been in some elegant casino in Europe. She'd probably been wearing diamonds and satin at the time, looking all slinky and sophisticated. An image of Grace Kelly in *Philadelphia Story* came to mind.

"Is it hot in here?" he asked suddenly.

"I hadn't noticed," Aunt Delia mumbled.

She barely glanced up from her papers. A little furrow of concentration lined her brow. Her reading glasses had slipped to the tip of her nose. Kevin observed her with tolerant amusement, laughing out loud when he noticed that she'd worn her fancy white sneakers with the rhinestones on them in honor of their outing. She was such a joy. It truly was a shame no man had seen that and dared to take her on for a lifetime.

"It's four minutes till post time," Kevin reminded her. "Have you made up your mind?"

She nabbed a little slip of paper from the pile beside her

and jotted down some numbers. "A trifecta," she announced. "In this order. Don't mess it up. I've put a lot of thought into getting it right."

"I won't mess it up."

"What about you? You planning to bet?"

"I thought I'd put a little down on that number eight."

Aunt Delia hurriedly glanced at her notes, scribbled all over the past performance listings. "Eight? That horse will go off at fifty-to-one. Why that one?"

"The name reminds me of someone," he said, and walked away.

"Scottish Lass," she murmured.

The sound of her laughter followed him over to the betting window.

"I just don't understand it," Aunt Delia complained after Kevin finally managed to drag her away after the eighth race. "That three horse was sired by a distance runner. His mama had speed. He should have blasted past every other horse on the track."

"Maybe he was a little too taken with that mare swishing her tail in his face in the homestretch. Hormones will distract a male."

"So I've noticed," his aunt retorted. "Are you planning to swing by the house?"

"I wasn't. Why?"

"There's something I left in that old bureau upstairs. I'd like to get it, as long as we're already in the vicinity."

"I thought you cleaned out every bureau and closet before you moved in with me."

"Well, I forgot this. Sue me."

"Okay, okay. We'll go by the house."

"Thank you," she said with a bite of sarcasm.

"You're welcome," he replied with the same edge.

Kevin knew there was something more going on with his

aunt than some forgotten personal item she couldn't do without. He had walked through every inch of that house with her a dozen times to be sure nothing of real or sentimental value had been left behind. No, she was up to something, but for the life of him he couldn't figure out what.

He began to get a worrisome idea when he noticed that the wrought-iron gate was unlatched. But how had Aunt Delia guessed that there might be a trespasser on the property, particularly the trespasser Kevin's gut told him was at this very moment trampling down weeds?

"Looks like someone's here, doesn't it?" his aunt said, not sounding especially surprised or worried by that fact.

"Probably kids," Kevin retorted, though he didn't believe any such thing. More than likely it was Ms. Gracie Mac-Dougal, up to no good. Kids were scared to death of the place. He'd planted several hints that the old house was crawling with ghosts. Kids hadn't been near it since, according to the neighbors who kept an eye on it for him. They huddled outside the gate, occasionally slipped inside and went as far as the front step on a dare. But at the first creak of the old, rotting wood, they dashed for safety.

No, the only person with the curiosity and the pure gall to be sneaking around was Gracie.

"Go visit Mrs. Johnson," he instructed his aunt.

"Why on earth would I want to do that? You know she hates people dropping by unexpectedly."

"Not as much as I hate the prospect of both of us getting clobbered over the head with something if we're wrong about what's going on here. Please, just apologize and stay with her until I come for you."

"You think it's that MacDougal girl, don't you? And you don't want me to meet her."

"Okay, yes. I think it's probably Gracie. And I don't want you to meet her. What puzzles me is how the heck you knew she'd be sneaking around here."

"Me?" she protested. "I've been with you all day. How

could I know anything? I resent you thinking I would do something sneaky and lowdown like luring you over here just so you could bump into her again."

Which, of course, was a little too emphatic and detailed a denial not to be the exact opposite of the truth.

"We'll discuss your scheming later," he said. "Just go see Mrs. Johnson and stay there."

"Fine," she said with an indignant little huff and headed off toward her longtime neighbor's house.

Kevin watched her departure with admiration. She was quite an actress. The local theater group could have used her skills in their recent production of *Arsenic and Old Lace*.

Once he saw that Mrs. Johnson was, indeed, home and had invited his aunt inside, he stepped through the open gate into Aunt Delia's yard. It really was a disgrace, he conceded, though at the moment the tall grass, dandelions, and butter-cups allowed him to pinpoint exactly which way the intruder had gone. He turned to the left and followed the trampled weeds.

He'd give Gracie MacDougal credit for being brazen. She'd probably found a way inside and was already measur-ing for curtains.

The path she'd left took him around the back of the house. Sure enough, it stopped right beside the steps to the glassed-in back porch, which his aunt alternately described as her sunroom or her garden room. Once it had been filled with pots of blooming plants, but now those very same plants were decorating her parlor at his place. He'd had to knock out a whole damned wall practically and replace it with win-dows until the lighting suited her and her philodendrons, or whatever the hell they were.

Of course, at the moment, that was neither here nor there. At the moment, he needed to figure out exactly where his quarry had slipped off to. It didn't look as though she'd bro-ken in. Every window was intact and the door was firmly closed. He tested the lock and it held. So where the dickens was she? Surely she hadn't vanished into thin air.

Suddenly his eye caught a glimpse of bright yellow where it had no business being, right on the bottom branch of the oak tree shading the side of the house. He shimmied up the tree and reached for the scrap of cloth. Silk, either from a blouse or a scarf. It was a nice, sunny shade, too, perfect for Ms. MacDougal's coloring. He'd bet she looked like a million bucks when she'd left home. He wondered if she looked half as good now that she'd scaled a tree and shredded her clothing.

He glanced up a little higher and saw what had attracted her. The second-floor window was wide open. He had left it cracked himself, to allow some air to stir in the place and keep it from getting musty. It had never occurred to him that anyone, not even the neighborhood kids, would spot it and break in. But, then, he hadn't known about Gracie MacDougal a few months ago.

Kevin considered scrambling down and using his key to go in the back door, but concluded that would be a tactical mistake. Though she probably didn't know it yet, Gracie was trapped inside. All the doors had deadbolt locks requiring keys to open them from inside or out. If he entered the same way she had, he could corner her and scare the living daylights out of her. Or he could save himself the trouble and just wait for her under the tree. Either way, he hoped it would be a good lesson.

After a few minutes waiting, he opted for joining her inside. Grateful that he'd worn sneakers, he climbed the rest of the way up the tree, stepped onto the porch roof, then tiptoed over to the open window. Whether she'd heard the commotion outside and decided to beat a hasty retreat or whether she'd simply completed her unauthorized tour, Gracie picked that precise moment to try to back out of the window.

Kevin paused and enjoyed the view for several seconds before asking quietly, "Going someplace?"

She rose up too fast and whacked her back on the edge of the window, let out a muffled exclamation, then hesitated as if torn between going back inside or completing her ignominious exit. He heard her heavy sigh of resignation. Then she backed the rest of the way out.

"Fancy meeting you here," Kevin said when she was standing toe to toe with him, her expression defiant, the bottom edge of her yellow blouse ragged where she'd snagged it.

"You scared me half to death," she retorted. "How dare you creep up on a person like that!"

"Excuse me? You're not exactly in the best position to be hurling accusations at anybody."

"I saw the window was open and I thought someone might have broken in," she said.

Kevin was impressed. She hadn't wasted a single second coming up with an explanation, even though on close examination it defied logic. "You're quick on your feet, I'll give you that. Did you consider calling the cops?"

Color crept up in her cheeks. "Not exactly."

"Or shouting for Mrs. Johnson to call the cops?"

"No."

"No, you decided to investigate all on your own."

"It seemed like the neighborly thing to do," she insisted, her expression daring him to question her motives. "Besides, you didn't call the cops or tell Mrs. Johnson to call them, did you? No. You did exactly what I did."

"Because I was just about one hundred percent sure who was inside," he said.

"It's the tiny one percent of uncertainty that will get you killed," she pointed out.

"A fact you'd do well to remember," he retorted. "Honestly, Gracie, if you wanted a tour of the place, all you had to do was ask."

She regarded him skeptically. "Would you have taken me through the house?"

"No. What would be the point, when the owner's not prepared to sell?"

"If I liked what I saw, maybe I'd up my offer so it would be irresistible."

"You can't go that high."

"You know absolutely nothing about my financial situation."

"Want to bet?"

"Meaning?"

"We live in the computer age, Gracie. It isn't hard to get a line on someone's credit rating."

She stared at him with stunned disbelief. "You investigated me?"

"Of course."

"Why, you no good, rotten scum. How could you? You don't even know me."

"Precisely the point of an investigation, wouldn't you say?"

"Oh, go to hell."

"Darlin', that's no way to win over an adversary."

She sighed and looked at him with those huge, golden-flecked eyes. "Is that what you are, an adversary?"

"When it comes to selling you this house, yes. On the other hand," he began and allowed a fascinated gaze to slide over her, "I can think of all sorts of other subjects about which we could get downright friendly. Care to discuss them over supper?"

"You're inviting me to dinner?"

"Sure. Why not?"

"But you won't discuss the house with me?"

"That's right. The topic's off limits."

"Then I can't imagine what we'd have left to discuss."

"Use your obviously fertile imagination. I'm sure you'll think of something. Call me when you do."

With that, Kevin stepped to the edge of the porch roof and lowered himself to the ground. When he glanced up, he saw Gracie staring after him incredulously.

"You're leaving me up here?"

"You got up there all by yourself. Surely, you know the way down. Call me when you've decided about supper."

"Kevin Patrick Daniels, don't you dare walk away and leave me up here."

"Later, darlin'."

"Kevin, dammit! Come hack here."

He waited around the corner of the house until he heard the rustle of leaves and the creak of branches in the oak tree. When he heard her thud to the ground with a muttered curse, he grinned, then hightailed it between the hedges and into Mrs. Johnson's yard.

Safely hidden by the high boxwoods, he was still chuckling to himself when Gracie stormed off down the sidewalk as if someone had lit a fire under her. Since he knew perfectly well that his aunt and Mrs. Johnson had watched the entire drama unfold, he could hardly wait to hear how the local gossips would manage to twist the story.

Five

"Of all of the lousy, rotten, lowdown things to do," Gracie muttered as she charged down the street toward her own house. "I could have broken my stupid neck getting down from there, but did he care? Oh, no. And whoever heard of putting deadbolts on all the doors? That's the first thing that'll go when the house is mine. I can't have a houseful of guests all trapped inside. Didn't he ever stop to think what could happen in a fire?"

Of course not, she thought, answering her own question. He obviously wasn't the kind of man to put a lot of thought into anything. Otherwise he'd never have left her up on that roof, where she could slip, break her neck, and then sue the pants off him.

She ignored the fact that she was the one who'd climbed up on that roof to sneak into the house in the first place. He hadn't lured her up there. Even so, a gentleman would have helped her get down. Kevin Patrick Daniels was the lowest form of pond scum, an insensitive, inconsiderate jerk. She wouldn't have supper with the man if he promised to fly it in from Paris.

Not that she wouldn't enjoy a little pâté de fois gras about now. Maybe some escargots or the local seafood, for that matter. She was tiring of fastfood hamburgers and scrambled eggs. She might have managed some of the finest kitchens in all of Europe, but her own culinary skills were sadly lack-

ing. Why cook when she could eat gourmet cuisine every
night free?

Actually, that was the one sticking point in this bed-and-
breakfast idea. If her guests ate food she'd prepared, they'd
probably die within hours. They'd certainly never come back
again.

Well, if there was one thing she was good at it, it was
hiring the best chefs available. She wondered exactly what
caliber of chef she could get on a shoestring budget. Maybe
it wouldn't hurt to see if the bookshop in town had a few
decent cookbooks, just in case. How difficult could it be to
master a few breakfast selections?

Not until she'd slammed into her house and poured herself
a very large glass of iced tea did she stop to consider the
pure coincidence of Kevin Patrick Daniels showing up at
that house at the same time she had. Now that she thought
about it, it didn't make a lick of sense. It was obvious from
that overgrown tangle of weeds she'd traipsed through that
he never came near the place, so why today?

She thought back to the call she'd had earlier, from a Mrs.
Johnson. In a quavery voice, the woman had said she feared
there was someone inside the Daniels house next door to her.
Supposedly she'd checked with other neighbors and no one
had been home to investigate. Would Gracie mind coming
over?

Naive jerk that she was, she hadn't recognized a set-up.
In fact, she'd jumped at the chance to have a legitimate reason
for poking around on the property. Now, belatedly, she realized there was no logical reason on earth for Mrs. Johnson
to have called on her. They didn't even know each other,
though she supposed by now everyone in town at least had
some idea of her name and where she lived. Still, if Mrs.
Johnson had been truly worried about an intruder, it would
have made far more sense to call the police than to call a
woman she'd never even met.

Which suggested to Gracie that Mrs. Johnson had been

motivated by something other than concern for her neighbor's property. Gracie's guess, with the twenty-twenty vision
of hindsight, was that Mrs. Johnson had wanted her to be
caught by Kevin. But why? Had she been in cahoots with
someone? The answer to that eluded her.

Maybe the woman was just old and housebound and bored.
Maybe she was just plain sneaky and conniving. Or maybe
Gracie's imagination was running away with her and Kevin's
arrival was a coincidence, after all.

Gracie didn't much believe in coincidences.

She did believe that Kevin Patrick Daniels was not above
using an old lady to do his dirty work. Maybe he was the
one who'd suggested Mrs. Johnson lure her there with that
cockamamie story of an intruder.

But why? She was back to that again. That was the sixty-
four-thousand-dollar question. He hadn't looked especially
pleased to find her there. He hadn't even looked triumphant,
as if he'd caught her in an act he could hold over her head.
He'd looked . . . amused, as if she'd fulfilled his expectations
in some way. He'd dangled that patch of yellow silk in front
of her as if it were surprise evidence in a trial.

While she was still trying to puzzle it out, the phone rang.
It was Max again. It had to be. Since she'd interceded with
the florist, he'd called twice more to get her to smooth over
the pastry chef's ruffled features and to ask which plumber
in town to call to fix a clogged drain. He probably figured
she'd see sooner or later that she was desperately needed and
come back to France without him having to beg.

Actually, the prospect of supercilious Max Devereaux begging cheered Gracie considerably The prospect of caving in
and going back to Worldwide Hotels did not. She let the
answering machine pick up, then smiled with satisfaction
when she heard Max's muttered oath, then the irritated crash
of the phone. She could practically see his exasperated expression as he realized he was going to have to deal with
whatever crisis it was this time without her assistance.

Okay, so it was only a tiny step toward distancing herself from Max and Worldwide, but it was a step. If she intended to take a giant leap toward a new life, it meant dealing with Kevin Patrick Daniels, she concluded with a sigh of resignation. Telling her no had been tantamount to throwing down the gauntlet. She wouldn't let up now until that house was hers. She'd worry about the details of running a bed and breakfast later.

Perhaps supper wouldn't be such a bad idea. Perhaps if they managed to get through it without skewering each other with the silverware, she could discover his greatest weakness and use it to get that neglected old Victorian away from him.

Reluctantly, she dialed his number. The phone rang and rang before he grabbed it up.

"Hey, Gracie," he said, as if he'd been as sure of her call as she'd been of Max's.

"How'd you know . . . Never mind. Caller I.D., I presume."

He chuckled. "Nope, lucky guesswork. Maybe a little wishful thinking."

She ignored that. "About dinner?"

"What time shall I pick you up?"

"Did I say yes?"

"You wouldn't be calling if you weren't going to say yes," he said reasonably. "Seven o'clock. How does that sound?"

"You mean you don't already know?"

"Darlin', sarcasm doesn't suit you. Settle down or you'll ruin your digestion."

"You let me worry about my digestion," she said grimly, already regretting her decision to call. "Seven will be fine."

"Dress casual. We're going for crabs and it's going to be messy.

"What if I don't like crabs?"

"Then it must mean you've never had 'em here. See you soon."

He hung up, which was just as well since she didn't have a smart retort to his confident comment.

She dressed in the most casual outfit she owned, linen pants and an expensive, starched cotton blouse. Kevin shook his head when he saw her.

"What's wrong?"

"Don't you own a T-shirt and some jeans?"

"No."

"We'll stop at the bargain store."

"Kevin, I'm not buying a cheap T-shirt to go to dinner. I'm not a messy eater."

"Whatever you say. I suppose it'll give the dry cleaner in town some business."

Gracie scowled. She set out to hate the crabs. She really did. But the next thing she knew she was up to her elbows in shells and butter and sweet, rich crabmeat. Kevin was right. She'd never had anything quite like them before.

He was also right about the T-shirt. There was no tidy way to eat the crabs. Picking them was messy and slow, but the reward was wonderful. There was also a certain amount of stress reduction in wielding that mallet she'd been given. Kevin, to his credit, didn't give her a single reason to want to use it on his head. Of course, the conversation had been mostly limited to his patient explanation of the best way to go about getting all the crabmeat out of the shells.

When there was a mound of red shells in front of her and she'd emptied two bottles of the locally produced ginger ale, Gracie sat back with a sigh of pure contentment.

"Enjoy yourself?" Kevin asked.

"Oh, my yes."

"Told you so."

"Are you one of those annoying men who has to be right about everything?"

"I don't have to be, but I usually am." He grinned at her.

"How about dessert? Homemade pie, maybe? There's almost any kind you could want."

"Not a chance," she insisted. She looked at the pile of shells in front of him. It was at least double her own. "What about you?"

"I wouldn't miss a slice of the strawberry pie. Are you sure you won't change your mind?"

"Absolutely."

"You'll be sorry," he warned.

Gracie couldn't imagine ever being hungry again. "I don't think so."

Naturally, though, when the pie came, with its huge strawberries and its whipped cream topping, her mouth began to water. Kevin took a first bite and then a second, before glancing her way and grinning.

"Change your mind?"

She scowled at him. "Yes, dammit."

"You want a bite of this or your own slice?"

The thought of sharing whipped-cream-coated strawberries with Kevin aroused images that were way too provocative. "I want one all my own," she said quickly.

His knowing expression made her regret her decision. "Never mind. I'll share yours."

Still grinning, he stabbed a huge strawberry, made sure it was dipped in the whipped cream and held it out. When Gracie reached for the fork, he shook his head. His gaze locked with hers as he waited for her to take a bite.

Two could play at that game. Swallowing hard, Gracie reached out a hand to cover his and hold the fork steady. She was pretty sure his skin heated a good ten degrees at the contact. She oh-so-slowly licked every trace of cream off the berry, then bit into the sweet, juicy flesh. By then there was no mistaking the rapid acceleration of his breathing. She ran her tongue over her lips.

"That was—"

"Exhilarating?" Kevin suggested, that amused expression firmly back in place.

"I was going to say wonderful," she contradicted.

"Same difference"

Gracie didn't like the gleam in his eye or the direction of the conversation.

"About the house—"

"Off limits," he reminded her.

"But—"

"Ms. MacDougal, surely you are not so conversationally challenged that that's the only thing you can think of to talk about."

"It's all we have in common."

"You don't know that."

"Mr. Daniels, I'm a workaholic. As near as I can tell, you avoid anything remotely resembling work. All you do is laze around in a hammock."

"I'm surprised at you. Don't you know appearances can be deceiving."

"I doubt it in this instance. The state of that house proves my point."

He sighed heavily. "We're back to that again. I'm beginning to think you don't have a very vivid imagination."

"My imagination is just fine."

"One-track mind then?"

"I have a lot of varied interests."

"Name one," he challenged.

Gracie desperately searched for something unrelated to the hotel industry or at least something that could be perceived as unrelated.

"Flowers," she said finally. "I love flowers."

Kevin looked skeptical. "You do much gardening?"

"I didn't say I gardened. I said I like flowers."

"Looking at them, smelling them, what?"

"Mr. Daniels, this isn't getting us anywhere."

"Sure it is, darlin'. We're getting to know each other."

"But I don't want to get to know you," she said.

"Then you have a lot to learn about business. It always pays to know the man sitting across the desk from you when you're doing a deal."

"As if I'd take business advice from you," she muttered.

"Maybe you should. You might learn a few things." He leaned back and looked her over as if assessing her. "For example, I already know that for the past eight years you've devoted all your energy to Worldwide Hotels, that you've left your job, that you're at loose ends, and that you want to turn that old Victorian into a bed and breakfast. That makes you anxious to deal, which improves my odds of getting top dollar for that house, assuming I decide to sell."

Gracie's heart sank. He was right. He had done his homework and she hadn't. She'd assessed and labeled him based on a single meeting and concluded she could wear him down eventually by throwing more and more money at him. She wasn't even taking advantage of this dinner to pump him for information or to search for any weaknesses she could exploit in her own behalf.

"Okay, Mr. Daniels, why don't you tell me a little about yourself?"

He chuckled at that. "No way. I'm not making it that easy on you. If you want information, you're going to have to work for it."

"Dammit, can't you just give me a straight answer?"

"Sure," he said agreeably. "As soon as you ask me a straight question."

Gracie sighed.

"Relax, darlin'. This won't be half as painful as you're anticipating."

"It's already way past painful. It's excruciating."

"You must not have gone on many dates, Gracie."

"What makes you say that?" she asked, instantly defensive.

"If you don't mind my saying so, you're not very good at small talk," he observed.

The accusation stung. She'd heard it before. She could see to the comfort of hundreds of hotel guests a month, but she couldn't make small talk with a man sitting across the dinner table from her. How many times had she been told she was too serious, too focused, too uptight? More times than she could count. The only reason she and Max had gotten along halfway decently was that he'd had a singletrack mind as well.

It was ironic that she was so good with the hotel staff, so deft at handling the vendors who supplied everything from soap to mushrooms. She made it a point to learn and remember little details about all of them, so she could ask about family members, favorite hobbies, whatever. Obviously she needed to apply the same skill to Kevin.

"Okay, let's start over," she suggested. "Tell me about your family. Any brothers or sisters?"

He took another sip of the same beer he'd been nursing all evening. "Nope."

"Parents alive?"

"Nope."

"You rattle around in that big old house all by yourself?"

"Nope."

Gracie fought her exasperation. His deliberate, single-word responses were not going to derail her attempts to get to know him. She was just going to have to become more clever at phrasing her questions.

"Who lives there with you?" A horrifying thought struck her. "Your wife?"

He grinned at that. "It's a little late to be panicking that I might be married, don't you think? We're already well on our way to getting downright intimate."

Gracie choked on a sip of ginger ale. She stared at him. "Are you crazy?"

"Nope."

"Would you stop that?"

"What?"

"Saying *nope* to everything I ask."

"If it'll make you happy."

"It will make me deliriously happy." She frowned at him. "Just don't go getting any wild ideas about the two of us, okay?"

"Sweetheart, I've been getting ideas about the two of us since you walked into my yard yesterday. I can't help it. It's just my nature."

"Well, put a lid on it."

"I'll do my best, but it won't be easy."

"Try." She worked to keep a pleading note out of her voice. "Now can I assume that there is no wife in the picture?"

"If it makes you happy."

"Kevin!"

"Okay, no wife. Not now. Not ever."

Because he sounded so fierce about it, she couldn't help taunting, "How come? Are you gay?"

That got him. He sputtered indignantly for a full minute before laughing. "Okay, you got me. I'll try to give you straight answers from now on."

"No pun intended?"

"Be still my heart," Kevin said with exaggerated astonishment. "The lady made a joke."

"You know, it's a wonder someone hasn't murdered you by now," she muttered. "Do you take anything seriously?"

"You'd be surprised at just how seriously I'm considering kissing you right now."

"Kevin!"

He grinned. "What's the matter? Hasn't anyone ever wanted to kiss you before?"

"I have been kissed plenty," she retorted, then regretted allowing herself to be drawn into such a ridiculous discussion.

"Care to do a little comparison test?" he inquired.

"I don't think so."

"How else will you know what you're missing?"

She drew herself up and declared primly, "In my experience, men who have to ask permission aren't very good at it."

He chuckled at that. "I'll remember that. Something tells me that catching you off guard might take a while, but it'll be worth waiting for."

The warning—or promise?—made her tremble. No man had affected her like this in a very long time. Why this man? she wondered irritably. She didn't even like him very much. He was annoying. He lacked ambition. He had absolutely no understanding of the rules of decorum. She might be overdressed, but the same surely couldn't be said for him. His jeans were marginally less revealing than the first pair she'd seen him wear, but his T-shirt looked as if he'd grabbed it out of the dryer.

All in all, she suspected that Kevin took his greatest pleasure in flouting rules of any kind.

So why was her gaze locked on his mouth? Why was she already imagining the feel of his lips on hers? Why was she guessing that he kissed with a kind of no-holds-barred lack of restraint?

Probably because that was exactly what he'd intended, she realized. He'd deliberately, sneakily, planted the notion in her head, then waited for her imagination to run with it. She wasn't wild about the all-too-vivid, X-rated results.

"Is it too warm in here?" Kevin asked mildly. "You look a little flushed."

"I'm fine," Gracie declared, gritting her teeth. Or she would be, if she could just gulp down a couple of glasses of ice water. Her last sip of ginger ale had done nothing to soothe her suddenly parched throat.

She was not going to let him see that he'd rattled her,

though. She forced a brilliant smile. "It's been an absolutely fascinating evening, Kevin. Thank you so much."

"In a hurry to get home all of a sudden?" he inquired in that lazy manner of his.

"No, of course not. I just don't want to take up too much of your time."

"Darlin', I have all the time in the world. You need to loosen up a bit, learn to relax, slow down."

"And do what?" she asked with genuine curiosity, unaware until too late how revealing the question was.

"Read a book. Stare at the sky and watch the clouds roll by. Go fishing. Pick daisies. Whatever comes to mind."

The last book Gracie had read was on hotel management. The only time she gazed at the sky was to check for rain. Her idea of fishing was a visit to the market to buy the day's catch. Obviously she had a lot to learn.

She sighed and caught the flash of amusement in Kevin's eyes.

"Don't know how, huh?" he said sympathetically.

"Afraid not."

"How come? Strict parents?"

"No, they just wanted me to have more than they'd had. They stressed the importance of education and hard work."

"What about family vacations?"

"Just one," she recalled wistfully. "Right here, as a matter of fact."

"Is that why you came here when you quit your job?"

Gracie nodded. "It was the last place I could remember being totally carefree."

"I guess you've gotten out of the habit since then."

"You could say that," she said, thinking of the sixteen-hour days she put in at the hotel, three hundred sixty-five days a year. No wonder Max missed her. She'd been a blasted machine, operating on automatic for years now. She hadn't just burned out. She'd incinerated.

"Don't worry. This problem isn't life-threatening," Kevin

reassured her. "I can have it corrected in a few weeks, tops. I'll give it my undivided attention."

Gracie was sorely tempted to give in. It might he nice to learn to play. It might be especially nice to be taught by an expert.

It would also be dangerous. Kevin Patrick Daniels rattled her. In no time at all, she might forget all about the house she wanted to buy so she could start a new life.

"Thanks anyway," she said. "I'm content with my life just the way it is."

He shrugged. "Whatever you say, sweetheart, but that wistful expression on your face suggests otherwise."

The man was entirely too intuitive where she was concerned. It made her nervous. If only she could read him as well. She was beginning to get the uncomfortable feeling that she'd sold him short, that there were depths to Kevin Patrick Daniels she hadn't even begun to see. Underestimating an adversary was very risky, indeed. She'd approached this whole project far too impulsively, just as Kevin had suggested earlier. She needed time to reassess, do a little of her own research.

She was competitive and driven by nature. She had foolishly assumed that getting her hands on that old Victorian gem was going to be a snap. Now she knew otherwise. Her blood raced in anticipation of the all-out battle ahead.

"Why the smile?" Kevin asked.

"Nothing," she assured him. She wondered how he'd react if he knew she'd been envisioning the day when she managed to steal that house right out from under him.

Six

There were a lot of provocative things about Gracie that Kevin couldn't forget during a long, restless night, but one particular thing lingered in the morning. He couldn't imagine a life as singlemindedly focused on career as hers had apparently been. Not that all work and little play had made her dull, but he'd never known anyone more in need of shaking up.

Fortunately, he'd grown very adept over the years at making the impulsive gesture, at doing the unexpected, at seizing the moment. Perhaps it was his way of compensating for the amount of responsibility that had been heaped on his shoulders. He'd been determined never to let it weigh him down. He'd learned to steal every minute he could for himself.

Plus, he'd discovered that it gave him a certain advantage over his more uptight competitors, whether in business or for the affections of some woman. Business opponents often misinterpreted his devil-may-care attitude for a lack of attention. Women simply enjoyed the spontaneity he brought into their lives.

After a rigorous workout in the gym he'd had installed off his bedroom, he showered and went down to the dining room to give the matter some more thought over his regular breakfast of scrambled eggs and country ham. He figured the workout just about balanced the cholesterol intake.

"You're on the go early," his housekeeper noted as she set

his plate in front of him. "You going to Richmond for business meetings?"

"Not today, Molly."

"Couldn't sleep, then?" She studied him worriedly. "Is something on your mind?"

He grinned ruefully at the woman who'd been watching out for him since he was barely toddling around the house. She was plump from too much of her own country cooking and unrepentantly gray-haired with curls like corkscrews, thanks to the home perms with which she periodically stunk up the whole house. No one on earth, though, had a bigger heart.

"Someone," he conceded with some reluctance, knowing exactly where the admission would lead.

Her expression brightened. "A woman?" she asked as she pulled out a chair and sat down opposite him. "Tell me."

"Not a chance. You're a worse meddler than Aunt Delia."

"I'll bet it's that pretty little thing who was here day before yesterday," she concluded without so much as a hint from him.

"How on earth did you know about her? It was your day off. I know for a fact that you were visiting your son in Washington."

"People talk."

"Aunt Delia, I suppose."

"She seems to think this one might have staying power."

"Aunt Delia needs to learn to mind her own business."

"She says you went out with her again last night."

"We had dinner, not an orgy."

Her gaze narrowed. "Watch your tongue. I don't want to hear about any orgies you might be having."

"I'm not having any," he protested, then gave up. "Tell me something."

Her expression instantly turned serious. "If I can."

"If you wanted a woman to learn to take time out to smell the flowers, what would you do? Send her roses?"

"Never," she declared at once. "Too ordinary." Her expression turned dreamy. "If I had the money, which you do, I'd plant a whole garden for her."

"You can't be serious." He studied her expression. "You are serious, aren't you?"

"Of course. If she has her own garden, she can't help but take the time to smell the flowers. And every time she does, you'll be on her mind."

Kevin chuckled at the logic. "Perfect. Molly, you are a treasure."

"Well, of course I am." She stood up and started for the kitchen, then paused. "One other thing, though."

"What's that?" Kevin asked distractedly, already making plans.

"Do the planting yourself. Don't go hiring somebody to do it."

"Molly, I don't have time to plant a garden, to say nothing of the fact that I don't have the first clue how to go about it. Besides, it sounds an awful lot like hot, sweaty work."

"A little sweat won't kill you. As for the rest, talk to Mr. Sparks. He can tell you what to do. He's been landscaping this place for fifty years. Keeps it looking like a showplace, if you ask me."

There was a note of defiant pride in her voice that caught his attention. "It sounds as if you admire Mr. Sparks."

She blushed furiously. "Well, of course I do. He does fine work."

"I was thinking of a more personal sort of admiration."

"Oh, get on with your foolishness. I'm too old for what you're suggesting."

"Molly, you'll always be young. That's your nature. Raymond walked off and left you on your own with those two sons of yours thirty years ago. You did a fine job of raising them, better than anyone in my family's done with their kids, that's for sure. If you're interested in Mr. Sparks, go for it.

He's been a widower for some time now. He'd probably appreciate an invitation to dinner every now and again."

"I couldn't," she protested.

"Of course you could. Do you know a finer cook in all of Westmoreland County?"

"No, but—"

"Ask him, Molly. If you don't, I'll put a bug in his ear about you."

"If you do, Kevin Patrick Daniels, I'll take a switch to the seat of your britches the way I used to. Given how threadbare they are, it'll hurt worse now than it did back then."

"Don't make threats you can't follow up on," he teased.

"I'm quicker now than I used to be." His expression sobered. "Ask him, Molly. I know he's spending a lot more time here than he needs to. There must be a reason for that, and I'm guessing that you're it."

"He does stop in for lemonade at the end of the day," she confessed.

"Well, then, next time he does, just ask him to stay on for supper."

She grinned. "Maybe I will. In the meantime, you ask him about planting that garden. He'll tell you what to do. He probably has everything you need in his greenhouse."

Before he could get on with his plan, though, Kevin had paperwork to finish up and a not unexpected visit from his cousin Helen. She almost always turned up after one of his more contentious encounters with her younger brother. Bobby Ray was a whiner and Helen always listened.

"Kevin, what on earth did you say to Bobby Ray the other day?" she demanded without so much as a greeting to preface it. "He's on the warpath. He thinks we should all hire an attorney to sue you for our money and an accountant to do an audit."

Kevin sighed. They'd been through this so many times, he had his response memorized. "If you want to waste your money that way, go right ahead. You know the terms of your father's will as well as I do. They're iron-clad. I ought to know. I've been hunting for a loophole to get out of it myself for years."

"As for an audit," he continued, "I provide you with one every year. You all pick the accountant, I don't."

"I know all that," she said dismissively. "So does Bobby Ray. What did you do to set him off?"

"I'm amazed he didn't tell you."

"Well, of course he did. I want to hear your version."

"I refused to give him the money for another one of his schemes."

Helen sighed. "I should have guessed he hadn't just asked for a piddly little advance on his trust funds. What was it this time? A hamburger franchise next to McDonald's?"

"Not quite that bad. I believe this one was a jewelry designer he wanted to back on one of those cable shopping channels."

"Must be that designer Sara Lynn is sleeping with."

Kevin held up his hands to ward off a full-blown discussion of the tale. "I don't want to know," he said emphatically. His opinion of Sara Lynn was low enough without fresh gossip.

"You're right. You don't. If Bobby Ray ever managed to marry the right woman, he might be able to get his life on track. He's not a bad person," she said in defense of her younger brother.

"Nobody ever said he was. And he was married to the right person: Marianne. He has a terrific kid. None of that's enough for him."

"He just needs a sense of direction, a goal."

"I agree. Maybe he could start by being a halfway decent father to Abby."

"You know he doesn't know how. Look at the example he had. Can't you help him, Kev? That's why Father left you in charge, you know. He thought you could straighten all of us out the same way you've been handling Uncle Bo and his brood."

"I doubt Dr. Joyce Brothers and a team of her peers could straighten all of you out. Your father knew that. He just wanted to keep you financially stable."

He regarded his older cousin fondly. Of all of them, Helen did have a head on her shoulders. She was brassy and pushy and, like her sister, a little too free with her credit cards, but she was insightful about human nature. She'd made the one solid marriage of all of them, to a man who had indulged her every whim. Maybe that was why she was also the only one who wasn't on Kevin's case about money all the time. Her husband had provided all she required, then left her with a nice insurance settlement when he'd died in a tragic boating accident a few years back.

"We are a dysfunctional lot, aren't we?" she said. "And you're right. We can thank Father for that. He never encouraged us do a thing for ourselves. He bailed us out of every single jam we got into. He bought Bobby Ray's college diploma by promising the school a new liberal arts building. Then he wondered why none of us took responsibility for our actions."

Kevin had given a lot of thought to his uncle's handling of his five children. With a little guidance from Aunt Delia, he'd finally reached a conclusion. "Maybe bailing you out was the only way Uncle Steven knew to stay involved in your lives. It made him feel needed."

"With Mama dying so young, all we ever needed was his love. Maybe if he'd loved us more, he'd have taught us to fly and kicked us out of the nest sooner." She sighed. "Oh, well, that's water under the bridge now, I suppose. We have to deal with the hand we were dealt. Or should I say, you do. He didn't do you any favors, dumping us into your lap, did he, Kev?"

"I've cursed him a time or two," Kevin conceded.

"More than that, I'll bet." She regarded him sympathetically. "Don't worry about Bobby Ray. I wanted to warn you about him stirring everyone up, but he'll settle down. He always does."

"I'm not worried," Kevin assured her. "There's no dirt for Bobby Ray to uncover, so he can't possibly make trouble for me."

"One of these days, he'll try, though. You know he will. The rest of us won't be able to stop him."

Kevin sighed. "I know."

"We may not want to, but we'll have to side with him, too," she warned.

"I know that, too."

She stood and rounded the desk to brush a casual kiss across his cheek. "Watch your back, darling. That's really all I came by to say."

"Thanks, Helen."

She opened her mouth, but this time Kevin knew exactly what she was going to say and beat her to it. "I won't tell Bobby Ray we had this conversation," he promised.

She smiled at him. "Never thought you would."

And then she breezed out as rapidly as she'd entered, leaving behind an expensive French scent and an atmosphere choked with tension. Kevin knew his cousin meant well, but she'd pretty much ruined his mood with her dire warnings. He could think of only one way to recapture his earlier optimism.

"Molly!" he shouted at the top of his lungs.

When the housekeeper appeared in the doorway, he ignored the scowl that his ill-mannered shout had spawned. "Get Mr. Sparks for me, will you?"

"You're going to plant the garden?" she asked, her expression brightening.

"I'm going to plant the garden."

When the pickup pulled up in front of her house, Gracie assumed it was for one of the neighbors. When Kevin emerged and began unloading huge sacks of something or other, she bolted through the front door and down the steps.

"What on earth do you think you're doing?"

He paused only long enough to shoot one of those irrepressible grins over his shoulder. "What does it look like?"

She read the label on one of the bags as it passed by. "That's mulch. What are you doing delivering mulch?"

"You're not too quick this morning, darlin'? Rough night?"

"My night was just fine," she lied. She'd tossed and turned, kicked off the covers, tugged them back into place, counted hundreds of infernal sheep, then finally gotten up and prepared a glass of warm milk. Nothing had been able to rid her mind of sexy images of the man who was currently ignoring her and going about doing whatever the heck it was he was doing.

She finally planted herself squarely in his path. "I didn't order any mulch."

"I know."

"I didn't order any dirt, either," she said when she spotted the bags of top soil.

"I know."

She peered past him into the back of the truck. It was filled with flats of flowers. Vivid pink petunias, red-and-purple impatiens, yellow marigolds, and a few things she didn't recognize. The one thing they all had in common was that they were blindingly bright. Cheerful, she concluded, smiling despite herself.

"I didn't order those, either," she said.

"That's true."

"So what are they doing here?"

"It's a present."

"A present?" she repeated.

"There you go again, going blank on me. Surely you've gotten presents before."

"A dozen roses is a present. A corsage is a present. This is a whole damned garden."

"Precisely." He beamed as if she'd finally grasped a very critical point.

"Nobody gives a garden as a present," she protested.

"I do."

She had to scramble to keep up with him. "Kevin—"

"You're not going to waste time arguing with me, are you? I could use some help deciding what goes where."

For a full sixty seconds she stared at his retreating back and tried to summon up the argument that would get him to go away. In the end, though, the image of her backyard filled with all those flowers held too much appeal.

"This is a waste of perfectly good flowers," she finally shouted after him.

"Why is that?"

"They'll have to stay behind when I move into that Victorian."

He laughed. "In your dreams, sweetheart. Now go away or prepare to get dirty." He surveyed her white slacks and shook his head. "You're hopeless, you know that. Do you have an apron in the house? Maybe some coveralls?"

"Why would I need those?" she inquired tartly. "You're doing all the work, aren't you? Isn't that part of the present?"

"I had this image of the two of us working companionably, side by side."

"Now who's dreaming?"

Eventually, though, curiosity got the better of her. She followed him into the backyard. "Do you have any idea what you're doing?"

"Not exactly."

"Terrific."

He dragged a dirt-streaked piece of paper out of his pocket. "I have instructions, though. It pretty much amounts to digging a hole and sticking one of these little suckers into it."

Gracie regarded him doubtfully. "Are you sure about that?"

"Cross my heart. Mr. Sparks says it's so simple, any fool can do it."

"And Mr. Sparks is . . . ?"

"My groundskeeper."

"Why didn't you just send him around?"

"And give him the pleasure of your company when I could be here myself? No way. Like I said, working together is going to be half the fun. I have an image of myself sitting in that chair over there and watching you bending over to put these little guys into the ground."

"I don't think so."

He shrugged. "Oh, well, you can't blame a man for hoping."

"Why are you doing this?"

"Isn't it obvious?"

"Not to me."

"It's simple enough. Every time you glance out your kitchen window from now on and see the flowers, you'll think of me."

Since he was stripping off his shirt as he said it, Gracie was pretty certain he was right. There was no way she'd get that image of bare flesh out of her mind. The man's lightly tanned body was a sculptor's dream. That much muscle definition didn't happen lazing around in a hammock all day long.

"Anytime you're through ogling the help, you can pick up a shovel and get to work," he said, bringing a flood of heat to her cheeks.

"I wasn't staring at you," she lied.

"Whatever you say."

She grabbed a shovel and jammed it into the ground, turning over a chunk of rich, black soil. It was more difficult than she'd expected. By the time she'd dug up a small three-foot square, Kevin had finished a patch twice as large along the fence. His shoulders were glistening with sweat, his muscles bunching in a totally fascinating way. Her gaze locked on the sight and lingered.

"Gracie?"

"Hmm?"

"You're staring again. Not that I mind, but it's not getting the garden dug up."

"I don't think I can dig anymore," she admitted. "I've got blisters."

A stricken expression passed over his face. "The gloves," he muttered. "Dammit, I was supposed to give you gloves. Let me see."

He took her hand in his and turned it over, palm up. He was so close, Gracie could feel the heat radiating from his body. He smelled of sun-warmed earth, sweat, and a lingering trace of some after-shave. The scent was so thoroughly masculine she forgot all about her injured hands. It was far more intriguing than the expensive cologne Max wore. There was something raw and primitive and real about it that no manufacturer could duplicate.

"Gracie?"

"Hmm?"

"I asked if you had any antiseptic in the house."

"What?" She blinked and tried to focus on Kevin's face. "Antiseptic?"

He grinned. "Yes. Do you have any?"

"There's a first-aid kit in the bathroom, I think. I'll get it."

"No, you sit down over there," he insisted. "I used to play with a couple of kids who lived here. I know my way around inside. I'll get it."

He came back after several minutes with a pan filled with hot, soapy water and the first-aid kit.

"Aren't you making an awful lot over a couple of blisters?" she asked, eyeing the first-aid kit warily. She had a pretty good idea whatever was in there was going to hurt worse than the blisters.

"They're broken. They could get infected. Now, hold still. This is going to sting."

With her hand cradled in his and his head bent in concentration, he poured half a bottle of peroxide over the wound.

"Holey moley!" she yelped, jerking her hand away.

"Don't be such a baby," he chided, taking her hand back and dabbing on the much cooler antibiotic cream.

"You have a lousy bedside manner," she grumbled.

"Darlin', you haven't let me near your bed. How would you know?" He covered the injury with a bandage, then brushed a kiss over it. "That should make it better."

"Or contaminate it with more germs," she said.

"Let me see the other hand."

She tucked it behind her back. "It's fine."

"Gracie . . ." he chided.

"Oh, for goodness sakes, you'd think I'd slashed it open," she complained. "It's just a couple of teensy little blisters."

"Let me see." He held out his hand and regarded her patiently.

Finally, reluctantly, she put her other hand in his. She heard his sharp intake of breath, then the muttered curse.

"Why didn't you say something sooner?" he demanded. "This hand's even worse. You should have quit when the first blister popped up. I hate to say it, darlin', but it's pretty obvious you're not used to a lot of manual labor."

"And you are?"

He grinned. "Is that it? Were you trying to compete with me?"

She shrugged. "What can I say? I have a very competitive nature."

Kevin shook his head and bent over her hand. This time she managed not to cry out when he poured on the peroxide. When he was finished with the bandage, though, he didn't let go of her hand. The gentle way he kept on holding it, the light caress by the pad of his thumb sent a very different kind of shock wave crashing over her.

How could that be? she wondered, trying to distance herself from the sensation so she could analyze it. Other men had made far more overt passes without stirring so much as a blip in her pulse rate. Kevin was barely touching her and her heart was thumping away as if she'd run a mile, which was several thousand feet farther than she'd ever run without panting.

"I don't know about you, but I'm starved," Kevin said in a way that suggested he was interested in something other than food.

"Me, too," she responded, a disgustingly breathless note in her voice.

"You stay put. I'll fix something."

He abandoned her so quickly, he left her head spinning. Gracie had the distinct impression he was anxious to get away. For a man who'd been making all sorts of provocative hints, he was very lackadaisical about follow-through.

"Now what do you suppose that was all about?" she murmured, staring after him. Since her own pulse was still scrambling, she supposed it was just as well. She wasn't interested in anything more than lunch. She couldn't be.

In no time at all, Kevin brought out a tray with two thick sandwiches and two glasses of milk. He took his and sprawled on the ground in front of her. He looked so thoroughly relaxed, Gracie couldn't help pondering if she'd imagined that instant of awareness that had shimmered between them.

"Have you given any thought to how you want the flowers arranged?" he asked.

"Not really."

"Are you in favor of the neat, symmetrical look or a wilder, more natural look?" he asked. "Let me guess. Neat, right?"

Because he sounded so blasted sure of himself, she snapped, "Wild. I want everything in there helter-skelter."

He stared at her. "That sounds mighty daring. You sure about that?"

"I said it, didn't I?"

His gaze narrowed. "Did I miss something here? You seem upset."

"I am not upset. I'm . . ."

"Frustrated?" he suggested, suddenly grinning.

"Oh, go to hell."

"That's it, isn't it?"

"I really could grow to dislike you," she warned.

"You wish." He scrambled to his feet, dropped a kiss on her forehead and began gathering up dishes. "Don't worry, darlin'. The wait won't go on forever. One of these days real soon, we'll wind up in bed."

"I have no intention of sleeping with you," she declared, leaving no room for misinterpretation—or so she thought.

He appeared undaunted. "You know what they say about the road to hell being paved with good intentions."

"You are the most annoying—"

"Sexy."

". . . exasperating—"

"Sexy."

". . . singleminded man I know."

"But when was the last time you had this much fun?"

The trouble was, Gracie couldn't think that far back.

Seven

When Gracie woke up the next morning, every muscle in her body ached. Her hands felt raw. But the minute she looked out the kitchen window, none of that mattered.

The garden was a riot of color. Kevin had taken her at her word when she'd said she wanted it wild. Purple was jammed up next to red, which bumped into orange. Taller snapdragons popped up amidst squat impatiens. Clusters of fragile daisies bloomed next to hardy hostas. By midsummer when everything was in full-bloom, it was going to be chaotic and wonderful. Songbirds had already started arriving and engaging in an astonishing turf war over the hollyhocks.

She still couldn't get over the fact that planting it had been Kevin's idea. No one had ever made such an extravagant gesture before just on impulse. She didn't inspire romantic impulses. Max had given her a gift certificate for Christmas for . . . luggage. She had a feeling if Kevin had had the same inclination, he would have chosen the luggage and tucked two tickets to Greece inside.

Comparisons, of course, were a waste of time. Max had never mattered. She had never let him. Kevin, however, had the sneakiness necessary to matter before she could stop him. She was going to have to stay on her toes to see that didn't happen. One good way would be to focus on stealing that old house out from under him.

She formulated her strategy on her brisk walk to the

Beachside Cafe for breakfast. She was pretty sure she could count on Jessie to give her straight answers or to point her in the right direction to find them for herself. Jessie was a very direct woman.

"Hear you have a new garden," Jessie said as she poured Gracie's first cup of coffee.

"News travels fast."

"How's your hand?" the waitress asked.

The memory of the bolt of awareness that had struck her as Kevin tended to her injuries brought a flush to her cheeks. To cover her embarrassment, she snapped, "Was somebody hanging over the damned fence?"

Jessie chuckled. "Actually, I just noticed the bandages. Now you've made me curious, though. What did go on in your backyard besides gardening?"

Gracie sighed. "Nothing. I'm sorry. I'm just not used to having my private life the subject of the morning news." Of course, in recent years she'd had very little private life. It had been easy enough to keep it discreet.

"Then you'd better stay away from Kevin," Jessie warned. "He's the kind of man who does draw attention. Half the women in town are fascinated. The other half are jealous."

"Believe me, I'd avoid him if I could. Unfortunately, he stands between me and that house I'd like to buy." She regarded Jessie intently. "You could help me change that."

"How?"

"Tell me everything you know about that house. Who owns it? How come Kevin's managing it and gets away with not doing anything to keep it up?"

"Have you asked him that?"

"Not exactly," she conceded.

"Why not?"

"Because when it comes to that old house, Kevin refuses to talk. He won't even let me mention it."

"Really? Now isn't that fascinating?" Jessie said thoughtfully.

"You see what I'm up against? Come on, Jessie, please. Help me out here. Think of it as your duty to the sisterhood of women."

Jessie chuckled. "Sweetie, I don't even get along all that well with my own sister. Sorry. I think I'll stay out of the middle of this one. I will bring you a big plate of scrambled eggs and bacon to help you keep your strength up, though."

"I don't need strength. I need answers."

"Sorry. You'll have to order those up from somebody else," Jessie said, not sounding sorry at all.

"Why? What do you owe Kevin?"

"More than you'll ever know," she said enigmatically, and retreated to the kitchen.

Gracie stared after her. She was still trying to figure out what to make of the waitress's comment when a man she'd seen once or twice around town slid into the booth opposite her.

"I couldn't help overhearing what you said to Jessie. I could help you out," he said.

"Oh?"

He held out his hand. "Bobby Ray Daniels. I'm Kevin's cousin."

Gracie studied him and saw a hint of family resemblance in the eyes, but the chin was weaker, the jaw less defined. One thing she would give Bobby Ray, he dressed a whole lot better than his cousin. She noted the well-tailored slacks, the expensive shirt with its monogrammed cuffs, the buffed Italian leather loafers. The outfit was as classy as anything hanging in Max's closet. She realized she'd recently developed a fondness for worn jeans.

"Why would you help me?" she asked.

"Just being neighborly."

"Shouldn't you be on your cousin's side?"

"I wasn't aware there were sides. You're not trying to cheat him, are you?"

"No, but—"

"Obviously you're not worried about hurting his feelings. You're already going behind his back."

"Just to pick up a little information," she said, feeling surprisingly defensive.

"So why not get that information from me?"

Because it didn't feel right to her. She couldn't explain it. "Thanks, but I don't think so."

"I could talk to the owner for you."

"You know the owner?"

"As well as Kevin does."

"Why not just give me the name, then?"

"And cut myself out? That wouldn't be smart business, would it?"

"So much for being neighborly," Gracie said.

He grinned. "A man's got to make a living."

Despite his willingness to sell out his cousin, there was a certain amount of charm about the man that was practically irresistible. He didn't sound as if there were a malicious intent behind the sneakiness, just good fun. A big joke on Kevin they could laugh about later. Gracie doubted Kevin would see it the same way.

"Okay, let's say I was willing to pay you to intercede in my behalf. What would you charge?"

"A finder's fee. Maybe fifty thousand," he said with every bit as much brazenness as Kevin might have under the same circumstances.

Gracie laughed at his audacity. "Never mind. I think I'll just go to the courthouse and check the property tax records."

"Go ahead. Won't tell you much."

"Why not?"

"The bills go to Kevin." He met her gaze with a friendly expression. "Bottom line, if you want to go around Kevin, you have to deal with me. I'll be every bit as fair as he would be."

Gracie stood. "Thanks all the same, but I don't think so."

He shrugged off the rejection. "That's okay. You'll change

your mind. Kevin's stubborn as a mule when he wants something, and I've got a pretty strong feeling what he wants is you. That house is his hold on you, isn't it?"

She didn't like Bobby Ray Daniels's insinuations, but she couldn't really deny them. She'd seen the gleam in Kevin's eyes when he'd looked at her. Would he be beyond holding that house just out of her reach to keep her coming around? Probably not. That didn't mean she had to deal with the likes of Bobby Ray to get what she wanted.

Ignoring Bobby Ray, she went to the counter to pay for her coffee.

"Steer clear of him," Jessie warned in an undertone. "Bobby Ray's okay in his own way, but there's bad blood between him and Kevin."

"So I gathered. How come?"

"It's a family thing."

"But I'd be willing to bet that you know every detail."

"Well, of course I do," Jessie agreed. "Doesn't mean I'd tell a stranger."

Gracie sighed. "How long will it take me to stop being an outsider around here?"

"Hard to say. Could be tomorrow. Could be you won't live that long. Folks are fickle about acceptance. There's no telling what'll turn the tide. I can't say if it matters, but I think you're going to do okay, as long as you don't push too hard. Take it a little slow. And whatever you do, don't antagonize Kevin. People around here think that man hung the moon."

"Because he was a high school basketball star?"

"Because he's a decent kind of guy, who'll come through for you in a pinch."

"You said something like that before, Jessie. What did Kevin do for you?"

"He came through for me, when no one else would. That's the long and short of it. And I'm not the only one. If you're looking for an example of someone who lives by the Golden Rule, you don't need to look any further than Kevin."

"Yet there's bad blood between him and his cousin. Why is that?"

"You'll have to ask Kevin or Bobby Ray about that. It's their business," Jessie said with finality and moved off to greet two customers who'd just come in.

Gracie struggled to grasp the distinction between spreading news of her activities far and wide and sharing a few insights into some apparently long-standing family feud in the Daniels clan. She didn't quite get it, but it was clear that Jessie had said as much as she intended to on the subject.

Back outside, Gracie debated the wisdom of going to the county courthouse in Montross to check property records. Bobby Ray had told her she'd be wasting her time, but the warning might have been totally self-serving. Or not.

It was such a beautiful day, too beautiful to spend indoors, looking through musty old records or even computerized ones if the county was up-to-date. The air was soft and warm, the sky a clear and brilliant blue. Maybe she should just go on back home and admire her new garden.

When she opted for the latter, she blamed it on Kevin's sorry influence and made a hasty detour to the bookstore to pick up those cookbooks she'd concluded she needed. She might spend the day lazing around in her own backyard, but the time wouldn't be totally wasted. She could choose recipes for the bed and breakfast. *Simple* recipes.

Two hours later, she was up to her elbows in broken eggs and flour. The kitchen looked as if a particularly nasty tornado had ripped through. Her version of the basic little soufflé she'd seen made a thousand times in the Worldwide kitchens was burnt to a crisp and had fallen in the middle. There were five others just like it in the garbage.

"Maybe you ought to switch to scrambled eggs," Kevin suggested.

Gracie glanced up from the mess and glared at him. "Where did you come from?" He was lounging in the doorway as naturally as if he belonged in her kitchen. She hadn't heard him or his car.

"I knocked on the front door. Obviously you were distracted by the explosion." He grinned. "That is what happened here, isn't it? something blew up?"

"Go to hell."

His grin broadened. "People only resort to cursing when they can't think of anything more creative to say."

Before she could think of a few dozen creative ways to tell him to get lost, he moved into the room and began moving pots and pans and bowls into the sink and running hot water over them.

"Sit," he instructed.

Gracie sat, because she was too exhausted to do anything else. She wanted to weep, but Kevin's presence kept her from indulging in a good cry.

"Exactly what were you trying to accomplish here?" he inquired as he expertly scrubbed the dishes, dried them and, after a little poking around in the cupboards, put all but one pan exactly where they belonged. He set the remaining pan back on the stove, surveyed the mess on the table and retrieved eggs, cheese, and butter.

"I was practicing."

"What exactly? Demolition work?" he inquired.

The butter began sizzling in the frying pan. Kevin whipped the eggs into a frothy mixture and poured it into the pan with smooth expertise.

"You're not all that amusing," she retorted, observing him enviously.

"Yeah, I suppose from your point of view I'm not. But darlin', if you can't laugh at yourself, life can get downright tedious."

"I suppose you laugh at your mistakes."

"You're assuming I make some."

Gracie let that remark pass. She suspected Kevin's ego couldn't be deflated with a pitchfork, much less any little jab she might take at it. Besides, her mouth was watering at the fluffy cheese omelette he was sliding onto a plate.

"I met your cousin this morning," she said instead.

He glanced over his shoulder at her. "Which one?"

"Bobby Ray." She noticed Kevin's hands stilled at the mention of the name and his shoulders tensed perceptibly.

"Oh? How'd that happen?"

"I was having breakfast and he stopped by my table."

Kevin sighed. "I imagine he offered to help you get the Victorian." He set the omelette in front of her, then pulled out a chair, turned it around backward and straddled it.

"How'd you know?"

"Believe me, I know all of Bobby Ray's moves. I'll bet he wanted a finder's fee for helping out, right?"

Because she was savoring the first bite of omelette, Gracie merely nodded.

"How much?" he asked. "Let me guess. Fifty thousand?"

"How'd you know that?"

"Because that's exactly the amount he was trying to get me to fork over. When I refused, he obviously started looking for other sources. It would suit him to take it from you for interfering in the business you and I have."

"What's he want it for?"

"He wants to go into business with his wife's lover."

Gracie nearly choked on her food. She stared. "He what?"

"I hear it's a long story. So far, I've managed to escape hearing the details. Bottom line? Stay away from him, Gracie. As much as I hate to say it, Bobby Ray's a conniving son of a bitch when there's something he wants, and right now it's a toss up whether he wants money or my head on a platter. He'll use you to get either one."

"I've already told him I'm not interested in his deal."

"That won't stop him. The word no is not in his vocabulary."

"Sounds like somebody else I know," she murmured.

"Okay, it's a family trait. I'll accept that. I still want you to steer clear of him."

"You don't sound as if you like him very much."

Kevin shot her a rueful look. "Does it sound that way? The truth is, I like him fine. I just wish he'd get a grip on his life and stop trying to take the easy way out. Biggest mistake he ever made was the first divorce."

"First?"

"There's been another one since. I'm hoping for a third. I don't much care for wife number three."

"What does he do?"

"As little as possible."

Given the disparaging nature of the accusation and his own apparent lack of regular employment, Gracie was surprised. "And you think that's a bad thing?"

"Of course it is."

"Maybe he's following someone else's example," she suggested.

"Whose?"

"Yours, for instance."

He chuckled at that. "There you go, making those assumptions again. Shame on you."

"I know what I see."

"Okay," he said agreeably. "Want to know what I see when I look at you? I see a woman who's hanging around the house all day long with nothing to do except scientific experiments that come damned close to destroying a kitchen that doesn't even belong to her. If I were the kind of man who jumped to conclusions, I'd say she has no practical skills whatsoever, no goals, no ambitions, and, judging from those bandaged hands, a dangerous lack of common sense."

Gracie bristled. "That's ridiculous."

"Is it? Not if I judge by appearances."

"But you know better."

"Because I did a little checking. Maybe you should consider doing a little investigating of your own before you reach any more hasty conclusions."

"Okay, okay, you've made your point." She regarded him curiously. "Why'd you come by anyway?"

"I was going to take you to lunch, but you'd already gotten a head start on me."

"I wasn't fixing lunch exactly."

"Then what was this all about?"

"I was practicing."

"For what?"

Before she could answer, comprehension obviously dawned. He stared at her incredulously.

"For the bed and breakfast?"

She nodded.

"Oh, my," he murmured, and started to chuckle.

"Stop it. Stop it right this minute."

"Can't help it," he said between laughs. "I was just envisioning the expression on the faces of your first guests when they come down and find a sight like this in the kitchen. Or were you hoping to serve them in the dining room and save them the trauma?"

"I'll be better before I open."

"Of course you will. In the meantime, though, maybe you ought to start thanking your lucky stars that I'm holding out."

"Why?"

"Because it seems to me you need another couple of years to practice your cooking skills."

Gracie considered whether it was possible to murder a man by whacking him upside the head with a cast-iron skillet. Fortunately for him, Kevin caught the direction of her gaze and her thoughts and made a hasty exit before she could find out.

Eight

Kevin had intended to stay the hell away from Bobby Ray for as long as humanly possible—or at least until he got over the absurd notion of backing his wife's lover in the jewelry, business. Unfortunately, his cousin's little meeting with Gracie required a response. Kevin wasn't exactly itching for a fight when he turned into the winding road that would take him to Bobby Ray's house on Monroe Bay, but he was in no mood to run from one, either.

There was a hodgepodge of homes tucked away on this side of the bay that fed into the Potomac. Some were doublewide trailers, some were small cottages that had been upgraded over the years with vinyl siding and fancy new decks. A few, like Bobby Ray's, were huge new homes with lots of glass facing the water and wide porches, lined with rockers or Adirondack chairs. To Kevin's regret, the garage at Bobby Ray's was wide open and there were no cars around, either inside the garage or in the driveway. Wherever he and Sara Lynn were, they apparently weren't together.

However, Kevin's favorite kid, a pigtailed, blond imp, was sitting on the porch with a book in her hands. She was so clearly absorbed in the story that he was almost beside her before Abby glanced up at him from behind the thick lenses of her glasses and grinned.

"Hey, Uncle Kevin!" she called out, using the honorary

title that had been easier for her to grasp than the concept of being second cousins.

"Hey, squirt. What're you reading?"

"It's about this girl who went all the way across the country in a covered wagon. Can you imagine getting over the Rockies way back then? It must have been awesome."

"Scary, more likely."

"That, too," she agreed, nodding solemnly. "How come you're here? Are you looking for Daddy?"

"Yep. Any idea where he is?"

"Probably sneaking around behind Sara Lynn," she said, sounding way wiser than any ten-year-old ought to be. "I figure they'll be together another month, tops."

"I see," he said carefully, trying not to let his disgust show. Abby shouldn't be this aware of her stepmother's sordid behavior.

She regarded him worriedly. "Uncle Kevin, can I ask you something?"

"Of course."

"How come Daddy can't stay married?"

"You ask the big ones, don't you, squirt?" He settled into the rocker beside her and gave the question some thought. Finally he shook his head. Answers that didn't involve labeling her father an irresponsible oaf eluded him. "I wish I could tell you, but I don't know. Sometimes things between grown-ups just don't work out."

"That's what Mom said, too. What I want to know is *why* they don't work out. Is it because Daddy changes jobs so much and never has any money? Mom told Aunt Emma he hasn't paid child support for me in the last six months."

Kevin bit back an angry retort. This was the first he'd heard that Bobby Ray wasn't making his payments. For a time he'd made them for his cousin, but Bobby Ray had claimed that was demeaning, that it showed a total lack of faith.

"Might as well cut off my balls and be done with it," he'd shouted during one of their more heated exchanges.

Kevin had actually seen his point. He'd relented and started sending all of the money directly to Bobby Ray. Obviously that had been a mistake.

Abby peered at him. "You're not mad at him, are you? Mom said not to tell you, that you had enough on your mind with all the rest of them without her bugging you, too. Besides, we do okay. Since she got that promotion, she's making real good money now at the bank."

Kevin forced a smile. "I know she is, but that's not the point. Your dad has a responsibility to pay his share. I'll talk to him."

Her lower lip quivered. "You won't yell, will you? Please, Uncle Kevin. I hate it when you and Daddy yell."

"Now, squirt, you know perfectly well that yelling is just something your dad and I do. Anything short of shouting doesn't register. It's the way we communicate." He glanced at his watch. It wasn't even three o'clock.

"What are you doing here all by yourself at this time of day anyway?"

"It was a short day at school, so I always come here 'cause Mom's still at work. Daddy was supposed to be here, but I guess he forgot. And Sara Lynn's never here in the afternoon. That's when she sneaks around with her friends."

Kevin saw red. He was going to kill Bobby Ray. He really was. And maybe Sara Lynn, while he was at it. Abby was safe enough here alone, but being forgotten by her father was lousy. He tried to keep his fury out of his voice. He even managed to force another smile. "How about coming home with me till your mom gets off? Aunt Delia'd love to see you. We'll call your mom and let her know where you are."

Abby hesitated. "What if Daddy gets back and I'm not here? He'll worry."

Kevin doubted that, but he wasn't about to say it. "We'll leave him a note."

"Okay," she said eagerly. "I'll get my schoolbooks. They're in the kitchen." She regarded him slyly. "Can we put the top down on your car?"

"You bet."

"All right! And turn the radio on real loud?"

"Is there any other way?"

Suddenly Abby threw her arms around his waist and buried her face against his chest. "You're the best, Uncle Kevin," she said, her voice muffled.

"No, you are," he retorted, lifting her into the air as he had from the time she was a baby. And why that damn fool of a cousin of his couldn't see what a treasure the child was, was beyond him. He put her back on her feet. "Now, scoot, and get your things."

Aunt Delia welcomed Abby with delight, even as she shot a questioning look at Kevin. He touched a finger to his lips and mouthed, "Later."

For a brief instant, her eyes glittered dangerously as she added up two and two and came to the obvious conclusion that once again Bobby Ray had let his little girl down. But the smile she managed for Abby was warm, and she led her off to the kitchen, already whispering conspiratorially to her. Kevin watched them go and sighed. He figured Molly would spoil both their dinners with sugar cookies, but Abby needed attention more than she needed a balanced diet at the moment.

Satisfied that his niece was in the best possible hands, he went into his office and called Bobby Ray's ex-wife. "Hey, Marianne, it's Kevin."

"Uh-oh, what's Bobby Ray done now?"

Her response was automatic, based on too many years of experience with her ex-husband's behavior. "You tell me," Kevin suggested.

"The list goes on and on," she said with an air of resignation. "That's nothing new."

"I hear he's behind with child support again."

"How'd you hear that? Not from Bobby Ray, I'll bet."

"No, I ran into Abby earlier. She was out at Bobby Ray's all by herself."

"By herself?" she said, clearly horrified. "Dammit, he knows her school schedule. Where was he?"

"No idea, but I brought her on home with me," he told her. "That's why I called, to let you know I'll bring her on home after dinner if that's okay with you. I'll bring the back support payments, too."

"You've already given that money to Bobby Ray," she protested.

"Don't worry. I'll get it back from him," he said grimly. "I'm not letting him off the hook."

"We're getting along okay without it."

"Okay isn't good enough. He owes you, Marianne. He owes both of you. Put it into Abby's college fund, if you don't need it now. Something tells me she's going to want to go to Harvard or someplace else that'll cost an arm and a leg to get into."

"She'll probably end up at UVA, like her uncle Kevin. She worships you, you know."

"It works both ways."

"Thanks, Kevin."

"No problem. I'll have her home right after supper."

"I wish . . ."

"Never mind. I know."

"You don't know. I still can't figure out how two people could share so much family history and turn out so differently. He wasn't always like this. Sometimes I wonder if it's not my fault."

"How the hell could you think a thing like that?"

"You know, because of us."

"You chose Bobby Ray, Marianne. He should have started

counting his lucky stars that day and never stopped." He hesitated, not sure how much his opinion was worth. Finally he asked, "Word of advice?"

"Sure."

"Don't let your bitterness over Bobby Ray ruin you for other men."

"I'm not. I just wish they'd cloned a few more of you."

"I'm no prize, either," he told her. "See you soon."

He heard her sigh as he hung up. It was true, there had been a time when he and Marianne might have had a shot at something, but that was long ago. She'd chosen his flashier cousin, fallen head over heels for him, in fact. They'd been divorced within a year, just weeks after Abby's birth.

If it had been left up to Bobby Ray, he and Abby probably would have had no relationship at all, but Marianne and Kevin had seen to it that they did. There were actually rare occasions when Bobby Ray showed a spark of interest in parenting his precocious daughter. Today hadn't been one of those days.

Kevin went in search of his aunt and Abby. Not that finding them was difficult. They were giggling like a couple of schoolgirls, which only one of them was. He found them glued to the TV and another one of those preposterous talk shows. He stole the remote right out from under his aunt's hand and flipped off the set.

"Aunt Delia, you should be ashamed of yourself. That's nothing Abby ought to be watching."

"She picked it," his aunt grumbled.

"I doubt that."

"I did," Abby insisted. "It pays to be informed."

To Kevin's deep regret, she sounded exactly like Aunt Delia. "You don't need to be informed about things like that for a very long time," he insisted.

"Sure I do. That way I can stay out of trouble."

"Just listen to your mom and your uncle Kevin. We'll keep you out of trouble."

Abby shook her head. "I don't know about you, Uncle Kevin, but I don't think Mom knows about stuff like this."

"One of her highest recommendations, as far as I'm concerned," Kevin declared. "Why don't we play Old Maid or something?"

"Old Maid?" Abby hooted. "That's a kid's game."

"You are a kid."

"I'm not a baby."

He grinned at her insulted air. "What would you like to play, then?"

"Poker," she said at once.

"Wonderful," Aunt Delia chimed in, always ready to do a little betting, no matter the stakes. "I'll get the chips. A penny apiece."

"Why not just use pennies?" Kevin asked. "Afraid we'll get raided and you'll be hauled away for contributing to the delinquency of a minor?"

"Just get the cards," his aunt ordered. "Unless you're too chicken to play with us."

He scowled at the pair of them, but he retrieved the cards, then pulled a chair up to the card table and sat. "I'll play," he said grimly. "Just to be sure you don't steal the child's lunch money."

As it turned out, the two females took every bit of change he had in his pockets along with another five dollars. If Bobby Ray ever discovered Abby's skill, he'd probably have her on the next flight to Vegas.

"Enough," he declared finally. "Molly probably has dinner ready by now."

"You wish," Abby taunted. "One more hand, winner take all."

"You have a smart mouth, young lady," he retorted. "And I'm not throwing one more penny into the pot."

She grinned unrepentantly. "I thought you wanted me to grow up smart."

"Brain smart, not sassy."

"Leave the child alone," Aunt Delia told him. "She won that money fair and square."

"Maybe she did," he conceded, gathering up the cards and feigning a count. "You, I'm not so sure about. Maybe I ought to check to see how many cards you've got tucked up those sleeves of yours."

"That's a fine way to talk to your elders," Aunt Delia chided. "Abby, pay no attention to your uncle. He's setting a very bad example."

Abby giggled. "You two are so funny. I wish I could come here all the time."

"You can come here anytime you want to, darling child," Aunt Delia declared, hugging her. "You just call and Kevin will come for you. Isn't that right, Kevin?"

"Anytime," he agreed.

An hour and a half later, after a dinner of Abby's favorite chicken and dumplings, he dropped her off at home, declining Marianne's invitation to come in for coffee.

"I've still got a couple of places to stop tonight," he told her, avoiding any specific mention of Bobby Ray.

"I really appreciate you rescuing Abby this afternoon."

"Not a problem. If it happens again, she knows she's to call me. She's probably safe enough at Bobby Ray's by herself, but I don't like it."

"He called here a little while ago to apologize for forgetting."

"Too little, too late," Kevin declared, then dropped a kiss on Marianne's forehead. "You're doing a great job with her. She's a terrific kid."

Marianne smiled. "Yeah, she is, isn't she? I wish her dad could see it. I wish . . ."

She shook her head. "Never mind what I wish," she said.

She turned away, but not before Kevin detected the sheen of tears in her eyes. He regarded her worriedly. "You don't still have a thing for him, do you, Marianne?"

"Of course not," she said with an obviously forced smile. "What kind of fool do you take me for?"

"Never a fool, sweetheart. But sometimes Cupid takes lousy aim."

She didn't have a snappy comeback for that, so Kevin decided to leave well enough alone. He waved and took off once more for Bobby Ray's.

Again, though, his cousin wasn't home. He'd probably guessed that Kevin would be gunning for him and decided to lay low until his cousin's temper cooled. He couldn't stay out of sight that long, Kevin thought grimly.

An image of Bobby Ray hitting on Gracie to make a deal behind his back fueled his black mood. He debated paying a visit to Gracie, but concluded she didn't deserve to have to put up with his lousy company. Besides, she might actually cheer him up and then Bobby Ray wouldn't get the full effect of his anger. Nope, better to let it simmer overnight and take his cousin on first thing in the morning, when he was still mad enough to strangle Bobby Ray with his bare hands.

"Max, how many times do I have to tell you? I am not coming back," Gracie declared wearily. It was just past dawn in France and nearly midnight in Virginia. Not that she'd been asleep when he called. She was once again in the middle of a kitchen that looked like a war zone. "Fill my job. Eliminate it. Do whatever you want with it."

"You are needed here."

"There are other hotel executives who would kill to work for Worldwide and the legendary Max Devereaux."

"I need you," he repeated emphatically. "I am at a loss without you."

"Only because you have no idea how to deal with the tradesmen in town or the staff. I'm sorry that the asparagus farmer refuses to deliver any longer, but there's not a thing I can do about it from here."

"Actually, there is one thing," he suggested meekly. "You could call him."

The meek tone was a nice touch, but she wasn't moved. "Pierre refuses to install a phone. He uses the public one at the end of his lane when he needs to make a call."

"What if there were an emergency?" Max demanded, clearly bewildered.

"I'm sure he's taken that possibility into account. I never questioned him about it. He's a very private man. You would know that, if you'd ever bothered to get to know him."

"That's true. I confess it. We made the perfect team, you and I. You know exactly how to handle everyone to keep the hotel running smoothly. I know how to keep it operating in the black. Things are falling apart without you here."

There was a distinct note of panic in his voice that she'd never heard before. "Are you groveling, Max?"

The question silenced him for a full minute, before he sighed heavily. "Yes, I suppose I am."

"Good," she said happily. "It suits you."

"Gracie, if begging will get you back here, I'll beg."

"It won't, but thanks for trying."

"Why not? What are you doing in Virginia that is so all-fired important?"

"You wouldn't understand."

"Try me."

"Okay. For once in my life, I'm doing exactly what I want to do."

"What the devil does that mean?"

"I told you you wouldn't understand. Bye, Max. Good luck with Pierre."

He was still blustering—begging, she thought cheerfully—when she hung up. It made the fact that she had just ruined her fourth straight souffle almost bearable.

Nine

"Well, well, well, look what the wind blew in," Jessie said as she was pouring Gracie a second cup of coffee at breakfast the next morning.

Gracie glanced up from her plate just in time to see Kevin coming through the door, the scowl on his face changing to a brilliant smile at Jessie's greeting.

"Hey, doll, how're you doing?" he asked, planting an enthusiastic kiss on her cheek. He ignored Gracie. "Any sign of Bobby Ray in here this morning?"

"Not today," Jessie said. "Are you staying? Shall I bring you a cup of coffee? Maybe some scrambled eggs and grits?"

"Coffee sounds good, but I've already had breakfast." He glanced at Gracie for the first time. "I'll just slide in here and torment Ms. MacDougal for a while."

"Thanks so much," Gracie said when the waitress had gone. "Am I supposed to be honored that you've taken notice of little old me?"

He grinned. "Uh-oh, what has your drawers in a knot this morning, darlin'? You jealous because I kissed Jessie?"

"Don't be absurd."

"I could rectify the situation," he offered, beckoning to her. "Lean across the table and meet me halfway. I've got plenty left over for you, if you're interested."

"I don't think so," she said, ignoring the little flare of excitement his taunt aroused. One of these days the flirting was going to end and he was going to follow through. She prayed she had the kind of resistance it would take to keep from falling for him.

"What brings you in here at this hour anyway?" she asked in an attempt to get the conversation onto safer turf. "Shouldn't you be crawling into your hammock about now?"

"Not quite yet. I have a little business to take care of, as soon as I catch up with Bobby Ray. I thought he might be in here again."

"Sneaking around behind your back, trying to finalize that deal with me?" she guessed.

"Exactly."

"You don't need to worry about that. I told you I had no intention of dealing with him."

"And I know you meant it. I just want to be absolutely sure he got the message. I also have another message to deliver to him regarding his daughter."

His expression was so fierce that Gracie was intrigued. "His daughter? What do you have to do with his relationship with his child?"

He gave her a terse and appalling summary of his cousin's neglect. "He doesn't figure he has to answer to Marianne or to Abby. I want to make sure he knows he has to answer to me," he concluded.

"Won't a confrontation with you in a public place just make things worse?" Gracie asked. "Apparently he already thinks you humiliate him every chance you get."

"Don't worry, darlin'. I have no intention of making a scene in here. I'll drag him outside before I beat him to a pulp."

"That'll be helpful," she said dryly. "Maybe if you just tried to look at things from his perspective once in a while, you could get through to him."

He stared at her, his expression incredulous. "You're taking his side?"

"I'm not taking anybody's side, especially that of a man

who virtually abandoned his daughter," she said. "But you're not going to solve anything your way. You'll just make matters worse." She shrugged. "Of course, it's none of my business."

"No, it's not."

They sat glaring at each other for a full minute before Kevin sighed. "Okay, let's hear it. How would you handle this?"

Gracie realized belatedly that she'd stumbled into a quagmire. The bad blood between these two men obviously went back a long way. Who was she to think she could waltz in and offer an easy solution? Obviously Max's high praise for her tact and diplomacy the night before had gone to her head.

"Maybe I should stay out of this," she said.

"Oh, no, darlin'. Don't go all shy on me now. You have something to say, say it."

"Okay, here goes." She leaned forward and gave him a penetrating look. "Have you ever really sat down with him and listened to what he's feeling? It sounds as if his father put you both in an untenable position. It doesn't help that you throw that in his face every chance you get. How many times have you quoted the terms of that blasted will to him?"

Kevin squirmed, looking vaguely uncomfortable. It was answer enough.

"Too many, right?"

"I suppose," he muttered.

"Maybe you should try sympathizing with his position once in a while. Try to figure out a way to make it work so that he has a little more control of his own destiny. Surely there are ways to bend the rules."

"There are, and I've been tempted to bend them a few times, but each time he manages to prove once again why his daddy wanted the will drawn up that way. If Bobby Ray knew how to exercise any control over his own destiny, he wouldn't be married to a woman who was cheating on him before the ink was dry on the wedding license."

"Could be that love blinded him to her faults," she suggested. "Have you ever been so crazy in love that you wouldn't listen to anything anybody said?"

"No," Kevin conceded, then regarded her intently. "Have you?"

"Well, no, but that's beside the point. We're not talking about me."

"Let's change the subject and talk about you," he challenged. "You've mentioned this Max guy a couple of times. Tell me about him."

"He was my boss. End of story."

"And that's all?"

"Absolutely.'

He appeared unconvinced. "Talked to him since you left France?"

"Yes," she admitted.

"How many times?"

"I don't know. A few, I guess. But it was always about business," she added defensively.

"Such as?"

"Look, why are you interested in this?"

"Because everything about you fascinates me. Come on, tell me. Why does Max call?"

"Last night he called because the asparagus farmer refused to deliver."

Kevin stared at her. "You're kidding, right?"

"I am not kidding. If you knew how much asparagus we served, you wouldn't think it was such an insignificant little problem."

"So it was a really important crisis?" Kevin said, his expression skeptical.

"Yes."

"Did you solve it?"

Now it was Gracie's turn to squirm. "Not exactly."

"You didn't jump in and help him out of this terrible business jam?"

"No, but—"

"Tsk, tsk, Gracie. I'm surprised at you. Where's your compassion? Your sense of duty?" He grinned. "I'll bet you told him where he could stick those asparagus, didn't you?"

"It wasn't amusing to Max," she said, smiling despite herself.

"No, I'm sure it wasn't." His expression sobered. "Gracie, does Max have a car?"

"Of course."

"Then he could have driven to the farmer's and picked up the asparagus, correct?"

The image of Max's impeccable Mercedes filled with vegetables was so outrageous that Gracie chuckled. "You don't know Max."

"No, but my point is, he didn't need to call you to handle this crisis. It was an excuse, Gracie. How many others has he dreamed up since you took off?"

She refused to answer. She'd been so pleased with the evidence of her indispensability that she'd never questioned whether Max might have ulterior motives for those calls.

"That many, huh? He must really have it bad."

"Max is not interested in me," she protested, "except as the manager of his hotel in Cannes." Now who was bending the truth? she thought guiltily.

"We could make a bet on that, but it would be easy money," Kevin said. "I'll let it pass."

"How noble of you."

He glanced over at her half-eaten, congealing breakfast. "Are you finished?"

"Yes. Why?"

"Let's go."

"Where?"

He gave her a lazy once-over that left her head spinning.

"It's a beautiful day," he responded. "I feel like taking my boat out, maybe doing a little fishing."

The prospect of being alone all day with Kevin rattled her.

He was far more disconcerting than Max would ever be. She was way too susceptible to this man she'd just met. Maybe all his attention would be on fishing, maybe it wouldn't. She concluded it wouldn't be smart to take any chances.

"I don't think so."

"We can talk about the house," he said, dangling the possibility before her.

The tactic was totally unfair. Downright sneaky, in fact. Naturally, she bit at once, throwing caution to the wind. "You have life preservers on board?"

"Of course."

"An extra fishing pole?"

"Absolutely."

"Let's go."

He kept his boat at the Colonial Beach Yacht Center. He picked up bait on the way. Gracie decided she didn't want to know exactly what kind.

Within minutes he was guiding the surprisingly modest twenty-foot boat away from the dock, through the calm waters of Monroe Bay and into the Potomac. With the wind mussing his hair and his hands steady on the wheel, there was a quiet confidence about him that Gracie found intriguing. He was usually all bluster and wit, but at the helm of the boat he seemed more at peace with himself and with nature.

"You love it out here, don't you?" she said eventually, breaking the silence.

"Sure I do. What's not to love?"

"I mean really love it," she said, not certain how to explain. "I'll bet you were a pirate in another life."

"You don't actually believe in all that reincarnation stuff, do you?"

"Watching you at the helm of this boat, I do. There's something different about you."

"Wait till you see me with a fishing pole in my hand.

You'll think I grew up on the Mississippi with Tom Sawyer and Huck Finn."

"That reminds me, exactly what did you get for bait?"

"Blood worms."

She choked back bile. "I was afraid of that."

He grinned. "I'll bait your hook for you if you're squeamish."

She gritted her teeth. "I can do it. I may not like it, but I can do it."

And she did, too. More than once, as it turned out, since Kevin seemed determined to stay on the water until they had enough fish for twenty meals.

When the subject of the house hadn't come up by midday, Gracie brought it up herself.

"I can't concentrate on business out here," Kevin claimed. "Besides, why spoil all this peace and serenity? Wait till we get in out of the hot sun."

Gracie frowned at the delay. "When will that be?"

"You tired or just impatient?"

"I'm just trying to avoid feeling as if I've been lured here under false pretenses," she retorted.

"Quiet, Gracie. You'll scare the fish."

She sighed and tossed her line into the water again. After a few more catches, Kevin concluded they had enough fish for the day.

"I'm starved. How about you? We can eat at Dockside, when we bring the boat in. Okay with you?"

"And we'll talk about the house?"

"Absolutely."

The subject still hadn't come up by dessert, which was an incredibly decadent combination of Oreos and cheesecake that Kevin insisted they deserved after their hard morning on the water.

"Okay," she said, when she'd licked the last bite off the fork. "About the house . . ."

"You want some coffee?"

"No. Stop avoiding the subject."

"I'm not avoiding anything. Talking business right after a meal is bad for the digestion," he declared. "Let's go for a walk. A nice lazy stroll will clear out the cobwebs."

"My head's clear as a bell now," Gracie protested.

"Then indulge me. You don't have anything pressing you need to get home to, do you?"

She thought of the recipes she had yet to master and sighed heavily, but she went for the walk. The only thing pressing on her agenda these days was getting her hands on that blasted house. Learning a dozen recipes wouldn't matter if she didn't have a kitchen to cook them in or guests to cook them for. Sooner or later, Kevin was going to have to talk about it. He'd promised, hadn't he? And wasn't every southern gentleman supposed to be a man of his word?

On the leisurely walk through Colonial Beach, Kevin pointed out several landmarks, spun a few tales about the oyster wars that had been fought in these waters, then showed her the Victorian house where Alexander Graham Bell had spent his summers. It was almost as lovely as the one Gracie wanted to buy.

But even though the Bell house had been spiffed up and its grounds were impeccable, it wasn't the house she wanted.

"Kevin—"

"I know. You want to talk about the house."

"You did promise."

"Okay, let's go take a look at it."

She stared at him in astonishment. "Do you mean it?"

"Why not? Unless, of course, you saw all you wanted to see when you slipped inside the other day."

"I didn't see anything, really," she swore. "I just checked to see if there was any evidence of an intruder."

"Then I'll give you the twenty-five-cent tour."

"Why?" she wondered, unable to keep a suspicious note out of her voice.

"You sound as if you're afraid I'll lock you in the attic and leave you there."

"Not that, but you have been pretty adamant about keeping me away from the place. Why the turnaround?"

"Because you've been very patient and you kept me from murdering Bobby Ray today." He grinned. "Don't let this little concession go to your head, though. It doesn't mean I'll sell the place to you."

Gracie didn't care. For the moment, poking around inside and imagining how she could convert the house into a bed and breakfast would be enough.

The rooms were dusty and mostly empty. What furniture remained was shrouded in sheets.

"I wonder if there's a ghost?" she asked in a whisper.

Kevin hesitated, then shook his head. "Not that I've ever heard about."

"Too bad," she said with genuine regret. "A ghost would be a great selling point."

Kevin regarded her with tolerant amusement, then led the way upstairs. There were half a dozen bedrooms, including one that opened onto a widow's walk. Gracie stepped outside and stared out at the wide river, imagining a time when someone had stood in this very spot and watched for a ship to make its way up from the Chesapeake Bay. The scent of lilacs wafted up from the overgrown bushes below.

"This is wonderful," she said dreamily. "I could stay out here all day long." She could feel the heat of Kevin's gaze on her and turned. "Or turn it into a honeymoon suite. Then again maybe I should keep it for myself. Turn it into an office."

"Don't let your imagination run away with you. The whole point of this was to show you how impractical it would be to try to turn this place into a bed and breakfast."

"Impractical? Why?"

"The rooms are too small, the floors are a mess, and wait

until you see the kitchen. I doubt there's anything in there
less than thirty years old."

"The rooms are fine, the floors are oak and could be polished and buffed in no time. As for the kitchen, a little renovation work doesn't scare me. Buying appliances won't take
more than one trip to a discount superstore."

"Trying to fit them in will provide the challenge."

"Let me see."

Kevin sighed. "You're not discouraged, are you?"

"Not a chance. If that was your plan, it backfired. Now
that I've seen it, I think this place is more perfect than ever."
She grabbed his hand and tugged. "Come on. I want to see
that kitchen you're so worried about."

"If you insist," he said, and led the way.

The kitchen was a bit of a mess and surprisingly dark. Not
that Gracie would ever admit to it. "It's perfect," she declared. "It's huge, or it will be once we knock out that wall
to the dining room. Then we could knock out part of that
outside wall ind put in more windows. It would be a great
area for serving breakfast to guests."

Her imagination took flight, replaced all of the old appliances with shining new ones, painted the walls a bright yellow, and added curtains. Something country French, she
thought. She could call some of her old suppliers in France
for the perfect fabric.

Of course, if she was going to redesign this room with
fabulous French decor, she'd better master that blasted souffle in a hurry. A menu of plain old scrambled eggs wasn't
going to cut it.

She described her idea to Kevin, who regarded her with
amused tolerance. "Can't you just see it?" she demanded,
wanting him to be caught up with her enthusiasm.

"No, but I can see that you do," he said.

He reached out and slowly brushed a tendril of flyaway
hair back from her cheek. Then his fingers lingered in a
gentle caress that stole her breath.

Before she realized what he intended, he leaned down and touched his lips to hers, softly at first and then with a hunger that stunned her. Gracie had never in her entire life been kissed with such consuming urgency. Her body swayed toward his, toward the heat radiating from him. Her hands came to rest on his chest, then slid slowly up until they encircled his neck.

And all the while his mouth and tongue were working magic, tasting, savoring, devouring. She was weak-kneed and dizzy by the time he finally pulled away. She was certain only his hands at her waist kept her upright. Otherwise she would have sunk to the floor, maybe made a fool of herself by dragging him down with her.

As a distraction, it was a hell of a kiss. For several very long moments, she had completely forgotten the business at hand: buying this damned house.

When she was certain she could manage it without stumbling, Gracie backed out of his embrace and scowled at him. "It won't work, you know. You're not going to dissuade me or sidetrack me from trying to get my hands on this house."

He grinned. "I know that," he conceded. "But wouldn't you say the stakes just got a whole lot more fascinating?"

Ten

"He had lipstick on his collar when he came in last night," Molly reported to Delia, her expression gleeful. "I checked the shirt he tossed into the laundry."

"Must have been Gracie's," Delia concluded happily. "I heard he swooped into the Beachside Cafe yesterday morning and practically carried her right out of there. Downright romantic is what it was."

"Do you think we'll finally get to plan a wedding around here?" Molly inquired wistfully.

"I wouldn't go getting your hopes up," Kevin said lightly, interrupting all of the merry speculating going on in his own kitchen. "Gracie doesn't especially want me. She wants that house of Aunt Delia's."

"You could make it a package deal," his aunt suggested.

A little bit insulted that she didn't think he could win Gracie purely on his own, he shook his head. "That's downright pitiful. Don't you two think I can catch a woman without offering a bribe?"

"Haven't shown any evidence of it so far," Molly observed.

He scowled at the housekeeper. "You can be replaced."

"Not likely," she retorted.

"Leave the woman alone," his aunt said. "You should be grateful she's put up with you all these years."

"What is this?" Kevin demanded irritably. "A blasted conspiracy? Never mind. I'll eat in my office. Bring my eggs and ham in there, please, Molly."

"You'll get bran flakes and be grateful," she retorted, and dumped some in a bowl. She then proceeded to drown them in milk . . . skim milk, at that. "You can take them with you."

Kevin accepted the sodden mess and turned to his aunt. "This is your fault, you know. Molly used to be docile as a lamb. Did everything I asked without a bit of sass. You're behind this insurrection and don't think I don't know it."

He heard them laughing as he headed for his office and couldn't hold back a grin of his own. Nothing could spoil his mood this morning, even if his life was being run by a couple of sneaky old women. That kiss he'd shared with Gracie was memorable enough to take the edge off his anger at Bobby Ray, too. Hell, he might even give his cousin that loan he wanted . . . right after he reminded him that he had a daughter he ought to be thinking about once in awhile.

He'd barely settled at his desk and eaten his soggy bran flakes when his cousin strolled in, his expression defiant.

"I heard you were looking for me," Bobby Ray said, bracing his hands on Kevin's desk and staring him straight in the eye. "What's the problem?"

Kevin drew in a deep breath and changed his mind. He might pummel Bobby Ray into a bloody mess, after all.

"Let's start with Abby," he said, managing an icy calm.

"I've already called and apologized. I talked to Marianne."

"So I heard."

"How? Did you go running right over there so she could cry on your shoulder like always?"

There was no mistaking the nasty insinuation behind the accusation. Kevin struggled to ignore it, kept his temper in check. "Never mind that. Your apology was a little late, don't you think? You should have been there when Abby got home from school, if that was the deal."

"Dammit, Kevin, how I deal with my daughter is none of

your business, unless, of course, you and Marianne kept fooling around after she picked me over you and there's some question about which one of us is Abby's daddy?"

This time his temper kicked in with a vengeance. Kevin came out from behind his desk so fast, Bobby Ray didn't have time to get out of his way. Kevin grabbed his cousin's fancy silk blend shirt and lifted him off his feet.

"Don't you ever make a lowdown, rotten comment like that again. Abby's yours, more's the pity. But we're family and she's my business when you forget all about her and leave her by herself. She's also my business when you're hanging onto the support money you're supposed to be sending for her every month." He stared deep into his cousin's eyes. "Are we clear on that?"

"Yes," Bobby Ray said, barely managing to choke out the word.

"Fine," Kevin said, letting him drop.

Bobby Ray sank into a chair, rubbing his neck where his collar had cut into it.

"Damn, Kev. You've lost your sense of humor entirely. Maybe you ought to take a vacation."

"I don't find anything funny in what you suggested. Marianne wasn't the unfaithful party in your marriage and you damned well know it."

Bobby Ray winced guiltily. "Okay, you're right, but not even you can deny she always had the hots for you."

"Maybe once upon a time, way back. She chose you to marry, though." He shook his head. "But it was never enough for you, was it? You never believed she made that choice because she loved you." His gaze narrowed. "Or did you simply choose her to prove you could take her away from me? Was that it, Bobby Ray?"

His cousin turned red at the accusation. Kevin stared at him and wondered why he'd never guessed that before. He'd always assumed it was nothing more than Bobby Ray's philandering that had come between him and Marianne. How could he have missed the obvious that way? Marrying Marianne had just been another form of payback aimed at Kevin. He wondered how soon after the ceremony Bobby Ray had let Marianne figure that out.

"You lousy son of a bitch," he said quietly. "How could you do that to her? Or did you even give her a thought?"

Bobby Ray remained stonily silent, which was answer enough. It was also warning enough to Kevin not to bring Gracie's name into the conversation. If he told his cousin to stay away from her, it would be like waving a red flag under his nose. Bobby Ray could charm the devil, if he put his mind to it. There was no telling what he'd do if he thought Kevin cared about Gracie. Kevin wouldn't have her caught in the crossfire between them.

"Get out," he said finally.

"Not just yet," Bobby Ray said, facing him stubbornly. "I still need that cash."

"You'll get it when pigs fly."

"Blast it, Kevin, that money's mine."

"And you'll get every penny . . . eventually."

Bobby Ray looked as if he might explode again, but he reined himself in. "What if I brought the paperwork by so you could check it yourself? It's a sound business decision, Kev. You'll see that."

Recalling what Gracie had told him about giving Bobby Ray the benefit of the doubt once in awhile, he nodded reluctantly. "Okay, bring it by." He met his cousin's gaze evenly. "Just tell me one thing, though. Why would you want to do business with a man who's sleeping with your wife?"

Bobby Ray came up out of his chair like a boxer heading for the center of the ring. "Where'd you hear that? It's a damned lie."

His quick reaction only confirmed Helen's report, as far as Kevin was concerned. "Where I heard it's not important," Kevin said. "I can see it's true. Is she worth it?"

His cousin's expression turned rueful. "Yeah, she is. Isn't

that a kick in the pants? I walked out on Marianne to make a point. Ginny was just a plain, old mistake. Now I've finally found a woman I could stay married to and it turns out she's got a wandering eye."

"Maybe that's the fascination. You don't have a hold on her. She's a challenge."

"Could be," he agreed. "But it feels like love to me and I'm going to fight for her."

"Is it love or pure cussedness?"

"Could be a little of both," Bobby Ray conceded without rancor.

"And you think going into business with her lover will help?"

"If I can tie him up designing jewelry to meet the demand on the shopping channel, maybe he won't have any time left for her," Bobby Ray explained.

"An interesting strategy," Kevin agreed. "Risky, though. What if he gets enough money to take her away to some fancy Caribbean island for a quickie divorce?"

"At least I'll have given it my best shot." He grinned. "And if he makes that much, then I'll be rolling in dough myself. I've got the deal worked in my favor."

Kevin actually chuckled at that. "Damn, Bobby Ray, maybe you have some business sense in that thick head of yours after all."

"Always told you I did," he said, as he headed for the door. "If I'd stayed in school, I'd be head of a multinational corporation by now, instead of running to you for pocket change all the time. I'll bring the papers by later today."

When he was gone, Kevin sighed. He didn't envy his cousin being so hung up on a woman that he'd let her tie his life into knots. In fact, he couldn't imagine letting anyone get under his skin like that.

Of course, Gracie MacDougal's kiss had been mighty tempting. Downright irresistible, in fact. He could see how a thing like that might sneak up on a man. He'd have to be very, very careful how often he indulged himself.

Gracie discovered she liked digging in the dirt. After years of spending her days in prim little suits, neat as a pin from head to toe, she thoroughly enjoyed getting filthy. She'd started spending every morning after breakfast weeding her garden. She'd even gone to the bargain store for some cheap shorts and a few T-shirts.

She gardened with abandon, too. She got on her hands and knees and poked around between the flowers Kevin had planted, looking for those clever little weeds that had dared to spring up overnight. She plucked them out and tossed them aside with startling ferocity. It felt good to have control over something. Goodness knew, the rest of her life was out of her hands.

At the moment, Kevin Patrick Daniels controlled her destiny and she didn't like it. She didn't like it one bit. If she'd run across another available house that was half as interesting as that old Victorian, she would have snatched it up in a heartbeat and avoided all future dealings with him.

Except, maybe, for an occasional kiss. She really hadn't minded that kiss at all. It had been an explosive experiment. In fact, she'd thought of little else for the past twelve hours. She'd even dreamed about it and awakened as hot and bothered as if it had just happened.

Let that be a warning, she told herself. Dealing with Kevin from now on was going to be very tricky. The man apparently had enough time on his hands to plan all sorts of sneaky strategies for distracting her from her goals.

Even this garden was a distraction, she thought, wiping perspiration from her brow and leaving behind what she imagined was a streak of dirt. She ought to be inside plotting strategy of her own. She ought to be dressing up and slipping down to the county courthouse to pore over property records.

Something was bound to give away the information she needed about the real owner of that house.

In fact, the more she thought about it, the more convinced she became that if she was ever to get her hands on that property, she was going to have to do some down and dirty investigative work.

She yanked one last weed out of the garden, then wiped her hands on her shirttail, grimacing at the mess. She would kill to be able to ship her clothes off to the hotel laundry about now, instead of having to do them all herself.

"Get used to it," she muttered as she headed inside to shower. If she opened that bed and breakfast, she was going to be doing more laundry than she'd ever dreamed of . . . personally.

An hour later she was all dressed up in a pair of linen slacks, a silk blouse, and leather flats. Casual but business-like, she concluded, surveying herself in the mirror. She added her favorite Cartier gold earrings and a matching bracelet, a set she'd splurged on one Christmas. Now she just had to practice her charm to see which little birdie in the courthouse she could coax into singing.

The drive to the county seat in Montross along Route 3— Historyland Highway, as it was dubbed—took her past the entrance to George Washington's birthplace, then past the turnoff to Stratford, birthplace of Robert E. Lee. She was in Montross with its oak-shaded town square in less than a half-hour.

She studiously avoided the temptations presented by a couple of antique shops and a display of bedding plants. She found the new courthouse complex a quarter-mile or so behind the impressive old courthouse with its faded brick facade and white pillars. The modern structure was far less interesting, far more institutionalized. Still, there was the promise of computerized information inside, and that was all that mattered. Maybe later she'd take the time to poke around in the local museum for some historical perspective on the property she wanted to buy.

A Mrs. Wilkes, according to the nameplate on her desk, offered to help her in the tax assessor's office.

"Do you have the location? A plot number?"

"No, just an address," Gracie said.

"Okay, let's see if we can work from that."

Her eyes seemed to widen ever so slightly when Gracie gave her the address. "Yes, of course. One moment, please."

Rather than going to the computer, Mrs. Wilkes disappeared behind a closed door. When she returned, empty-handed, she smiled brilliantly at Gracie. "It won't be long now."

"Aren't you going to check it on the computer?"

"I have someone checking in back," she assured her. "Why don't you have a seat?"

Since she couldn't think of any alternative, Gracie sat. She tapped her foot, glancing repeatedly at her watch and the clock on the wall. Ten minutes passed. Twenty.

Twenty-two minutes later precisely, the main door opened and in strolled Kevin. He winked at Mrs. Wilkes. "Thanks, Etta Mae."

He slipped onto the seat next to Gracie. "Hey, darlin'."

Gracie shot a wicked look at the woman she'd previously thought to be so kind. "I suppose she called you," she said sourly to Kevin.

"Of course she did."

"Why?"

"I figured you'd be turning up here sooner or later. I asked her to call."

"And naturally, like all women, she couldn't wait to do you a favor."

"Etta Mae and I go way back, don't we, Etta Mae?"

"Way back," she agreed, beaming at him. She stood up. "Think I'll go to lunch now."

"Good to see you," Kevin called after her.

"You, too. Anything else I can do, you let me know."

"I surely will."

"Is there anybody in this entire county who doesn't owe you a favor?" Gracie grumbled.

"None I can think of," he conceded. "How about some lunch? There's a place that serves the best North Carolina barbeque you've ever put in your mouth not too far from here."

"I don't want to have lunch with you."

He relaxed in the chair next to her, crossed his legs at the ankles, and seemed pretty much settled in. "Suit yourself."

"I'm going to get that house, Kevin. Get used to it."

He grinned. "If you say so."

"I never back away from a challenge."

"Me, either."

She slanted a sideways look at him. "North Carolina barbeque, huh?"

"The best."

"You lead. I'll follow in my car."

"I don't think so, darlin'. It's just down the road apiece. We might as well go in one car."

"You don't trust me, do you?"

"Not from here to the door," he agreed.

"That's insulting."

"That's the honest-to-goodness truth. If I left here ahead of you, you'd slip right back in and go poking around in that computer all by yourself, wouldn't you, especially without Etta Mae here to put a stop to it?"

Gracie sighed at the accuracy of his guesswork. "Come on, then. This barbeque had better be very good."

"It'll make your mouth water," he promised.

Gracie was less concerned about the tastiness of the barbeque than she was about how soon she could shake Kevin and get back to the courthouse and give old Etta Mae Wilkes a piece of her mind. Maybe she could point out the error of her ways in conspiring with a lowdown sneak like Kevin.

"She won't change her mind, you know," Kevin commented as he drove through Warsaw, crossed the Rappahannock River and headed into Tappahannock.

"Who won't?" Gracie asked, feigning innocence.

"Etta Mae."

"Who said anything about trying to change her mind?"

"You didn't have to. I know how you think."

"You do not."

"You were going to plague her with some song and dance about sisterhood and women sticking together and all that hogwash. It won't work. Etta Mae's very liberated. She makes up her own mind about things."

"I don't know about that. She fell for whatever story you fed her, didn't she?"

"Nope. She was just doing her job."

"Reporting my presence to you is her job?"

"Doing what a county supervisor asked," he corrected.

"You're on the board of county supervisors?"

"Yep."

"Well, hell." She frowned at him. "Etta Mae's not the only one in that courthouse on the lookout for me, is she?"

"Not by a longshot. Hers was just the first call I got. Not the last."

It was definitely a complication she hadn't counted on. But, in the long run, it would just make things more interesting. She smiled at him, clearly disconcerting him.

"What's that gleam in your eye all about?" he asked suspiciously as they walked into Lowery's.

"Nothing," she insisted in a way that suggested exactly the opposite, that she had all sorts of devious things in mind.

"Nothing, my patootie," he retorted. "You're up to something. What?"

"Just you wait and see," she said cheerfully and proceeded to concentrate on the biggest, juiciest minced barbeque sandwich she'd ever had in her life. That and the bemused, worried expression on Kevin's face almost made up for the morning's failure.

Eleven

As she was finishing up her walk the next day, Gracie spotted an old woman sweeping her porch next door to what she'd come to think of as her Victorian. Mrs. Johnson, no doubt, the woman who'd called her about that supposed intruder.

Gracie saw an opportunity to get a little information about exactly how that turn of events had come about. She waved. "Good morning."

The woman's gaze shot up and something that might have been worry creased her brow. "Morning, miss."

"Are you Mrs. Johnson?"

"Who's asking?" The woman's expression was suspicious.

"Gracie MacDougal. I believe you called me the other day when you thought someone had broken in next door."

She nodded then, but her expression was no more welcoming. "You're that gal who wants to buy the place and turn it into some sort of fancy hotel."

"A bed and breakfast, actually."

"I'm not sure I like the idea of a lot of strangers coming and going next door. Always been a quiet neighborhood. I'd like to keep it that way."

This wasn't a reaction she'd expected. Gracie opened the gate and stepped inside. "Do you have a minute? I could explain what I have in mind. I don't think you'll find it half so troubling once you understand."

Mrs. Johnson seemed to be debating the wisdom of letting her set foot on the porch. Finally she nodded. "Okay, come on up and sit a spell. I'll get us some iced tea."

"That's not necessary. I don't want to put you to any trouble."

"No trouble," she said, and disappeared inside.

She was gone so long, Gracie anticipated seeing Kevin turn up any second, just as he had the day before at the courthouse. Eventually, though, Mrs. Johnson returned with two glasses of tea and a plate of cookies on a silver serving tray. She put it onto the table between two rockers.

"Help yourself. Baked the cookies this morning. Doctor doesn't like me eating sugar, so I'm taking most of them over to the church later. You turning up gives me a chance to sample one." She chuckled. "Have to prove to my guest they're not poisoned, don't I?"

Gracie grinned at her, relieved that the old woman's attitude seemed to be mellowing. "Absolutely."

"Okay, then, tell me about this bed-and-breakfast thing. Never been to one myself."

"Basically, you're right about it being a hotel, just a very small one," Gracie explained. "In this case, probably four rooms, by the time I enlarge a couple of the bedrooms and add private bathrooms."

"You ever run one of these before?"

"No, but I've run several hotels in Europe."

"In Europe? You don't say. Which ones?"

"Most recently, the Worldwide Hotel in Cannes, the Maison de Sol."

"Lovely place. I was there once, years ago, of course, before your time. Any others?"

"Before that, I was at the one in Baden-Baden, and before that in Geneva."

"And Worldwide, that's the chain that prides itself on luxurious surroundings, isn't it?"

"It did," she said, unable to hide the trace of bitterness.

Mrs. Johnson regarded her intently. "That why you left? Were they paying too much attention to the bottom line and not enough to the comfort of the guests?"

"Exactly."

"That's the way the world's going these days," Mrs. Johnson lamented. "Fast food, inexpensive motels, economy cars, fake copies of great art. Nobody cares about the finer things in life the way they used to. In my day, it was better to have a few nice things than to load up on cheap knock-offs. My Charles, rest his soul, always wanted the best for me."

She reached out and rubbed her gnarled fingers over the silver tray. "You see this? He gave it to me on our silver wedding anniversary. How many people do you see nowadays using silver to serve? Not many, I'll warrant. They fire up their barbeques in the backyard and serve everything on plastic."

"I won't be using plastic," Gracie said quietly. "I want my bed and breakfast to have an old-fashioned elegance."

"Proper bed linens, ironed fresh?"

"Absolutely."

"Flowers from the garden in every room?"

"Of course."

"You collecting antique china or using whatever you can get from the department store?"

"I actually hadn't considered that."

"Go with antiques. Won't matter if the sets match. It'll still be a nice touch. Now, what about the breakfast part? You plan on dumping cereal and sliced bananas into a bowl and calling that breakfast?"

"That depends," Gracie conceded ruefully.

"On?"

"Whether I can master cooking. It's not my strong suit. All the hotels had very fine chefs. I never had to learn to cook. Now I'm starting from scratch, and I must admit, my attempts have been pretty disastrous."

Mrs. Johnson looked appalled. "You can certainly read, can't you?"

"Of course."

"Then all you need is a good cookbook and a little daring."

"I have the cookbook, but you should see the results of my experiments. Most of them are inedible," Gracie confessed. "Even the cats that wander by turn up their noses."

"Then what you're missing is the daring," Mrs. Johnson declared. "You can't be afraid. You come over here this afternoon at four o'clock, after my shows go off. I'll teach you."

Gracie regarded her with astonishment. "You will?"

"Why not? I don't have anything exciting going on in my life. You'll be a challenge."

"Does that mean you approve of my plans?"

"Can't say yet. All depends on how quick a learner you are."

"I may not be quick, but I'm determined."

Mrs. Johnson gave her a nod of approval. "That'll do for a start. We'll begin with blueberry muffins. I'll pick up the ingredients. You can pay me later."

"I don't know how to thank you."

"No thanks necessary." She grinned. "I'll get to keep one or two of the muffins."

"You may change your mind, after I'm finished."

"Now, what kind of self-confidence is that?" Mrs. Johnson chided. "Bring a notebook. You can write down the recipe."

"I can't just make a copy?"

"Not of this one. It's all in my head." She stood up and waved Gracie off. "Now, get along with you. I have to get to the store. You be back here at four and not a minute earlier. I don't like missing a single second of my shows. Never can tell what Reva and Josh and them good-for-nothing Spauldings are going to be up to."

"I'll remember," Gracie promised. She would be here on

the dot of four, notebook in hand and filled with more questions than Mrs. Johnson had ever anticipated.

"She was here," Bessie Johnson reported to Delia.

"Exactly as I expected," Delia said with satisfaction. "What's she like?"

"Pretty, smart, open to suggestions. I think she'll do for Kevin just fine. Told you that the other day after I talked to her on the phone. I liked the way she didn't waste time on a bunch of silly questions. She just came straight over when I called about that intruder we invented."

Delia gave a little nod of approval. She'd thought as much. Gracie MacDougal had struck her as a no-nonsense kind of woman. Clever, too. She'd been smart enough to go down to the courthouse and dig around. Delia had heard that story from Kevin last night. It was too bad Kevin had been one step ahead of Gracie and even more unfortunate that Etta Mae had seen fit to conspire with him. That silly old woman didn't have a romantic bone in her body.

Not that Gracie would have gotten the answers she was after, anyway. All the tax records were in Kevin's name. So was the deed, for that matter, though he'd insisted that as long as Delia lived she would make any decisions when it came to selling or keeping her home.

"Was she asking a lot of questions this time?" she asked Bessie.

"Didn't give her a chance to," Bessie replied. "I was asking too many myself. Got her to talking about that bed and breakfast. She's got a head on her shoulders, all right. One thing you ought to know, though. She claims she can't cook a lick."

"Oh, dear. Won't that be a problem at a bed and breakfast?"

"I was thinking more of Kevin's stomach. That boy always did have an appetite. Don't you worry, though. I'm taking care of it. I offered to teach her. She'll be back at four to learn how to bake blueberry muffins."

Delia chuckled at her friend's deviousness. "Kevin's favorite."

"You think I didn't remember that? He used to beg enough of them off me."

"You're not to tell her I own the house just yet," Delia reminded Bessie.

"You think I don't know how to keep a secret, Delia? I've kept yours all these years, haven't I?"

Delia sighed. "Yes, you have. You've been the best friend a person could ever ask for."

"Well, then, you just leave Gracie MacDougal to me. Your job is to work on Kevin till he's primed to marry the woman."

"He's a stubborn one, though. He's lived his whole life around bad examples. Saying 'I do' won't come easily to him."

"Then you'll just have to be a little sneakier, won't you?" Bessie said. "It's what you want for him, isn't it?"

"More than anything," Delia said wistfully. "More than anything in this world, I want to see him settled before I die."

"Then we'll make it happen," Bessie said confidently. "Make no mistake about it, Delia. Kevin's days as a bachelor are numbered."

After she'd hung up, Delia sat back, closed her eyes and smiled. It was all going exactly the way she'd envisioned from the moment she'd spotted Gracie MacDougal with her nephew. She'd seen the way they'd argued, seen the way Gracie had peeked at Kevin's body when she was sure no one was looking. Most important of all, she'd seen the too-rare sparkle of sheer delight in Kevin's eyes when he'd talked about her.

Thanks to the mess those in her generation had made of their lives, Kevin had had all too little to smile about. She

intended to see to it that he got a woman who could change
that.

Kevin pounded on Gracie's door, then fought disappointment when there was no response. He'd gotten it into his
head in the middle of the afternoon that he needed to see
her. He'd battled the urge for an entire hour, told himself he
was behaving like a lovesick adolescent, then finally stopped
pretending it was a battle he could win.

He'd driven into town to see her without bothering to call.
He enjoyed taking her by surprise. She struck him as the
kind of woman who'd had far too few surprises in life. In
some ways, that made them more alike than she probably
knew. Most of the surprises in his life had been bad ones.

"So, where are you, Gracie?" he wondered after checking
out the backyard to make sure she wasn't sitting out there
admiring her new garden. She was probably sneaking around
trying to get information on the property she wanted.

He liked that about her, liked that she didn't give up, that
she was totally convinced she could eventually wear him
down—or bypass him completely—and get what she wanted.

He tapped on the backdoor one last time, then turned the
knob. She'd left the stupid thing unlocked. Okay, Seagull
Point was a small town, but folks didn't just go off and leave
their doors unlocked even here. The locals might be fine
people, but a person never could tell who might be passing
through.

He stepped into the kitchen, which was the tidiest he'd
seen it. Either she'd given up entirely on cooking or she just
hadn't experimented today. Thinking of the mess he'd seen,
he hoped for the former, but laid odds on the latter.

Though he wanted to, he couldn't quite bring himself to
venture beyond the kitchen. Everybody deserved their privacy. He had no reason at all to go poking around the rest
of her house, not even to see if he could discern what tricks

she might have up her sleeve for snatching that house of Delia's.

That didn't mean he wasn't filled with curiosity when the phone started to ring. Probably that guy from France, the one she was so adamant was nothing more than an ex-boss. He paused beside the answering machine and waited for it to pick up. He figured he could tell a lot just by hearing the man's voice.

"Gracie, *chérie,* where are you? This is Max. What could there be in that little podunk place to keep you away from home so often?"

Kevin couldn't help it. He found that supercilious tone very annoying. Without giving the matter any thought, he grabbed the phone. "Hey, Max, this is Kevin Daniels."

"Who?"

"Gracie's friend."

"I was not aware that Gracie had any friends in Virginia," he said stiffly.

"She does now," Kevin replied. "What's up? Another little crisis you need her to solve? I can give her a message."

"Never mind. I will explain it to her when we speak. Let her know that I will call back later. Tell her, please, that it is very important that I speak with her today."

"Sure thing," Kevin agreed. "Who knows, though? Maybe between now and then you'll figure out a solution all by yourself."

"Good-bye, Mr. Daniels," he said, his tone chilly.

"Au revoir, Max."

He hung up feeling decidedly cheerful. He didn't even bother erasing the partial message Max had begun before Kevin picked up. He figured Gracie wouldn't be pleased with the derisive little comment about the podunk town she was about to adopt as her home, not if she was serious about staying.

As far as he'd been able to determine, Gracie wasn't a snob, even if she had jumped rather quickly to the conclusion that he was little more than a lazy slacker. He hadn't done much to disabuse her of that notion. He kind of enjoyed the fact that she was starting to like him despite her initial bad impression. Definitely not a snooty bone in her body, unlike old Max.

So where was she? Max was right about one thing. For a stranger, she did seem to get around. On foot, too, since her flashy red car was parked right out front.

It didn't take a lot of imagination to guess she'd probably headed over to take another peek at Delia's. Kevin walked the few blocks, fully expecting to find her up on the roof, sneaking in the window again. To his surprise there was no sign of her.

Then he heard her laugh. There was no mistaking that bright, pure sound. It was coming from Mrs. Johnson's. As he drew closer, he realized it was also accompanied by the familiar scent of blueberry muffins.

Rather than knocking on the front door, he went around to the back, just as he had a hundred times as a kid. Mrs. Johnson spotted him before he could set foot on the back stoop. She was grinning when she opened the door.

"There you are, Kevin. I've been expecting you."

He didn't doubt Mrs. Johnson's claim. He'd almost never missed a batch of her blueberry muffins. She baked on Wednesday mornings like clockwork and he always showed up. This was an off day and an odd time, but he just figured luck was with him.

Gracie, however, clearly hadn't anticipated him turning up. She regarded him with suspicion, then turned her gaze on Mrs. Johnson. "You knew he was coming by?"

"Hasn't been a time since he could walk that Kevin didn't turn up here for my blueberry muffins. Always did have a sixth sense about when I was baking."

"Is that right?" Gracie said, still scowling.

"Don't look so suspicious, darlin'. It's pure coincidence, me turning up."

"I'll bet," she muttered, turning her back on him to open the oven door. "Oh, my."

"You didn't burn them, did you?" Kevin asked, unable to keep a plaintive note out of his voice.

"No, I didn't burn them," she retorted, sliding the pan out. "They're perfect."

"Look good," Mrs. Johnson confirmed. "I told you you could do it."

"Must be a foolproof recipe," Kevin observed.

"If you came by to beg a muffin, you're getting off on the wrong foot," Mrs. Johnson chastised.

"Just experience talking." He regarded the muffins intently. "Could be the tide's about to turn, though. Those look pretty good. I'll test the first one."

"I shouldn't let you have a single one after that remark you made," Gracie said. "But maybe it would be better to let you take the risk, rather than one of us. It'll serve you right, if you get sick."

"On second thought—"

"Oh, no you don't," Gracie said. "You volunteered." She popped a muffin out of the pan and put it on a fancy porcelain dessert plate, then slid it in front of him. She sat down across from him and watched him anxiously. "Do you need a knife? Butter?"

"If you've done 'em right, I won't need anything," he said, breaking off a chunk. The texture was light and fluffy. It was filled with plump blueberries. "Looks okay."

Actually, it looked better than okay. His mouth was watering, but he wouldn't give her the satisfaction of telling her that. He waited a full minute for the chunk to cool before popping it into his mouth. He closed his eyes. It was heavenly.

"Well?" Gracie prodded.

"Not bad."

"Kevin Patrick!" Mrs. Johnson chided.

He grinned. "Okay, it's sensational."

Gracie studied him worriedly. "Really? You're not just saying that?"

"Have you ever known me to be diplomatic?"

"Hardly."

He ate another chunk. "Delicious. Every bit as good as Mrs. Johnson's."

Gracie jumped up and threw her arms around the older woman. "Thank you," she said fervently.

Her face flooded with embarrassed color, Mrs. Johnson quickly extricated herself from the embrace and patted Gracie's hand. "You're the one who did the work."

"But Kevin was right. Your recipe had to be foolproof."

"Aren't you going to taste one yourself?" he asked, amused by her enthusiasm.

"I guess I should," she said, eyeing the muffins cautiously. Clearly, she thought he might be exaggerating the quality.

Finally she took one, neatly broke off a tiny piece and ate it. A smile broke across her face. She tried a second bite, then sighed contentedly. "It is wonderful, isn't it?"

"Don't even think about resting on your laurels," Mrs. Johnson said briskly. "Tomorrow we'll do scones."

"Cranberry-orange?" Kevin asked hopefully.

Mrs. Johnson sighed. "I suppose you'll be back here begging a sample, if they are." Despite the sigh, she didn't look particularly displeased by the prospect.

"You bet." He glanced at Gracie. "That is, if Gracie doesn't mind."

"Whatever," she mumbled, her mouth stuffed with another chunk of muffin.

Kevin grinned. "If I'd known what it took to make you so agreeable, I'd have arranged for cooking lessons days ago."

"Okay, you two, get along with you," Mrs. Johnson said. "I'm tired."

"We can't go until I've cleaned up," Gracie protested.

"Leave it be. It won't take me but a minute. I'll do it after

I've fixed supper. No point in cleaning up, only to mess it up again an hour from now."

"Are you sure?" Gracie asked.

"I said it, didn't I?"

"Come on, Gracie. I recognize that tone," Kevin said. "She's fed up with both of us."

"Okay, if you're sure," Gracie said, taking one last look at Mrs. Johnson.

"Go," she said succinctly, then glanced at Kevin with a tolerant smile. "Take the muffins along with you, why don't you? You know I'm not supposed to have them."

Kevin grabbed a paper sack from the drawer where they'd always been kept, then dumped all but one of the muffins into it. He dropped a kiss on Mrs. Johnson's weathered cheek.

"Thanks. If I could have found a woman who baked like you, I'd have married her years ago."

"Give Gracie a little time," she suggested with a wink. "Maybe she'll fill the bill."

"Could be," he agreed, and turned to find the woman in question blushing furiously. "Come on, Gracie. On the way back to your place, I'll explain the function of locks."

"Locks? I know what locks are for."

He winked at Mrs. Johnson as they left. "Then why don't you use them?"

He saw the precise instant when Gracie figured out the implication of the question. Bright patches of color appeared in her cheeks and her eyes flashed sparks.

"You've been in my house, haven't you?"

"That unlocked door was the next best thing to an invitation," he replied unrepentantly. "By the way, your buddy Max called."

She stared at him indignantly. "You answered the phone, too?"

"Not until after he'd started his message. I didn't like his attitude."

"What's wrong with his attitude?"

"You'll see."

"Kevin, you can't just barge into other people's homes and start taking their phone calls because you disapprove of the caller."

"Not normally, no. You made it easy for me."

She sighed. "I suppose there was another crisis."

"So he claims."

"Did he say what it was?"

"Nope. I suggested he try to solve it all by himself."

She stared at him. "You didn't."

"I did."

A smile began working the corners of her mouth. "And what did Max say to that?"

"Let's just say I doubt we'll ever be buddies."

"That was a given," she said, chuckling. "You and Max are as different as night and day."

Kevin nodded. "One question, darlin'. Does that work in my favor or his?"

She reached up and patted his cheek. "I think I'll keep the answer to that to myself."

Twelve

Though torture couldn't have forced her to admit it to Kevin, Gracie was delighted with the pattern that was developing. Every afternoon precisely at four, she went to visit Mrs. Johnson for another cooking lesson. An hour later, Kevin showed up to taste the results.

So far, she'd mastered two different kinds of scones, a second type of muffin, and a pecan coffee cake that was to die for. She'd lengthened her walk every morning just to burn off the extra calories. Given his apparent lack of energetic pursuits, she had no idea why Kevin hadn't turned into a blimp. That he hadn't raised all sorts of fascinating questions about what he was up to when they weren't together.

She studied him as they walked back to her house after consuming most of that pecan coffee cake. His stomach was flat as a pancake. Though she couldn't see his abs at the moment, she knew exactly what they looked like—taut and well defined. She allowed him to get a step ahead of her and assessed his rear. Definitely calendar pin-up material.

"Enjoying the view?" he inquired lightly, not the least bit embarrassed by her blatant inspection.

Gracie, however, was humiliated at being caught. She tried feigning innocence. "Excuse me?"

"I asked if you were enjoying the view."

"Um, sure," she mumbled. "The water's lovely this time of day."

He glanced at her with that same tolerant amusement she found so infuriating. "Darlin', if you were looking at the water, you'd know a storm's brewing. It's choppy as the dickens out there."

She glanced at the Potomac. Sure enough, it was churning with whitecapped waves. "So it is," she acknowledged. "If a storm's rolling in, I guess you'd better hurry home before it breaks."

"I'm not scared of a little thunder and lightning." He peered intently at her. "Are you?"

"Of course not," she denied a little too vehemently, unable to hide the shudder that washed over her.

His eyes widened. "You are, aren't you?"

"I said I wasn't."

"It's just a little bowling going on up in the heavens," he offered.

Gracie wasn't going to be placated with that particular tale. She'd heard that one and more as she'd cowered in her bed as a child with the blankets pulled over her head. For reasons she'd never been able to fathom, storms had always terrified her. It was a weakness she hated in herself and wasn't about to admit to.

"I'll protect you," Kevin promised, just as the first rumble of thunder sounded in the distance.

"Don't be ridiculous," she said, feigning nonchalance. "It's just a silly old thunderstorm."

"Then why did you just turn white as a sheet?"

"Must have been something in the coffeecake."

"Gracie, there's nothing to be embarrassed about. Everybody's scared of something. Storms shake up a lot of people."

"I am not scared," she protested, then shivered unmistakably when lightning slashed through the rapidly darkening sky. The air was charged with electricity. She could practically taste it in the air, feel it in the prickling of her skin. She quickened her pace. She really, really wanted to be safely inside when this sucker broke, preferably inside a window-less closet.

Kevin kept pace with her easily over the last block, but instead of dashing for his car as the first scattered fat drops of rain fell, he followed her inside.

"You don't have to stay," Gracie insisted. "I'll be fine."

"You have any wine?" he asked, ignoring her protest.

"In the wine rack in the pantry," she said, more grateful than she liked that he wasn't leaving despite her protests.

"Candles?"

She chuckled. "I'm glad to see your priorities are in order. First wine, then candles."

"Where are they, sweetface?"

She couldn't recall for the life of her. "I think I saw some in the drawer by the stove."

He rummaged around in there for a minute, then held up a package of birthday candles. "I doubt these will last long. What about an oil lamp?"

She should have remembered that in the first place. After the first storm of the season, which had caught her off guard and lasted less than an hour, she'd searched high and low until she found one so it would be ready for the next such occasion. "In the living room."

"Any oil in it?"

"Yes. I saw to that right away."

"Matches?"

"Right beside it. There's a flashlight there, too."

"Good."

She worried over the implications of all the preparations. "Kevin, are you expecting the power to go out?"

"It's not a given, but I wouldn't bet against it."

Gracie sighed.

"Don't worry about it. I'll be right here. We'll be safe and cozy. Do you have any cards?"

"Cards?"

"You know, playing cards. It's either that or cuddling on the sofa."

She trembled at the choice, almost opted for the more dangerous one, the one that guaranteed the storm outside would pass by unnoticed. Eventually, though, common sense ruled. "I'll hunt for cards."

Kevin grinned. "Too bad. Cuddling's a lot more distracting, especially if it leads to something more."

Oh, yes, Gracie thought. She'd bet her dream house on that. She practically tore the kitchen apart looking for a deck of cards. She finally found an old, grease-stained poker deck in the back of a drawer.

They were playing their first hand when the rain began in earnest. This wasn't the soft rain of spring. It was a hard, driving rain, accompanied by increasingly loud crashes of thunder and brighter slashes of lightning.

The power went a half hour later with a cracking sound, the explosion of a nearby transformer, Kevin assessed. Though it was still daylight—or should have been—the sky was so dark with rolling clouds, it could have been late evening.

Even so, Kevin laid down his next bet before getting the oil lamp and lighting it. The man had the concentration and competitive instincts of a cardsharp.

"Where'd you learn to play like this?" Gracie asked when she lost the fifth straight hand, either because the cards were all falling his way or because she wasn't paying nearly enough attention to the ones she'd been dealt.

"Family hobby," Kevin said, dealing the next hand.

"You come from a family of poker players?"

"It's not a career, darlin'. Like I said, it's a hobby." He gestured toward the pile of cards in front of her. "Pick up your hand."

Gracie picked up the cards and looked them over, then discarded two, accepting two more in return. Nothing, absolutely nothing. Not even a piddly little pair. Even so, she bet to win. Kevin wasn't fooled. He raised her bet.

"Do you all take your hobbies so seriously?" she asked.

"Yep," he said, as he spread a full house onto the table and raked in yet another pot.

"Do you think it's fair, then, to be taking advantage of a rank amateur?"

"Absolutely. I almost never win at home. Those people play for blood. Took me for five bucks and change the other night."

Gracie grinned. "That much, huh? I'm astonished you didn't have to declare bankruptcy."

"If I ever let 'em raise the stakes above a penny, I might have to. My niece is particularly bloodthirsty."

"Is that Abby?"

"Yeah. You'll have to meet her one of these days. She's an angel, though I'll deny I ever said it if you tell her. Just don't play poker with her."

The next flash of lightning lit the room as bright as noontime sun. Thunder shook the house and set Gracie to trembling just as violently.

Kevin reached across the table and clasped her hand. "Hey, darlin'."

Thoroughly embarrassed, Gracie refused to meet his gaze. If the gesture had been meant to steady her nerves, it had backfired. She was shivering uncontrollably now, though the blame for it couldn't be placed entirely on the storm.

"Look at me," he commanded softly.

She finally dared a glance up and into his eyes. She saw compassion there and something more, the kind of heated look that inspired a renewed trembling all its own. She swallowed hard and wished desperately she were the kind of woman who could indulge in sex for the sheer fun of it. The offer—the desire—was plain enough on Kevin's face, in his touch. No matter that the caress of his hand on hers was only slightly less innocent than a handshake, the vibrations it sent through her were pure sin. Her blood raced.

"I'm fine," she said firmly, extricating her hand from his.

"Any idea why you're so afraid of storms?"

"None," she said, seeing no point in further denials. "It's silly, I know. I probably saw some report on TV once about somebody getting struck by lightning or a house burning down and the image stuck."

She glanced outside, hoping to see clearing skies. Instead, the vicious dark clouds went on as far as she could see, dumping out torrents of hard rain. "How long is this supposed to go on?" she asked plaintively.

"There's no telling."

"And the power?"

"Could be hours before it's restored. Do you have anything in the refrigerator that's likely to spoil?"

She thought of the pricey ice cream she'd discovered and become addicted to in recent days. It was filled with cherries and chocolate and nuts.

"Just some ice cream."

Kevin's eyes lit up. "Can't waste that. I'll get it."

He came back with the carton and only one spoon. Gracie grinned at him and reached for both. "Thanks," she said.

Kevin held the ice cream out of reach. "Back off, kid. Nothing gets between me and my ice cream," he warned. "Especially this flavor."

"It *is* my ice cream," Gracie pointed out.

"And I'm a guest."

"I suppose it shouldn't surprise me that no one ever taught you to share."

"Okay, okay," he grumbled, scooping out a spoonful and holding it out for her.

Gracie reached for the spoon, but Kevin held on. "Just take a bite," he said, as if he feared relinquishing the spoon would be the end of his claim on the rest of the carton.

Remembering the effectiveness of her tactic with the

strawberry pie, a streak of pure devilment came over her once again. Rather than simply eating the offered ice cream, she wrapped her hand around his to steady it, then slowly began to lick the ice cream as if it were in a cone. She ran her tongue around the melting edges, then took the spoon into her mouth and sucked. She turned the eating of that little mound of ice cream into an erotic adventure, one step more dangerous than the strawberry pie he'd fed her.

Kevin's skin heated more quickly than the burner on a stove. Beneath her clasp, she could feel his pulse buck. His breath fanned against her cheek and seemed to come more rapidly.

She took a very long time to finish, and only when she was done did she dare to meet his gaze. She was shocked by the raw hunger she saw in his eyes. For a second she feared she had unleashed something primitive and untamable in him, but he blinked and it was gone, replaced by that familiar, irrepressible grin.

"That was . . ." He hesitated. ". . . interesting," he said finally.

Gracie was too stunned by the yearning thrumming through her to reply. She had to wonder just which one of them had been caught by the game's snare.

Kevin dipped another spoonful of ice cream from the carton and offered it. "More?"

Her gaze rose to clash with his and she saw the laughter and the dare in his eyes. "Sure," she said bravely. "Why not?"

She took a little less time with the second bite and the third. Somewhere around the fifth, Kevin glanced into the carton and realized what had happened.

"Why, you little sneak," he muttered. "It's gone. You ate the last of the ice cream."

Gracie grinned at him. "Yeah, I did, didn't I? Thanks for sharing."

"Sharing? I never got so much as a single lick."

"Really? I'm sorry."

"I should go off and leave you to sit out this storm all by yourself."

"But you won't," she said confidently.

"Why is that?"

"Because you're a southern gentleman."

"Something at the moment I am deeply regretting," he said. "That's what cost me that blasted ice cream."

"Oh, no," Gracie said. "That was lust, pure and simple. Watching me eat that ice cream was turning you on. Admit it."

"I don't think you want to go too far down that particular path, darlin'. Somebody might accuse you of being a tease. Somebody might decide to claim what you were so clearly offering."

Gracie swallowed hard at the lightly-spoken warning. Some part of her wanted him to do exactly that, wanted him to take matters out of her hands and persuade her straight into bed. If he'd known how little effort it would require, no doubt he'd seize the opportunity.

But the sensible, practical side of her knew better than to open that particular door, knew that if she didn't change the subject in a heartbeat, one of them was going to make a move from which there'd be no turning back. As long as Kevin stood squarely between her and the future she wanted for herself, she couldn't allow anything else to develop between them. It would be asking for trouble.

Unfortunately, she didn't exactly feel like resisting too hard. Nor could she come up with another topic that was half so fascinating.

Fortunately the ringing of the phone saved her.

"Max, no doubt," Kevin said dryly. "It's just about time for his daily crisis."

"It's not even dawn in France," Gracie pointed out as she crossed the kitchen toward the phone.

"Which means he must roll out of bed thinking of ways

to get you back over there," Kevin replied. "Sure you don't want me to take the call? I enjoy dealing with old Max."

"Much as I would like to delegate the responsibility for dealing with Max to you, I think I'd better handle him myself."

"Suit yourself." Kevin rocked back on his chair and watched her, clearly intent on making the conversation his evening's entertainment.

"Hello," Gracie said, wishing she'd bought a portable phone, instead of one that necessitated standing right in front of Kevin. And, of course, a portable wouldn't have worked with the power out, which would have been better yet. "Yes, Max, I was still up. What is it this time?"

Her tone was more impatient than usual thanks to her awareness of her audience.

"You sound upset, *chérie*. Is everything okay?"

"Everything is just peachy. And stop calling me *chérie*. I'm not your dear and you're not French."

"You *are* having a bad day," he concluded.

"I'm fine, Max. Why did you call? I haven't heard from you for a couple of days now. I'd hoped you were handling the crises on your own."

"Everything is running smoothly, yes."

Gracie was taken aback by that announcement. She found the reaction more telling than she liked. Could it be that she had enjoyed Max's little crises, invented or not? Could it be that she had actually craved those daily reassurances that she was missed?

"I'm delighted," she said through gritted teeth, unsure whether her sudden annoyance was directed at Max or herself.

"Yes, I can hear that in your voice."

"Why did you call, Max?"

"I called only to say hello, to see if you are getting along okay."

"I'm fine. Terrific, in fact."

"And this man who answered your phone the last time I called, who is he?"

Suddenly—finally—Gracie got an inkling of why she hadn't heard from Max for a few days. He'd been sulking. He'd actually been sitting over in Cannes stewing over Kevin. Was it possible she had actually misjudged the level of his interest in her? Would it matter if she had? Truthfully, no.

"He's a friend," she said, refusing to meet the fascinated gaze of said friend.

"That's all?"

"Max, I've been here a few weeks," she said, her exasperation plain. "What more could it be? Besides, what business is it of yours?"

"I worry about you," he confessed. "You were very vulnerable and unhappy when you left here. I would not like to see someone take advantage of that."

Max's insight startled her. She'd never suspected he was capable of thinking beyond his precious bottom lines.

"Max, you don't need to worry. I can take care of myself."

"Perhaps I should come and see for myself."

The announcement startled her so badly, it took her a minute to gather her composure. "You want to come here?"

Kevin's increasingly smug grin broadened. "Told you so," he murmured.

"Oh, go to hell," she muttered back.

"What?" Max asked, sounding shocked.

"Not you, Max."

Max sighed heavily. "He is there, then?"

"Yes, more's the pity."

"If you don't enjoy having him there, why don't you insist that he leave?"

"We got caught in a bad storm," she began, then broke off. She didn't owe Max any explanations at all. "Never mind. Max, I appreciate you offering to come, but it's not necessary."

"I think it is. In fact, I am more convinced of it than ever.

I will call you when I have made the arrangements. Expect me within a week or so, sooner if I can get matters here under control."

"Max!"

"All revoir, ma petite."

He hung up before she could try to talk him out of coming. "Well, damn," she muttered.

"So," Kevin said, still grinning. "Max is coming?"

"It appears he is," she said, and began pacing.

"You didn't try very hard to talk him out of it."

"I didn't think he was serious until it was too late. Besides, nobody talks Max out of anything. He's a very stubborn man."

Before she realized what he intended, Kevin reached out and snagged her hand, toppling her into his lap. The next instant, his mouth covered hers in a bruising, heady kiss that couldn't be mistaken for anything other than a branding.

He released her as abruptly as he'd claimed her, setting her on her feet and standing himself. He walked to the door, then turned back. "Remember that, when Max comes calling," he said lightly.

Before Gracie could gather her wits, he was gone, the door slamming behind him and another crash of thunder adding its emphasis to the moment.

She touched her fingers to her swollen, tender lips and felt the tug of something powerful in her belly. Forget the prospect of Max's unwanted arrival. The more immediate problem was what to do about Kevin Patrick Daniels and his unnerving ability to make her head spin.

Thirteen

Kevin was hotter than a sidewalk at high noon in August. His temper, not the heat, was responsible. In fact, it was only a pleasant eighty-degrees outside with a breeze that actually made lying in the shade in his favorite hammock almost chilly. He'd been mulling over that phone call from Max the night before and getting more worked up over it by the second.

Unfortunately, with his usual lousy sense of timing, Bobby Ray chose this precise moment to show up and interrupt his already dark mood. When Kevin caught sight of Sara Lynn and a ponytailed man with Bobby Ray, his annoyance tripled. Perhaps if he feigned sleep, they'd go away.

"Hey, Kevin!" Bobby Ray shouted as they approached.

"Not now, Bobby Ray," he said without opening his eyes.

"Yes, now," Bobby Ray said, his tone fierce and just a little desperate.

That panicked note got Kevin's attention. He sighed and rolled out of the hammock. "Inside," he said, and led the way.

In his office Sara Lynn regarded him warily, while the stranger, Daniel Featherstone, grabbed his hand and pumped it enthusiastically.

"You're not going to regret this," he claimed.

Kevin glanced at Bobby Ray. "Oh, really," he said wryly.

"Everything was spelled out in those contracts I left for

you," Bobby Ray reminded him. "You've looked them over, right?"

"I looked them over," Kevin confirmed. Bobby Ray had managed to tailor the deal in his own favor without it being obvious. Too bad he hadn't used that business acumen in some of his other pursuits.

"It's a great deal, right?" Featherstone enthused. "Bobby Ray and I are going to get rich."

Kevin doubted it, but the prospect of arguing with the man hardly seemed worth the effort. He regarded Sara Lynn intently, then exchanged a pointed look with Bobby Ray. "You're sure you want to do this?"

"I'm sure," his cousin insisted, keeping his gaze fixed on his wife.

Kevin sighed and pulled out the checkbook for the estate account. He scribbled in the exorbitant amount Bobby Ray needed to hang on to his wife, then handed it over. Everybody beamed, including Sara Lynn. Kevin scowled back.

"Out!" he ordered. "Now."

Sara Lynn and her friend didn't waste a second bolting from the room. Bobby Ray lingered.

"Thanks, Kevin."

"Don't thank me. I just pray you won't live to regret it. For the life of me, I can't figure out how you can choose a woman like that over Marianne."

For an instant Bobby Ray's expression turned wistful, then the flash of vulnerability was gone, replaced by his more typical cocky expression. "You always did have a soft spot for Marianne, Kev. Get over it. I did."

For the first time in all the years since the messy divorce, Kevin wondered about that.

The meeting left him in a foul mood for the rest of the morning. He yelled at Molly, snapped at Aunt Delia, and told his secretary in Richmond not to bother him with things she could handle herself.

Why was he in such a lousy mood and taking it out on

everyone around him? He knew better than to lay all the blame on Bobby Ray. The bulk of it belonged to Gracie.

Blame it on that smoldering kiss they'd shared right before he'd walked out on her. Blame it on the untimely call from Max and the promise—no, threat—of Max's visit.

Blame it, ultimately, on the fact that he was losing his head over a woman he barely knew. He sighed and sipped his lemonade, wishing for once that it was something stronger, something that would dull his mind and make this hot ache in his loins go away.

"Okay, young man, what has you in such a snit?" Aunt Delia demanded, standing next to him, hands on hips and fire in her eyes.

Kevin opened one eye and peered at her. The effect of all that indignation was ruined a bit by the whimsical addition of a hot pink baseball cap someone had given her from the Saratoga racetrack and her matching hot-pink sneakers.

"Go away," he ordered.

She stood her ground and impaled him with a blistering look. "Not until you tell me what's going on. It's one thing for you to bark at me or Bobby Ray, but Molly and that sweet lady in your office don't deserve it."

"I know it," Kevin conceded with a sigh. "I'll apologize. I'll buy Molly that new food processor she wants and I'll send Jane flowers."

"And I'm sure they'll appreciate the gesture, but I'd prefer it if you'd just tell me why you're in such a mood." She regarded him craftily. "Is it Gracie? Did you two have a fight?"

"No."

"I don't believe you. You were always a lousy fibber, Kevin Patrick. What's Gracie done to upset you?"

He sat up with an air of resignation. "You aren't going to leave this alone, are you?"

"No," she said as emphatically as he had a moment earlier.

She sat in a nearby Adirondack chair, folded her hands in her lap and regarded him patiently.

"Gracie's having company," he finally said.

"I see."

"Her old boss. She thinks he's just coming to try to persuade her to come back to work for him."

"And you disagree?"

"The man has invented more crises than the Middle East has had since the beginning of time."

"Maybe he depended on Gracie."

"I'm sure he did. In fact, I know he'd be crazy if he didn't want her back running that hotel of his."

"Are you afraid she's going to go?"

"Of course not. It doesn't matter to me one way or the other whether she goes."

"Nonsense. Of course, it matters. Any fool could take one look at you and see that it does."

"I'm telling you I don't give a damn what she does," he repeated, as if saying it often enough could make it so. "I just don't want her to get bamboozled into thinking that Max only wants her for her competent brain."

"What makes you think he's interested in something more?"

"Other than all those lame excuses he's come up with for calling every day? I heard it in his voice."

"You've talked to him?"

"Damn straight I've talked to him. I answered the phone the other day while he was leaving a message about our podunk little town."

Aunt Delia grinned. "Yes, I can see why that might set your teeth on edge. What did he say to you?"

"Not too much, really. He seemed surprised, maybe a little irritated." He paused thoughtfully. "Obviously he was a lot more than irritated since he's flying over here to protect his turf, so to speak."

"I'd say he must have responded to you picking up that

call the same way you're reacting to the news of his impending arrival," Aunt Delia observed slyly.

Kevin scowled at her. "You don't know everything, you know."

"Sure, I do. I'm old. I've been around."

"Oh, really? I thought you were a sweet, innocent spinster."

"Show a little respect for your elders and don't try to change the subject. What is it you're really worried about? Are you scared this Max is going to win, that Gracie's going to pack up and go back to France with him?"

"Okay, yes. The thought has crossed my mind," he admitted reluctantly.

She shook her head, scowling at him with impatience. "Kevin Patrick Daniels, I am surprised at you. You are the most confident man I've ever known. Surely you're not scared to compete with this Max person."

"Of course not," he snapped. "I just don't know if I should."

"Why not?"

"It's not as if I have an alternative to offer her."

"You could propose," she suggested.

He stared at her incredulously. "Are you nuts? I've already got more people depending on me than I can cope with. How can I ask any woman to share that?"

"Maybe she wouldn't view it as a burden at all. In fact, maybe having her in your life would lighten your load, give you more strength."

"I am not going to ask Gracie MacDougal to marry me and put up with Bobby Ray and all the others, so you can just get that crazy idea right out of your head."

"If you say so." She hesitated, her expression thoughtful before she finally said, "You could sell her the house. That would keep her here."

"I'm not selling her the damn house, either," he retorted, walking away.

Delia watched him go, then smiled to herself. Everything was moving along quite nicely.

Gracie no more wanted Max Devereaux in Seagull Point, Virginia, than she wanted to dye her hair pink and take up skydiving. Unfortunately, his arrival seemed inevitable. He'd bought plane tickets three days earlier, rented a car, and, if she knew Max, had enough maps to guide him through the most uncharted territory on earth. Max was a very methodical man. Like it or not, he'd be at her house before nightfall.

She might not have been half so worried about his upcoming visit if there hadn't been this nagging little suspicion that Kevin was right and Max wanted more from her than instructions on dealing with French tradesmen. He'd been awfully persistent for a man who only wanted to know how to get the hotel toilets cleaned efficiently.

The knock on her door jolted her. It couldn't possibly be Max already. His plane had barely touched down a half hour ago. She knew. She'd checked, hoping it had been diverted to Alaska. She doubted it was Kevin. He'd made himself scarcer than hen's teeth ever since he'd kissed her silly and walked out a few nights before.

The doorbell chimed again, a trifle impatiently, it seemed to her. She opened the door and stared at the woman on the front porch. She was slender and made up as artfully as if she'd just come from the cosmetics counter in some very exclusive shop. Her hair, which had been streaked with blond highlights by an expert, shimmered in the morning sun. Its upswept style could not possibly have been created anywhere other than a very fancy salon. Gracie would have bet it was a two hundred dollar hairdo, minimum.

She might have moved on to stare at the clothes—definitely off a designer rack—if she hadn't been caught off guard by the grin. It was a feminine version of the one she'd spotted all too often on Kevin's face.

"Can I help you?" she asked instead.

"I'm Helen Monroe, Kevin's cousin. Has he mentioned me?"

Gracie shook her head, which only broadened that smile.

"It figures. I'm the good cousin. I'll bet you've heard all about Bobby Ray."

Gracie couldn't resist grinning back. "As a matter of fact, Bobby Ray's name has come up a time or two. He and I have met."

"Yes, well, Bobby Ray can be a trial. I can say that because he's my baby brother. May I come in?"

"Yes, of course." Gracie stepped aside, then followed Helen into the living room. She seemed to have an unerring sense of where to go. "Have you been here before?"

"In this house? Oh my, yes. My best friend used to live here during the summer. Of course, that was years ago. She married a plastic surgeon and moved to Los Angeles. Hasn't been seen on this coast since."

"Turned into a snob, did she?"

"Either that or she's gotten fat and lazy and doesn't want us to see. I prefer to think it's the latter."

Gracie chuckled. "Would you like something to drink?"

"I'll bet you have lemonade, right?"

"Yes, as a matter of fact, I do. What made you think I would?"

"It's Kevin's favorite."

Gracie went absolutely still. It sounded as if Helen Monroe had gotten some very bad information about her relationship with Kevin. "Mrs. Monroe, I don't know what you're thinking—"

"It's Helen, and I'm thinking that it's about time someone came along and turned Kevin's life upside down, someone other than one of his relatives, that is."

"I am not turning Kevin's life upside down, not intentionally anyway."

"That's even better," Helen said.

"Is that why you came by? To give me your blessing?"

"Curiosity, actually. I've been wondering about all the rumors."

Gracie handed her the lemonade before her shaking hand managed to spill it all over the just scrubbed kitchen floor. "Rumors?"

"About you and Kevin."

"Exactly what rumors are we talking about?" she asked, her tone flat and—if Helen had only been listening—deadly.

The woman waved off the question. "Nothing to worry about. It's a small town. People talk. Maybe speculate a little."

"Speculate about what?"

"How long it will take him to catch you or vice versa." She grinned. "You have to understand, Kevin has been inspiring this sort of speculation for years. Something told me, though, that this time might be different."

"Why is that?"

"Because he actually gave Bobby Ray some money for one of his outrageous schemes. That suggests he's either very mellow or very distracted. Either way, there had to be a woman behind it. You're the obvious candidate."

"And you wanted to see what I was like?"

Helen shot her an unrepentant grin. "Like I said, curiosity."

Gracie wanted to be furious. She had a feeling under other circumstances she might have been, but she couldn't help liking Kevin's cousin. There was nothing devious or sneaky about her. She was blatantly nosy and not the least bit apologetic about it. She was also polished and sophisticated and just sassy enough to be a more than even match for any man.

Struck by an inspiration, Gracie checked for a wedding ring. To her relief, Helen wasn't wearing one. Yes, indeed, Helen Monroe would be a more than even match for a man like Max Devereaux. With any luck she could keep her around for another couple of hours.

Gracie beamed at her. "More lemonade?"

"You're not kicking me out?" Helen asked, clearly surprised.

"Heavens, no," Gracie assured her, thinking that there was another little matter about which Helen might prove helpful. "Now that you're here, maybe you can fill me in on that house Kevin refuses to discuss with me."

"House?" Helen repeated in the worst attempt at feigning innocence on record.

"Yes. It's an old Victorian, right on the river just a few blocks from here. Kevin manages it, though he does a lousy job of it from what I've seen."

Polished, sophisticated Helen Monroe actually squirmed ever so slightly. "I don't really keep up with Kevin's business affairs."

Gracie sighed. "You're not going to discuss it, either, are you?"

Helen smiled. "Sorry. Family loyalty and all that. I have no idea why Kevin's keeping mum about that house, but I have to respect his decision."

"And I suppose I should admire you for that," Gracie conceded glumly. "I really want to know more about that place."

"Have you met Aunt Delia?"

Gracie shook her head. "No, who's she?"

"Actually, she's Kevin's great-aunt on his mother's side, but all the rest of us claim her, too. She's a wonderful woman. She's living with Kevin. I'm amazed you two haven't met."

"I was only at Kevin's the one time, and most of our conversation took place in the yard while he lazed in a hammock."

"Yes, Kevin does love that hammock. He claims he does his best thinking there."

"It must get chilly out there in winter or does his mind take a sabbatical?"

Helen chuckled. "I like you, Gracie MacDougal. You may

be precisely the breath of fresh air this stale, dysfunctional family needs."

"I told you, there is nothing going on between Kevin and me," Gracie protested.

"That's what you think," Helen countered. Her expression turned gleeful. "In my experience, romance is all the more fascinating when neither party expects it to erupt into fireworks."

Gracie thought of the flares and rockets that had already gone off. She couldn't deny, at least not to herself, that the possibility of an entire, spectacular display was more than likely. That was hormones, though, not emotions. She might not be the most experienced woman on the face of the earth, but even she recognized the distinction.

She couldn't prevent Helen or the rest of the town from speculating about her and Kevin, but she could turn the tables on her guest.

"Obviously you think you know me pretty well," Gracie said. "However, I don't know a thing about you. Tell me about yourself, Helen. Are you married?"

Helen's expression sobered at once. "Widowed," she said softly. "I married early and we were together for fifteen wonderful years before Henry's tragic death."

Regretting the impulse to snoop, Gracie said, "I'm so sorry. I had no idea."

"It's okay. Henry died three years ago and I'm getting on with my life slowly but surely. The last thing he told me before he died was that he didn't want me pining away for him for the rest of my days." She smiled ruefully. "Not that I ever did what he told me to."

"This time, though, his advice was sound," Gracie said. "You should take it."

"I just don't know if I'll ever find anyone who could make me as happy as he did. He was a remarkable man."

As if Gracie had planned it, the doorbell rang again, this time with a distinctive hint of impatience. Max, no doubt.

"Excuse me. I'm expecting company."

"Your friend from France," Helen guessed.

"My, my, word does travel fast, doesn't it?" Gracie replied as she went to the door. Opening it, she found Max on the threshold, dressed impeccably as always, every hair in place. No one could have guessed that he'd been on a plane for hours before making the two-hour drive down from Dulles Airport.

"Gracie," he said, his gaze surveying her from head to toe, his scowl revealing his reaction to her tight blue jeans, loose T-shirt, and bare feet.

She had meant to change, but maybe this was better. He was seeing her as she actually was—or as she was rapidly becoming. And she provided a startling contrast to the well turned out woman watching with blatant curiosity from the archway into the living room.

Helen glided—Gracie had never actually seen it before, but Helen accomplished it—toward Max as Gracie made the introductions. She saw the unmistakable flare of interest in Max's eyes. She'd seen him regard a work of art with much the same appreciation for its beauty. He was definitely a connoisseur of fine things.

"Helen Monroe, this is Max Devereaux. Max, Helen."

"It is my pleasure," he said, bending over her hand to brush a kiss across her knuckles with continental flare.

Max was the only American Gracie knew who could do that without looking absurd. Helen seemed pleased, but not unduly stunned by the gesture. Gracie nodded with satisfaction, pleased that she wouldn't be a knockover. Max needed a challenge in his life, especially one who wasn't her. She smiled brightly at the pair of them.

"Lemonade, anyone?"

Max stared at her as if she'd lost her mind.

"Perhaps Max would prefer to have a glass of wine," Helen suggested mildly. "A nice Bordeaux, perhaps?"

"Perfect," he said, gazing at her with frank approval.

"I'm afraid my wine cellar is a little low on Bordeaux," Gracie said without much regret. As if struck by a sudden brainstorm, she said, "Maybe you could show Max the best place in town to buy wine."

Helen laughed. "You mean the only place. Max, I would be happy to take you, if you're not too tired from your trip."

Max demurred with a frown. "I cannot leave so soon after I've arrived. Gracie and I have important matters to discuss."

"Oh, believe me, Max, those can wait," Gracie assured him. "I'll be right here when you and Helen get back."

He seemed puzzled by the response. "You would not mind?"

"Of course not. Take your time. I should have thought to have the Bordeaux here myself."

"But this is such a short visit and we have so much to discuss," he repeated worriedly.

Even so, she noticed, his gaze kept straying to Helen.

"I'll be here when you get back," Gracie assured him. "Our business won't take all that long."

"You could call Kevin," Helen suggested slyly. "We could make it a party."

At the mention of Kevin, Max's lips thinned. "Yes, do. I would like to see this man for myself."

Gracie wouldn't have drawn Kevin into this little gathering for a million bucks, but rather than say that, she just nodded, hoping that an indication of acquiescence would keep Helen from calling him herself.

"We'll be back in no time," Helen promised, dashing down the walk with Max in tow.

That had been easy, almost too easy. Either Helen was awfully eager to be alone with Max or she simply wanted him away from Gracie to protect her cousin's interests. Whatever her motivation, it suited Gracie just fine. She watched them go, and carefully covered a smile of pure delight.

When they were out of sight, she went back inside, hid all the Bordeaux she'd bought in anticipation of Max's arrival, poured herself a glass of inexpensive chardonnay that would have appalled Max and headed for a rocker on the porch. It promised to be a long evening, and with any luck she wanted her nerves dulled for most of it.

She offered up a silent toast to Helen, thanking the gods for her timely appearance. So far, keeping Max occupied had been disgustingly easy. If his visit were short enough and luck was with her, she might never spend a single second of it alone with him.

Fourteen

The call was so hushed that Kevin thought at first it was from some sort of blackmailer. It wouldn't have been the first time one cousin or another had been targeted by someone hoping for easy money.

"Whatever you want, I'm not in the mood," he snapped, and hung up when he couldn't understand the hissed, urgent message. He almost tossed the portable phone across the yard, but instinct told him it would be ringing again. Sure enough, it rang again, almost at once. Somebody adept at speed-dialing, obviously.

"Kevin, don't you dare hang up," Helen whispered, this time more distinctly.

"Helen?"

"Yes, you idiot. It's me."

"Why all the cloak-and-dagger stuff?"

"Because I'm with Max Devereaux."

"Who?"

"Gracie's friend. I've abducted him. We're at the liquor store."

"Robbing the place?" Kevin inquired hopefully. Seeing Max locked away for a good long time in a windowless cell would cheer him up considerably.

"Heavens, no. We're searching for the perfect Bordeaux," she explained. "He finds the choices appallingly lacking in sophistication."

The comment confirmed his worst suspicions about the man. "He would," he said dryly. "How did you manage to get hooked up with him? Where's Gracie?"

"At home, and it's a long story. I suggested she call you, but something told me she wouldn't. I think dropping in about now would be a very smart idea."

"What for?"

"To protect your interests, of course."

"You're assuming I have any interests to protect."

"Kevin, stop arguing and get over there. I have to go."

She clicked off her cell phone and went back to whatever undercover operation she assumed she was masterminding. Thinking about it, he couldn't help grinning. Helen was as fierce as a doberman and clever as a cat burglar when it came to protecting those she cared about. Obviously he was to be the beneficiary of her latest scheme. The woman had had way too much time on her hands since Henry's death. If she wanted to keep Max occupied during his visit, who was Kevin to argue.

That didn't mean he was going to race straight over to Gracie's. He settled back in the hammock and set it to swaying. He closed his eyes . . . and envisioned Gracie in the arms of another man.

Two seconds later he was on his feet and heading for his car. Driving by wouldn't be the same as dropping in. He could survey the situation from a distance, maybe catch a glimpse of this man who was so all-fired determined to steal Gracie away from Virginia. Gracie wouldn't even have to know he'd been in the neighborhood.

Naturally, though, that would have been too easy. She spotted him right off from her perch in a rocker on her front porch. She was all alone and a little tipsy, judging from the rather vague wave she sent in his direction. Kevin braked to a stop in front of the house. He sighed and cut the engine. He didn't like the implications of Gracie's drunkenness one little bit.

"Hey, Kevin!" she called out as if she were actually delighted to see him.

He walked slowly toward her, pausing at the foot of the steps.

"Did I invite you over?" she asked, regarding him intently.

"Nope."

"Didn't think so."

"Gracie, are you drunk?"

Her eyes widened at the accusation. "No way. I don't drink."

"What's in the glass?"

"Just a little wine. Can't make me drunk."

"I beg to differ. Maybe we should try walking it off."

She shook her head at that, then clutched it as if the motion had made it spin. "Whoa," she murmured.

Kevin beckoned to her. "Come on. Let's go."

"Can't," she insisted.

"Why not?"

"Legs don't work."

"They will," Kevin said grimly and helped her out of the chair. "Put your arm around my waist."

"Okay," she said, and snuggled against him. "Nice."

Kevin's heartbeat took off like a 727 on a rapid climb. He gritted his teeth and concentrated on keeping her upright.

"Why are you drinking, Gracie? Does Max's visit have you that upset?"

"Haven't seen Max," she said, not unhappily. "Not for hours and hours. He left with Helen." She nodded. "Nice woman, Helen. Like her a lot."

"I had no idea you and my cousin were so close."

"Just met."

"When?"

"Today, right before Max got here."

"What fortunate timing," Kevin said wryly. He wasn't sure whether to kill his cousin or thank her. Obviously Helen had been a very busy woman. Maybe he should recommend she get a job so she'd stop meddling in his life.

He studied Gracie, who was concentrating intently on putting one foot in front of the other, the tip of her tongue caught between her lips. Another jolt of pure lust shot through him. He picked up the pace, which meant he wound up virtually carrying Gracie.

"Whoa," she murmured, a pleading note in her voice.

"Too fast?"

"Uh-huh."

"Gracie, if you have to get drunk to face Max, that should tell you something, don't you think?"

She lifted her gaze to his. "What?" she inquired dreamily.

Obviously this was not the time to try to make a point, he concluded. "Never mind."

"Kevin?"

"Yes, Gracie."

"You're a nice man," she said. She patted his cheek. "Very nice man."

"Thank you."

"You won't go away when Max comes back, will you?"

"No, Gracie, I won't go away."

She nodded. "Good."

Kevin didn't see anything good about it. She was testing the limits of his control.

"Don't want to go back to France," she said.

"Nobody's going to make you go back to France."

"Max could," she said, her head bobbing up and down.

"No, he can't. Not unless it's what you want."

"He'll offer me lots and lots of money."

Kevin had never before considered what Gracie's financial situation might be. She'd certainly seemed to be getting along okay. She was thinking about buying a very expensive waterfront house. She couldn't be flat broke.

Still, perhaps she did need to get a job. He supposed she couldn't live forever on whatever she'd saved. No wonder she was so anxious to get her hands on Aunt Delia's house in a hurry. She probably needed to get a business up and running before she ran out of cash.

"Don't worry about the money, Gracie. We'll figure something out," Kevin promised.

There were plenty of other choice properties available that might serve Gracie's purpose. He'd check them out himself first thing in the morning, then steer her toward one of those if she was determined to stay here and open a bed and breakfast.

If all else failed and Delia agreed, he'd have to reconsider selling her the Victorian that had been in his mother's family for generations. It was his one direct link to the side of the family that had never made any real demands on him. He hated the thought of giving it up, of seeing it turned into a commercial venture.

He glanced over and noted that Gracie seemed to be walking with a little less difficulty staying upright. By the time they had circled the block, she was almost steady on her feet. She still clung to him, though, which made him wonder. Was she as confused by her feelings for him as he was by his for her? The possibility offered some comfort.

As they turned toward her house, her steps slowed. Kevin glanced ahead and saw that Helen's car was parked in front of the house.

"Uh-oh," Gracie said softly. "They're back."

Kevin folded her hand in his. "Don't worry about a thing, darlin'. I'm right here beside you."

Gracie had only a dim recollection of the first meeting between Kevin and Max. Despite the walk that Kevin had dragged her on, she'd been surprisingly muddle-headed from her two glasses of wine. Maybe she'd just wanted to get drunk and willed it. She had noted that Max and Helen were getting along nicely, noted Kevin and Max were shooting daggers at each other, then politely excused herself and wandered off to bed.

Okay, it was the coward's way out, but no one had objected too violently. In fact, judging from the tension in the air, she wasn't so sure anyone had even noticed.

She'd slept straight through until morning, then awakened with just enough of a hangover, to make her wonder if it had been two bottles, not two glasses of wine. She vowed never to touch another glass of anything stronger than water. Obviously she did not have a head for alcohol. Apparently she'd sipped a lot less wine in France than she'd recalled.

When she went downstairs, she found Max already in the kitchen, sitting glumly at the table with a cup of coffee. Since she doubted he'd made it himself, it was probably yesterday's. At this point, though, any caffeine was better than none. She poured herself a cup and sat down opposite him.

"Feeling better?" he inquired tightly.

"Much," she lied, forcing a smile. "Did you enjoy your evening with Helen?"

"Helen and Kevin," he corrected. "I don't get it, Gracie. He doesn't seem your type at all."

"What do you know about my type?"

"You forget, I met several of the men you dated in France. They were all suave and sophisticated."

Yep, there was a contrast there, all right. "Kevin grows on you," she said simply. "Besides, we're not dating. He's a friend."

"Really? He seems to think it's more than that."

She stared at Max suspiciously. "What did he say?"

"In so many words, he warned me off."

"Tell me exactly what he said."

"Just that you were well taken care of, that you had plans for the future, that sort of thing."

"I see."

"So, what are your plans?"

For some reason, Gracie didn't want to tell Max about the

bed and breakfast. Maybe she feared some scathing comment. Whatever her reason, she kept silent.

"Is Kevin involved in these plans?"

"Yes," she conceded truthfully. He stood between her and attaining the house she wanted, though she didn't spell that part out to Max. Let him think what he wanted.

"I see. Then my coming here was a waste of time?"

"I told you that before you ever booked the flight."

He shrugged. "I thought I could change your mind."

Getting through to him had been easier than she'd expected. Now, though, he looked so despondent that Gracie took pity on him. She was certain that look had more to do with his dread of the search for a replacement hotel manager than with losing her, but she tried to cheer him up nonetheless.

"Stay, Max. Spend a few days now that you're here. I don't have many friends. I'd like to keep you in my life."

He stared at her, clearly startled. "You think of me as a friend?"

She grinned. "I imagine I could with a little practice." She studied him a minute, then added, "And it seemed to me last night that Helen was more than a little interested in getting to know you better."

"A lovely woman," he said, his expression softening. He regarded her closely. "Are you certain I wouldn't be in the way?"

"Not at all."

"Perhaps I will stay for a day or two then."

"Why don't you call Helen? I'm sure she'd love to show you the sights."

He eyed her skeptically. "There are sights?"

"Yes, Max. Not all of the world's beauty is tucked away in France. Just one thing, though."

"Yes?"

"If Helen suggests a picnic, lose the suit."

He actually laughed at that. "Before or after we are together?"

"I think I'll leave that decision up to the two of you." She stood up. "Now, then, what about breakfast? I've actually gotten quite good at it."

He stared at her incredulously. "You cook?"

"Believe it or not," she told him, and began making an omelet to prove it.

When she slid the plate in front of Max, his eyes widened with astonishment. "Very nice. Excellent presentation."

"Forget the presentation. Taste it."

He grinned at her. "Do I dare?"

"Try it, Max."

He took a forkful of the eggs, cheese, onions, and tomato and sighed. "Heavenly. Perhaps I have been a bit too hasty in giving up. I may have an opening for a chef quite soon."

"Forget it. I'm not coming back as a chef," she said, refusing to admit how flattered she was that he'd even made the absurd suggestion.

"What else can you cook?" Max asked anyway.

"Never mind."

"She's a whiz with blueberry muffins," Kevin chimed in, appearing at the back door. He walked in as if it were perfectly natural for him to show up at the crack of dawn. He even paused to drop an affectionate kiss on the tip of her nose. "Any more of that omelet, darlin'?"

"No, but I'll make one for you," Gracie offered, delighted with the chance to show off her skills. This would be good practice for the future, when guests were likely to be showing up at odd times to be fed.

"Any scones left?" Kevin asked.

"I doubt it," she said. "You eat them faster than I can bake them. Look in that airtight container on the counter."

Kevin picked it up, then sighed. "Just crumbs."

"Sorry."

"You make scones, too?" Max inquired. "I'm afraid I don't understand this sudden domesticity."

"I don't see why not," Gracie said defensively. "The same skills that are required to run a hotel are just as essential in running a home."

"I suppose. I just never thought you were interested in being a happy little homemaker." He studied Kevin. "Perhaps things have changed, however."

Gracie gritted her teeth. "Max, you only know one side of me, my professional side. You never knew me as a person."

"I thought it was all one and the same," he said.

"No, that's the way *you* live," Gracie said. "Not me."

"If you say so."

Kevin edged up behind her at the stove. She could feel his breath fanning across her neck, the beckoning heat of his body. She barely resisted the temptation to lean back against him, to let him literally lend her his support.

Of course, Kevin's only interest was in snatching a crisp strip of bacon from the plate she'd been preparing for him. He winked as he made off with his prize.

He leaned back against the counter and stared at Max with open curiosity. "How long are you sticking around, Max?"

"Gracie has persuaded me to stay a few more days."

Kevin's gaze shot to her, disbelief in his eyes. "Really?"

She beamed. "That's right. Max will be here a few more days."

"I see."

"Sit down, Kevin. Your breakfast's ready." Gracie put the plate on the table.

Kevin sat, but he didn't seem to have much of an appetite.

"Something wrong?" Max inquired cheerfully. "You object to my staying, perhaps?"

"It's Gracie's house."

"Yes," Max agreed. "It is Gracie's house."

The two men glowered at each other. Heaven protect her

from territorial males, Gracie thought, scowling herself at the pair of them.

"Max, I thought you were going to give Helen a call," she said.

"Why the hell would he be calling Helen?" Kevin demanded.

"I thought she might enjoy taking Max sightseeing."

Kevin stared at her blankly. "Why?"

She kicked him under the table.

"Ouch, dammit." He frowned at her.

"Call her, Max. Something tells me Helen gets out and about early."

"Actually, she does," Kevin said, still regarding her with evident confusion. "Max and Helen?" he mouthed when Max's back was turned.

Gracie nodded.

Kevin sighed heavily, but at least he kept his mouth shut while Max made the arrangements.

"We're going to see the birthplace of Robert E. Lee," Max announced when he'd hung up.

"Stratford Hall," Gracie said. "I hear it's wonderful."

"You haven't been?" Max asked.

"No, not yet. I've been busy."

"Doing what?"

"Spending time with me," Kevin said at once. His expression turned grimly determined. "Shall we tag along to Stratford, Gracie?"

Actually, that wasn't what she'd had in mind at all, but she could see that Kevin wasn't about to leave Max alone with his cousin, whether Helen might have preferred it that way or not. Kevin's wariness of Max apparently extended to what might happen between him and any of the women Kevin knew.

"Sure, why not," she said. "You don't mind, do you, Max?"

Max shot a look at Kevin that could have withered an

entire garden, but he forced out a terse agreement. "The more the merrier."

Gracie feared there was going to be nothing merry about the outing at all, but she hadn't counted on Helen's wiles. Helen managed to separate the two couples in the blink of an eye. Before Gracie knew what was happening, she and Kevin were headed on a long walk toward the river beyond the main plantation house, while Helen and Max went off on the tour.

"She's very good," Gracie said, staring after her admiringly.

"Good? She's a blasted sneak," Kevin grumbled. "I don't like her being off alone with that man."

"Max is harmless."

"That's not what you were saying last night."

"I don't recall half of what I said last night," she admitted. "The point is, Helen can deal with Max. You don't have a thing to worry about. Besides, there are a dozen other people on that tour. What could happen?"

"Pardon me for saying it, but your judgment where Max is concerned is not exactly top notch. And Helen is proving to be a very slippery woman. I am not reassured."

"Come on, Kevin. It's a beautiful June day. The flowers are blooming. The sky is blue. I'm sure you can think of something better to do than worry about your grown-up cousin and whatever passing fancy she's taken up with Max."

He'd been staring after Helen and Max, but he turned then and stared into her eyes. "Something more interesting to do, huh?" he said softly. "Only one thing I can think of that might distract me."

Gracie's breath caught in her throat. "What's that?"

He reached out and skimmed a finger along her cheek, then dragged it oh-so-slowly across her lips until they parted in a gasp. She swallowed hard as his head descended and his mouth met hers.

Oh, yes, she thought as a sweet thrill reverberated through

her. From her perspective, this was definitely better than worrying about Max and Helen. She opened her eyes and met Kevin's gaze. He smiled.

"Feeling better?" she asked.

"Not just yet," he said. "But I'm definitely getting there."

Fifteen

Throwing Helen and Max together might have been a mistake, Gracie concluded when Max was still ensconced in her tiny guest room after a week. His presence in the house might have been awkward enough by itself, but with Kevin inevitably thrown into the mix, the tension was sometimes thick enough to cut with a knife.

Lately she'd found herself caught in the middle of a turf war declared by two very possessive men. Max apparently couldn't help himself. Even though his interest in Helen was obvious, he couldn't seem to resist making a daily pass or two at Gracie. Force of habit, she suspected. She had no idea what Kevin was up to.

For some reason, though, Max's attempt to stake his claim annoyed her more than Kevin's did. She planned on analyzing that more thoroughly once Max went back to France.

She also planned on trying to figure out why, after all the opportunities she'd had over the past few days and several long walks right past it, she still hadn't shown Max the old Victorian house that was at the heart of her relationship with Kevin. She had a feeling she wasn't going to like the answer to that one bit.

Add to that general emotional confusion Kevin's casual touches, which were startlingly provocative no matter how innocently intended, and she was a nervous wreck. Kevin was the kind of man who stole every single legitimate opportunity to touch a woman. There was never anything overtly sexual about the quick brush of his fingers across her knuckles or the grasp of his hand on her elbow, but Gracie found the accidental contact astonishingly sensual. Her reaction to it was downright disconcerting. She had to keep reminding herself that Kevin was a totally unambitious, laid-back human being, not the sort of match for her own type-A personality at all. Obviously this was some sort of passing, hormonal quirk.

Even so, mix in a few bone-melting goodnight kisses and there was no telling where things would lead one of these nights when they were left alone to sit and wait for Max and Helen to finish whatever it was they were doing in Max's steamed-up rental car.

"Do you know how ridiculous this is?" she inquired late one night, breaking into the companionable silence as she and Kevin rocked side by side on her porch, sipping lemonade.

"How ridiculous what is?" Kevin asked distractedly, his gaze locked on that car halfway down the block.

"The two of us sitting out here, waiting up for a couple who are in their thirties. Don't you think Helen is beyond needing a chaperone?"

"Not if she's out with him," Kevin replied.

His grim tone startled her. "What exactly are you afraid of? That he'll seduce her? That he'll whisk her off to France? That they'll fall in love and get married?"

"Bite your tongue."

"Kevin, your cousin is old enough to decide whether she wants to go to bed—or to France—with a man." Gracie was delighted to discover that she didn't feel the slightest twinge of jealousy over either prospect. That confirmed what she'd been so sure of all along: she wasn't the least bit interested in Max as a lover.

Kevin sighed. "Okay, maybe I am being overly protective.

It's just that she's vulnerable. She has been ever since Henry died."

"And despite your complaining about your family, you have a white knight complex where each of them are concerned. Remember something, though. You thought I was vulnerable, too. I managed to handle Max just fine, didn't I?"

He scowled. "Sure, you introduced him to Helen, for which I may never forgive you."

Gracie grinned. "Actually, I thought that was a rather ingenious strategy."

"It was a lowdown, sneaky, rotten strategy. Now I have two of you to worry about around him. I've seen the way he looks at you. No matter what's going on between him and my cousin, he hasn't given up on you, Gracie."

"Don't be ridiculous."

"I don't trust him."

"There's nothing wrong with Max."

"If you like the pompous, snooty sort."

"Apparently Helen does."

"Yeah, well, what does she know? She hasn't met many men like Max before."

"Kevin, I thought her husband was a successful CEO of a multinational conglomerate."

"He was, but we'd known him all our lives."

"Who's being snooty now? Is Virginia blue blood the only blue blood good enough for a Daniels?"

He frowned at the accusation. "I am not a snob," he insisted. "But I am holding you responsible if Helen gets hurt or this turns ugly."

"Helen's a big girl. She's looked radiant to me the last few days. Maybe she's willing to risk being hurt. And the only way it's going to turn ugly is if you and Max start brawling one of these nights."

"Don't tempt me. I repeat, I don't like the way he looks at either one of you."

Tired of all this talk of Max and Helen, she regarded Kevin speculatively. "Kevin, don't you have something better to do than worry about your cousin?"

He finally turned his full attention on her then. A grin tugged at his lips. "You offering to distract me again, darlin'?"

She feigned a long-suffering sigh. "If that's what it takes to give the two of them some privacy."

He reached for her hand. "Get on over here then."

Warning herself of the dangers, she slipped onto his lap a little too eagerly. She didn't know what it was about this man that had allowed him to creep past her defenses, but the truth was, she had discovered recently that she enjoyed tempting fate.

Snuggling against his chest, her head tucked on his shoulder, she felt warm and safe and deliciously aroused. To keep her libido in check, though, she took the opportunity to make a renewed plea for more information on the Victorian.

"It's not for sale," Kevin repeated for the umpteenth time, though his heart didn't seem to be in it. In fact, he was busy nibbling on her ear.

"Rent it to me, then," she suggested, trying out a new angle. "I'll make all the repairs in return for a break on the rent and a long-term lease."

He pulled back. "Do you do all of your negotiating this way?"

"Of course not. This is a technique I reserve for special cases." Actually, she'd only just now discovered how stimulating negotiating with Kevin could be.

"No wonder you had such good luck with the asparagus farmer. I'm quite sure Max couldn't compete with this."

"Very amusing. Will you rent it to me or not?"

"Not."

She studied his face intently. "Kevin, what is it about that house that makes you so protective of it?"

"I'm not protective."

"Could have fooled me. What would you call it?"

"I am just trying to do my legal duty as manager of the property."

Gracie lost patience with the same old nonsense. "Then how come you don't cut the damn grass?"

"Maybe I will."

"When?"

"One of these days. School's almost out."

She tried to puzzle out the implication of that and finally gave up. "What does that have to do with anything?" she asked.

"Just an observation," he said evasively, then studied her intently. "Now it's my turn."

"Your turn for what?"

"To ask probing questions."

She eyed him suspiciously. "Such as."

"You didn't tell Max about your plan to open a bed and breakfast, did you? You haven't even pointed out the house to him. I know because I've been waiting and waiting for him to say something or insist on a tour."

She wasn't sure she liked the new direction of the conversation. This was an area she'd already found troubling. She shook her head.

"How come?"

"It was none of his business.

"Is that it or were you afraid he'd tell you exactly how crazy your idea was?"

"It is not a crazy idea, and Max's opinion doesn't matter to me one way or another."

"If you say so."

"I say so," she said firmly, but she couldn't help wondering if maybe that had been her concern. Was she afraid that Max, with all his years of hotel experience, would laugh at her plan or possibly denigrate the whole idea of exchanging a career with Worldwide for opening up a bed and breakfast in what he obviously considered to be the middle of nowhere?

She could say Max's opinion didn't matter, but the truth was she respected him, even if he was way too absorbed with the bottom line.

"Gracie?"

"What?"

"Maybe you should talk it over with him, get the perspective of an expert."

"I'm an expert," she responded testily. "I have the degrees and the resumé to prove it. Besides, this is my dream. I don't want Max Devereaux anywhere near it."

"And me?"

She gave him a rueful smile. "Like it or not, you're smack dab in the middle of it."

Kevin was worn out by the time Max Devereaux finally left town. This business of keeping an eye on Gracie was very tiring.

As for Helen, she'd made a blasted game out of eluding him to sneak off with Max. He couldn't imagine what his cousin saw in the man, but to each his own. Despite his grumblings to Gracie, he did recognize that Helen was an adult. She'd been walking around in a daze ever since Henry's death. If Max managed to distract her even a little, Kevin actually agreed with Gracie that there was no reason to get too worked up over it. It wasn't as if it was the start of something lasting. In fact, the very thought of Max as a cousin-in-law made him shudder.

Not as much as the thought of Max with Gracie, however. He smiled, thinking of how cleverly Helen had managed to keep those two apart. It hadn't been quite enough to allow him to relax his guard, but it had given him a few peaceful moments, when he'd been able to concentrate totally on Gracie and the fact that he'd suddenly become rather addicted to her kisses.

After several days of nonstop running around, he was finally back in his hammock, contemplating the meaning of life. Or, more specifically, the meaning of his reaction to Gracie. He couldn't think of the last time he'd thought so much about sleeping with a woman without actually doing anything about it. For some reason, though, Gracie didn't strike him as the kind of woman he should be fooling around with unless his intentions were totally honorable.

Which they weren't, he concluded emphatically. No way in hell was he drawing her into the circus of his life. It was bad enough that Bobby Ray had tried to use her and that Helen had poked her nose into their affairs. He was sure the rest of them would find some way to use or abuse Gracie's good nature if they knew she was important to him. Thankfully, most of the rest of them were out of town and, since it was summer, Uncle Bo was too busy fishing to get into much mischief.

As for Aunt Delia, he could only thank his lucky stars that she hadn't gotten it into her head to make his relationship with Gracie her own personal project.

"I'm surprised to find you here," the woman in question said, turning up just then and interrupting his peace and quiet. "Shouldn't you be off somewhere with Gracie?"

"Gracie's safe and sound at home, alone," he told his aunt with evident relief. "I'm taking a break. What brings you outside? It's hot out here."

"Jane called from Richmond. She's wondering if you have any intention of showing up at the office for the remainder of the century."

"Were those her words or yours?"

"Her thoughts, my spin," Aunt Delia conceded.

"Thanks to e-mail and the fax, I have no reason to go to Richmond in the middle of a heat wave."

"Kevin, it's eighty-five, not a hundred and ten. Besides,

it's demoralizing for your staff when you never actually put in an appearance."

"I'll show up when something comes up I can't deal with on the phone," he said. "Unfortunately, most of my clients are dead. I'm just left to deal with the beneficiaries, who have absolutely no desire to get together with me unless the checks are late. That's the joy of estate law. Most of the time, I don't even have to show up to submit the wills for probate. And thanks to dear old dad, the Daniels name will be on the letterhead for all eternity, no matter how much time I actually put in at the office."

His aunt glowered at him. "Listening to that nonsense, if I didn't know better, I'd conclude that you are the laziest man on the planet," she said.

He lowered his sunglasses and winked at her. "Maybe I am."

"No, you are not," she retorted sharply. "I know exactly how many clients you have, how many of them are pro bono, and you handle every one of them with the kind of compassion and attention they deserve. So why do you insist on acting as if you could give a damn about work?"

"Balance, Aunt Delia. Balance. Do you have any idea how much concentration it requires to achieve it?"

"I suspect quite a bit less than you devote to it," she said dryly. "Does Gracie have any idea what you actually do for a living or that you work at all, for that matter?"

"I certainly haven't told her. She likes thinking I'm a disreputable bum. It enables her to believe she's living on the edge just by associating with me."

"Well, that's certainly a dandy way to build a relationship," his aunt grumbled. "Whatever happened to old-fashioned honesty?"

"I am honest. I just avoid getting into the details. Besides, who said anything about trying to build a relationship? We've covered that. Gracie's just a friend."

"A very special friend, judging from the way you scooted

off to make sure she didn't go back to France with that Max person."

"Don't read too much into that. I just didn't want her to make a mistake she'd regret. She asked me to stick around and offer moral support."

"Which you absolutely detested doing, right?"

Kevin slid his sunglasses back into place. "That's enough meddling for one day. Go away."

"You can get rid of me if you want, but it won't stop you from thinking about her," Aunt Delia said smugly. "If you want my advice—"

"Which I don't."

She ignored him and went right on. "I'd tell you to snatch her up before somebody else comes along. You're not getting any younger, you know."

"Thanks for the update on my age. Mind telling me why it's relevant?"

"Babies, Kevin."

He sat straight up and stared. "Excuse me?"

"Babies," his aunt repeated emphatically, returning his startled gaze with a touch of defiance.

"What about them?" he asked cautiously.

"It's time you had some, if you intend to. I have to say I wouldn't mind seeing some toddlers scrambling around this dreary old mausoleum of yours. Molly feels the same way. We want some kids around before we're too ancient to enjoy them."

"Is this another way of reminding me that you're bored and that I owe you a trip to Fredericksburg to see a movie?"

"No, it's another way of reminding you that Molly and I aren't the only ones who are going to be too old to keep up with a toddler if you don't hurry up and get started."

He lay back down. "Okay, okay. I'll take it under advisement."

"Which means you'll forget about it, the minute you get me to shut up, I suppose."

"You suppose right."

His aunt sighed. "Then I guess it's up to me, after all," she murmured.

The enigmatic remark was more alarming than a shrilling smoke detector. Kevin shot up so fast, he almost rolled himself right out of the hammock.

"What was that?" he demanded. "What do you mean it's up to you? What's up to you?"

She gave him a vague wave, but no response.

"Well, hell," he muttered.

He had the sinking feeling he'd just made a very serious tactical blunder, but short of locking his aunt in her room or hiring a bodyguard to tail her and notify him if she came within a hundred yards of Gracie, he couldn't think of a single way to keep her out of mischief. Something told him his dear aunt Delia could wind up being more trouble than Bobby Ray, Helen, and the rest of them all rolled into one.

Sixteen

"Uncle Kevin, could you come and get me?" Abby asked, sounding more plaintive than frightened.

The phone call from his niece had prevented Kevin from sitting his aunt down for a nice, long, firm lecture about staying the hell out of his relationship with Gracie. Delia had drifted off toward the kitchen, no doubt to conspire with his housekeeper. He sighed and turned his attention to this latest crisis.

"Where are you, angel?"

"At Daddy's, except he's not home and Sara Lynn doesn't like me being here when Daddy's not here. I guess I cramp her style or something." She sounded world-weary when she said it, as if she'd been hustled out of the way one too many times.

Kevin gritted his teeth. Part of his deal with Bobby Ray for that investment money had been that he'd pay more attention to his daughter. He should have known Bobby Ray's promises weren't worth a hill of beans.

"I'll be there in fifteen minutes," he told Abby. "Tell Sara Lynn not to budge. I want to have a little chat with her when I get there."

"Not because of me, Uncle Kevin, please."

"It's okay, Abby. We won't argue." In fact, he didn't intend to let the woman get a word in. He'd be doing all the talking and she'd damn well better listen. "Bye, angel. I'm on my way. I'll see you soon."

Spurred on by his anger, he made the drive in ten minutes, a sheriff's deputy on his tail the whole way. When he turned off Route 3, the deputy followed and Kevin pulled to the side of the road. Prematurely gray-haired Otis Fowler ambled up to his car, thankfully without his citation book.

"Where's the fire, Kevin? Problems at Bobby Ray's again?"

"Not yet," Kevin told him grimly. He was all too aware that the sheriff's department had responded fairly regularly to domestic disputes at the house. According to the neighbors, Bobby Ray and Sara Lynn settled their disagreements at a volume a rock band would have envied.

"Then slow down," Otis warned. "You're setting a bad example for the other citizens."

"Sorry. Abby called and I was anxious to get over here and pick her up."

"She there by herself again?"

Kevin stared at him, startled by the direction of his guesswork. "Next best thing. She's with Sara Lynn. But how do you know she's been there by herself?"

"My girl's in her class at school. Abby's mentioned it a time or two when she's been over to the house. I've warned Bobby Ray that the girl has no business being left alone. I try to keep a lookout when I'm in the area, but I'm not always on this shift."

He shook his head, his expression sorrowful. "This ain't like the old days, when a kid was safe to play outdoors without a parent watching over him," he lamented. "Often as not in those days if one parent wasn't home in the area, another one was and everyone looked out for everyone else's kids. Now, just look at those kids killed up near Fredericksburg the last couple of years, all of 'em taken from their own front yards. We haven't had problems like that, but Spotsylvania

County's not so far away that we can lose sight of the possibility. No sense tempting fate."

"I'll see to it that it doesn't happen again," Kevin assured him.

"Abby's a cute kid. Smart, too. Why do you suppose Bobby Ray can't appreciate that?"

"I wish I knew, Otis. I wish I knew."

When he got to Bobby Ray's, Abby was sitting on the porch, her nose stuck in a book. The child did love to read, probably because fictional worlds were a whole lot less complicated than the real-life world she lived in. He stopped by and ruffled her hair.

"Good book?"

"Uh-huh," she said, barely sparing him a glance.

"Sara Lynn inside?"

"I guess."

"Okay, let me talk to her and then we'll get out of here and do something fun, okay?"

She nodded. Something about her response troubled him. She'd been pretty anxious for him to come and get her. Now it seemed his arrival didn't matter one way or the other.

"Abby?"

"Hmm?"

"Look at me."

She finally glanced up and he spotted the tears shimmering in her eyes. A lump formed in his throat. Hunkering down in front of her, he took her hands.

"Okay, baby, what's wrong?"

"I told you Sara Lynn was going to get mad if I told her you wanted to talk to her," she said, swiping angrily at a tear.

"What did she do?" Kevin asked, his tone deadly.

"Nothing. I swear it, Uncle Kevin."

"I know better. What did she say to you?"

Abby heaved a sigh. "She told me if I was going to be such a tattletale, she was going to see to it that Daddy never spent another second with me." She regarded Kevin anxiously. "She can't do that, can she, Uncle Kevin?"

"No," he said tersely. "She can't do that. You sit tight. I'll be right back."

He found Sara Lynn upstairs sitting in front of her dressing-table mirror applying makeup. Dressed—barely—in a silk-and-lace dressing gown, she looked as if she were getting ready for a night on the town. He'd never much liked her, but at this moment he was angry enough to start smashing all the pretty little crystal bottles in front of her. Losing her expensive French perfumes—paid for with Abby's child support money, no doubt—might get her attention.

"How dare you threaten Abby?" he said, barely containing his fury. "She's a kid, Sara Lynn. If you have a problem with me, you yell at me. If you have a problem with your marriage, you deal with Bobby Ray. You don't take it out on Abby."

She didn't turn, just glanced up at his reflection in the mirror. "Nice to see you, too, Kevin."

"Don't waste your sarcasm on me. I know your kind, Sara Lynn."

Her gaze narrowed. "And what kind would that be?"

"You're trash. You're a user. You married Bobby Ray because you thought he had money. It's galled you ever since that I control how much he has to throw around."

She turned around then and gave him a tight smile. "Well, well, well, I guess the gloves are finally off."

"You bet they're off. If I ever hear that you've threatened Abby again or that you've been anything other than kind to her, the money around here will dry up faster than you can blink. See how many lovers come sniffing around you then."

She paled. "You can't do that."

"Watch me."

Downstairs, he paused in the kitchen to let his temper cool before going back onto the porch to get Abby. Outside, he forced a smile. "Ready to go, angel?"

She regarded him seriously, but he noticed that there were no more tears.

"Is Sara Lynn still mad?"

"I suspect so," he admitted. "But at me, sweetpea, not at you."

"Maybe I shouldn't have called."

"Yes, you should have. That's our deal, remember. You can call me anytime." He draped an arm around her shoulder and led her to the car and helped her in. "Now, then, what would you like to do?"

She hesitated, then flashed him a bright smile. "Can we go to the old house? We haven't been there yet this summer."

"You want to go to Aunt Delia's? Why?" He grinned. "You hoping I'll put you to work so you can earn some summer spending money?"

"That, too," she admitted with a grin. "But mostly I just like it there. Mama takes me there sometimes, too. We sit on the porch and watch the water. Mama asked and Aunt Delia said it was okay."

"Of course it's okay. I'm just surprised."

"I like to watch the water, Uncle Kevin."

"Why is that?"

"It's always there, no matter what."

"Not like people, huh?"

Abby sighed. "Yeah, not like people."

It was funny, he thought now. He'd always felt that way about Aunt Delia's place himself. Years ago, his father had spent more time in Richmond than he had at home. When his father was around, there were always aunts and uncles and cousins in and out of his house asking for help with one crisis or another. The help had always been given, but usually not without a lot of shouting. After his mother died, Kevin had taken refuge at Aunt Delia's whenever Molly or his father would agree to take him.

Maybe that was why he was so opposed to Gracie's plan, he thought, startled by the unexpected insight. Maybe he just didn't want to think of that peaceful, serene house turned upside down by strangers. Maybe he was being totally selfish in trying to keep it for himself, when the odds of him ever living there were practically nonexistent. For some reason, though, he just liked knowing it was there, available, as steady and dependable as the flowing of the Potomac.

Then again, he thought wryly, maybe he just liked making Gracie a little crazy with his stubborn refusal to take her offers seriously. That had provided him with a whole month or more of pure entertainment.

"Why are you grinning, Uncle Kevin?"

"Just thinking about something."

"That lady, I'll bet."

He stared at her. "Which lady?"

"The one Daddy says you like, the one who wants to buy Aunt Delia's house. He called the house last night and told me about her. You know what else?"

"What?"

"He and Mama talked for a long time, too. They hardly ever do that. Do you think it means anything?"

Kevin doubted it. "I don't know, sweetpea."

"I was just thinking it would be nice if they got back together," she said wistfully.

"Every kid whose parents are divorced wishes that," Kevin told her. "Sometimes it's for the best if they don't, though."

"I guess." She grinned. "So tell me about you and this lady. Is she pretty?"

"You're entirely too nosy for a kid," he told her.

"Which means I should stop asking questions, right, 'cause I'm making you nervous?" she said, nodding sagely. "Can I meet her?"

"One of these days, I suppose."

"Why not today?" Abby prodded. "I'll bet she'd like to come to Aunt Delia's with us."

"I'm sure she would."

"Daddy said you caught her sneaking into the house one day. Is that true?"

"Actually she was sneaking out," he said, recalling the fascinating view.

"She sounds really cool. Can we get her, please?"

"Sure, why not," Kevin said eventually, making the turn that would take them to Gracie's. He braked to a stop, tilted Abby's chin up and looked directly into her eyes. "But you are not to mention that the house belongs to Aunt Delia, okay?"

"Why not?"

"Because I said so."

"Isn't that like a giant fib or something?"

"It's not a fib," Kevin declared. "It's an omission."

"Who does she think owns the house?"

"I haven't told her."

"Why not?"

"You ask entirely too many questions."

"Don't you know why?"

"Because I don't want to, that's why."

"You're weird, Uncle Kevin. You know that, don't you?"

"That's a fine thing to say to your favorite uncle."

"It's okay," Abby reassured him. "I love you, anyway."

He grinned. "Thanks, squirt. I love you, too." He shut off the engine, then tilted his head and pretended to study her. "Even if you do have freckles on your nose."

"Do not," she protested, instantly covering her nose.

"Do, too."

"You're teasing."

"Ask Gracie, if you don't believe me," he suggested as he led Abby around to Gracie's backyard. For once, he opted for a little formality and actually knocked before stepping into the kitchen. "Anybody home?"

When Gracie didn't answer, Abby said, "I'll bet she's at Mrs. Johnson's."

Kevin peered at her intently. "Exactly where are you getting all your information about Gracie's habits?"

"Never mind. I have my sources," she said, giving him a superior little smile. "Wanna bet that's where she is?"

"No, I do not want to bet," Kevin retorted. "If we hurry, though, she might have some muffins ready."

"Blueberry, I'll bet. Just for you."

Sure enough, they found Gracie in Mrs. Johnson's kitchen and there were scones, not muffins, just out of the oven. Chocolate pecan, this time. Kevin could smell the melting chocolate before he ever stepped inside.

"Told you he'd be here," Mrs. Johnson said with satisfaction.

Kevin grinned at Gracie. "Were you worried I wouldn't show up, darlin?"

"Afraid you would," Gracie contradicted, then focused her attention on Abby. "You must be Kevin's cousin."

"I'm Abby."

"And I'm Gracie. It's very nice to meet you. I've heard a lot about you."

"Probably next to nothing compared to what she's heard about you," Kevin muttered.

Abby shot him a grin. "I heard that, Uncle Kevin."

He tugged on her pigtail. "I'll bet if you ask Gracie nicely, she'll let you try a scone."

"You never ask nicely," Gracie pointed out. "You just grab."

"That's because I don't want to take the chance you'll turn me down."

"As if she would," Mrs. Johnson said. "All of you, take the scones and run along. I've got things to do."

Kevin regarded her closely. "Such as reporting in to Aunt Delia?"

"What I do with my time is none of your concern, young man. Now, scoot." She smiled at Abby. "You're growing up

too fast, young lady. Another inch at least since the last time
I saw you."

"I'm almost as tall as Mama now," Abby said proudly.

"Well, you tell your mama hello for me. Stop by next time
you all come over to sit on that porch next door."

Kevin noted Gracie's startled look at Mrs. Johnson's ref-
erence to the front porch of the Victorian. As soon as they
were outside, Gracie asked casually, "Do you and your mom
come over here often?"

"Lots in the summertime," Abby said. "We don't live by
the water. Sometimes we sit here until the moon comes up,
especially the full moon. It's totally awesome the way it
shines on the water."

"Yes, it is," Gracie agreed.

Kevin could practically see the wheels turning in that brain
of hers. He wondered how long it was going to take before
she began adding up two and two.

No sooner had they walked up the front steps at Aunt
Delia's than Abby asked, "Can I cut the grass, Uncle Kevin?
You let it go too long again. There's probably snakes and all
sorts of other critters hiding in it."

"Including baby bunnies," he retorted slyly. "You want to
scare them to death?"

"That's what you always say," she chided. "The bunnies
run away, you know they do. And they come right back the
minute the clover pops up."

Letting Abby cut the grass solved several problems. It kept
her away from Gracie, minimizing the risk that she would
let something slip. Just as important, it would get Gracie off
his back about the out-of-control lawn. He reached in his
pocket and took out the key to the toolshed in back.

"Be careful now," he instructed. "You might have been
joking about those snakes, but you never know when you
might stumble across one."

"Snakes?" Gracie said, staring at him with wide eyes, even
as Abby dashed off. She unconsciously drew her feet up onto

the bottom step, out of the way of any slithering creatures that might be in the vicinity.

Abby might have been totally unintimidated by his warning, but Gracie clearly was scared to death.

"You're not going to let that child cut grass when she might run across a snake," she protested.

"It probably won't be a big one," he said, enjoying her reaction.

"You ought to be ashamed of yourself. Cutting the grass is supposed to be your job."

"Nobody said I had to do it myself. Abby likes doing it."

"Which suits your purposes just fine, doesn't it?"

"Sure. It means I get to sit on the porch all alone with you. Can't get a better deal than that."

She remained silent for several minutes, pondering that and idly eating one of her scones. "How often do you get Abby to cut the grass for you?" she asked eventually.

"I *let* her do it whenever she wants. Obviously she has more time once school is out."

"Which is why the grass hasn't been cut before now," she guessed.

"That's one reason." And keeping Aunt Delia away from the place was another, one he didn't care to get into.

Naturally, though, Gracie promptly asked, "And the other reasons would be?"

"Do you really want to know all the details of the grass-cutting schedule around here?"

She nodded. "Yes, I think I do."

Kevin sighed. "The grass gets cut when it gets cut. End of story."

"Do you pay her?"

"In ice cream usually, though now that she's growing up, she'll probably want cash so she can buy more books. Abby's quite a reader."

"You planning on getting her to paint the place, too?

Maybe buying her a pizza in return for whitewashing the fence? Or maybe getting her a whole set of encyclopedias?"

"Now you're being sarcastic."

"Yes, I am," she confirmed. "That doesn't mean I don't want a straight answer."

"Abby will not be painting the house," he said, then hesitated. He grinned at her. "Unless she wants to."

"There's something about this that doesn't make sense," Gracie said, her expression thoughtful.

"You worry too much, darlin'. Can't you just kick back and enjoy the view?"

She set her rocker into motion. She even gazed out at the water. But there wasn't a doubt in Kevin's mind that those wheels in her head were spinning like roulette wheels in Vegas. Sooner or later she was bound to come up with a winning explanation. He found that downright worrisome.

"I thought it was time you and I got to know each other," Kevin's Aunt Delia declared to Gracie, pouring tea into lovely old china cups.

Gracie had been stunned by the message on her answering machine inviting her to tea at Greystone Manor. She'd recognized the name from Kevin's occasional mention of an aunt Delia, but until the call, she'd had no idea the woman actually lived with him. Very curious.

She'd been even more intrigued when she'd realized that she was to be the only guest. She'd called back immediately to accept the invitation for the next day.

Delia Winthrop was a lovely woman with her snow-white hair and still flawless complexion. Her eyes twinkled with pure mischief as she led Gracie into the living room where a teacart had been set up by French doors leading out to a rose garden. The sweet scent of roses was thick in the air.

"Does Kevin know about this?" Gracie asked.

Delia looked guilty for no longer than a heartbeat. "Heavens, no!" she confessed. "He'd have my head for meddling. He's gone to Richmond for the day."

"I see," Gracie said, though she wasn't certain that she saw at all.

"Why don't you tell me what you were thinking of doing with the house?" Aunt Delia suggested as she handed Gracie a plate of little sandwiches.

"You know about that?" Gracie asked, surprised that Kevin had discussed it with anyone. He certainly managed to avoid discussing it with her.

"Well, of course I do. It's my house, after all."

Gracie's hands shook so hard she had to set the plate down. "Yours?" she asked, wondering why she hadn't figured out before that the house belonged to someone in Kevin's family. No wonder he could afford to take such a lackadaisical attitude toward its upkeep.

Delia gave a satisfied little nod. "Thought so. Kevin hadn't mentioned that, I suppose."

"No, he had not."

"Well, it is. Lived in it for seventy-five years, right up until the day Kevin insisted I move in here with him. That was a good many years ago now and I've never regretted it for a minute, though I do miss that house."

"I'm going to kill him," Gracie muttered.

"Oh, my dear, you don't want to do that," Delia protested, chuckling. "Things are just getting downright interesting around here."

"Maybe from your perspective."

"Yours, too. I suspect. Who'd you think the house belonged to?"

"I wasn't sure. For a while I thought it was some mysterious stranger. Then I began to wonder if it actually belonged to Kevin."

"The truth is, I have transferred the deed into his name, but he refuses to think of it as his. He won't until I'm dead, and I've no intention of that happening anytime soon."

"Are you the reason he won't discuss selling it to me?"

"Goodness, no. I've told him to do whatever he thinks is best. If you ask me, he's being difficult for the pure enjoyment of tormenting you. That boy hasn't had nearly enough fun in his life."

Gracie couldn't believe her ears. It seemed to her that all Kevin ever had was fun. She'd certainly never seen him do a lick of work.

"What do you mean?" she asked carefully.

"He's been responsible for the whole lot of us for years now," she said. "There's me and his uncle Bo, that's his father's brother, and Bo's good-for-nothing boys. Plus his uncle Steven's brood. They depend on him for everything, too, thanks to Steven's will naming Kevin trustee of his estate. I believe you've met Bobby Ray and Abby, and Helen, of course."

Well, I'll be, Gracie thought. Delia's revelations certainly gave her a whole new perspective on Kevin. Obviously he managed to do something to keep all of those financial balls in the air. He just didn't make it look like work. Fascinating.

"Is Kevin in Richmond on business?" she asked.

"His law firm's there."

Gracie's mouth gaped. "Kevin is a lawyer?"

"Well, of course he is. Didn't he mention it?"

"Not exactly."

Delia shook her head. "That boy. Sometimes I just can't figure him out."

"Kevin actually practices law?" Gracie asked again, wondering if maybe he'd only gotten the degree without ever putting it to good use.

"Yes, indeed. Estate law, just like his daddy before him."

"Well, I'll be," Gracie murmured.

"Okay, enough about Kevin. I asked you over here for another reason. I want to hear all about your plans," Delia said again. "I want to hear every single thing you have in mind for that house."

Despite all the revelations she wanted time to absorb, Gracie was only too eager to finally talk over her plans with someone who seemed as enthusiastic about the bed and breakfast as she was. She practically talked herself hoarse, her excitement mounting with every word.

"Oh, my, yes. That sounds lovely." Delia's eyes sparkled. "We'll do it," she declared after an hour of bombarding Gracie with more questions.

Gracie stared. "Excuse me?"

"You and I, we'll do it. It will do me good to see that old house spruced up and filled with people again."

"But . . ."

"You think I'm too old to get involved in a project the size of this, don't you?"

"It's not that," Gracie protested.

"It's just that you don't want a partner then," Delia guessed, looking disappointed.

Actually, it was the fact that Kevin was going to have her hide for dragging his aunt into a scheme of which he disapproved. Besides which, this would effectively rob Kevin of a house that was legally already his.

"Don't worry about Kevin," Delia said as if she'd read Gracie's mind. "He'll come around when he sees it's something I want to do."

"But you said you'd already put the house in his name. How can you turn around and do something like this?" Gracie protested. "Is it even legal?"

"I told you, Kevin sees the name on the deed as a technicality. As far as he's concerned, that house is mine to do with as I choose. And I choose to see it turned into a bed and breakfast," she added with a touch of defiance. "You and I can work out an arrangement. Kevin won't mind at all. It'll just be one less worry. Goodness knows, he has plenty of them without me adding to the list."

Gracie wasn't even remotely convinced he'd see it that

way. "Maybe you should think this over," she said. "We both should."

Delia's disappointment was evident, but she nodded. "We'll talk tomorrow then." She winked. "But I can promise you I won't change my mind."

Seventeen

"Met your Gracie yesterday," Molly told Kevin at breakfast the day after his trip to Richmond.

He almost choked on his coffee. "Excuse me? Gracie was here?"

"With your aunt. Thick as thieves they were."

Kevin scowled at the housekeeper. She looked as if she were enjoying dropping this bombshell a little too much. He had a hunch she'd been chosen to be the messenger of this juicy tidbit. Even though his trips to Richmond were rare, he'd obviously made one too many.

"Any idea how this came about?" he inquired, facing the fact that such a meeting had probably been inevitable.

"All I know is I made them tea and some of those little cakes your aunt likes so much."

"So Gracie didn't just drop by unexpectedly?"

"No, indeed. She was invited, all right. Your aunt was busy planning it for days."

"Any idea what they talked about?"

"You, the house, this and that."

"If you were listening at the keyhole, the least you could have done was get more details."

"I didn't have to resort to that. Your aunt filled me in over supper. Told me as much as she wanted me to know."

"You and my aunt are entirely too chummy. You know that, don't you?"

"We have things in common."

"Such as?"

"This and that."

"I could fire you for insubordination," he mused speculatively. "Probably should."

"But you won't," she said with confidence.

"Why is that?"

"I know all your sins, going way back."

"Sins? What sins? You always said I was your precious angel," he retorted.

She grinned at him. "I'm biased. Doesn't mean the rest of the world would see you the same way."

"I'm not running for political office, Molly. Doesn't matter much what skeletons come tumbling out of my closet."

"If you say so."

Kevin turned serious. "Molly, what did happen here yesterday?"

"Ask your aunt."

"She needs looking out for. I don't want anyone, even Gracie, taking advantage of her."

"I know you love Delia," Molly soothed. "But she's got all her wits about her, Kevin. There's no need to worry. No one's going to take advantage of Delia. If you ask me, Gracie's the one who's in over her head. Looked downright bemused, when she left here yesterday."

"What the hell is that supposed to mean?"

"Ask your aunt," Molly repeated, and firmly shut the kitchen door behind her.

Kevin mulled over the enigmatic remark most of the morning. It turned out his aunt had slipped out of the house at the crack of dawn to get her hair done. A neighbor had stopped by to take her. Molly claimed to be as surprised as he was that Delia had made a clean getaway.

He was resting in his hammock, pondering the implications of Gracie's little tea with his aunt, when he heard a car door slam. He could have gone to investigate, but he suspected Molly would see to it that his aunt found him. Sure enough, a few minutes later she was heading his way. He got a subtle whiff of her lily of the valley perfume just before she arrived.

"I brought you a fresh lemonade," Delia said, handing him the glass.

"A peace offering?" he inquired, opening his eyes to gauge her reaction. He was so startled by the sight that greeted him, he almost choked on the first sip. "What the devil happened to you?"

Her hand fluttered up toward her shorn hair. "I like it," she said defensively. "It's stylish and easy to care for."

"It's red, for heaven's sakes."

"Strawberry blond, actually."

"What were you thinking?"

"I was thinking I ought to spruce up a bit if I'm going into business."

Kevin concluded he needed something much stronger than lemonade to hear the rest of this. He made do with a long, slow swallow of the beverage at hand. The tart drink only added to the acid already churning in his stomach.

"Maybe you'd better sit down and tell me exactly what's going on," he suggested quietly. "From the beginning."

She regarded him with a stubborn set to her chin. "I don't have to answer to you, you know."

"Humor me then. I'd like to hear what you're up to. I'm guessing it has something to do with Gracie's little visit yesterday."

His aunt beamed at him. "What a lovely young woman! No wonder you're so fond of her."

"How did she happen to be here for tea, when I specifically asked you to stay away from her?"

"Kevin, you are my nephew and I love you, but you do not get to run my life. If I want to make new friends, there's not a thing in the world you can do about it."

He gritted his teeth. "So you just happened to pick Gracie to become your new friend?"

"Well, of course, I wanted to get to know someone you're so obviously fond of. I just wish I'd insisted on inviting her out here sooner. She's been so many interesting places, had so many fascinating experiences."

"Couldn't you have waited until I introduced you?"

"I might not have that many years left," she said wryly. "You tend to be stubborn."

He sighed. "Okay, I suppose there's no harm done. Have you satisfied your curiosity? Is this the end of it?"

She toyed with her lace-edged hankie, twisted it nervously into a knot. She also avoided looking directly at him. Her reaction was not encouraging.

"Not exactly," she conceded.

The business, he thought with an impending sense of doom. How could he have forgotten? "Tell me," he said grimly.

"Gracie and I were talking," she began, then beamed at him again. "My, she does have same exciting ideas for that bed and breakfast of hers."

"She shared that with you?"

"Yes, indeed I asked about it, of course. I could just see how lovely it would be. Have you heard what she has in mind or have you been too stubborn about that, too?"

"There's not going to be any bed and breakfast," he said fiercely. "The details don't matter."

"Well, they did to me. Did you know I once envisioned operating a gracious old inn myself?"

"Did you really?" he asked skeptically. "This is the first I've ever heard of that."

"You know how it is. Life takes us down a different path and things change."

Something in her voice alerted him that there was more to this than he'd ever imagined. Delia had never talked about lost dreams before. "You're serious, aren't you? You actually wanted to operate an inn?"

"As a matter of fact, I did. I doubt you remember much about the old Colonial Beach Hotel, but it was something in its heyday. There were galas, famous guests from the cream of Virginia society." She sighed. "Of course I was much too young to attend such things, but I heard about them. Mama and Daddy went several times. I always thought how wonderful that hotel would be if it could become a family resort with old-fashioned games on the front lawn, croquet, badminton, that sort of thing."

Kevin was astounded by the amount of thought she'd apparently given the idea. "Did you ever consider buying it?"

"Women in my generation didn't do such things, but actually, yes, I did consider it. I even made a few discreet inquiries before it was torn down."

"What happened?"

Her expression clouded over. "This and that."

"Aunt Delia?" he prodded. "Tell me."

She reached over and squeezed his hand. "It doesn't matter now. It wouldn't have been the right thing for me, I'm sure. Still, I can't help imagining what it would have been like."

"So you identify with Gracie's dream, is that it?"

"More than you can imagine."

His gaze narrowed. "She didn't take advantage of that, did she?"

Aunt Delia looked startled. "Take advantage? What do you mean?"

"I mean, did she use it to try to get you to take her side, maybe sell her the house behind my back." His gaze narrowed. "Did you tell her you own the house?"

"What if I did?" she said defensively. "It's my decision to make."

"Yes, I suppose it is," he said wearily. "How'd she take the news?"

"Needless to say, she was surprised."

"And mad as a wet hen at me, no doubt."

"Truth be told, your name almost never entered the conversation, not until the very end anyway."

He wasn't sure whether to be pleased or insulted by that. "And what happened at the very end?" he asked.

She scowled at him. "Stop rushing me. I'm getting to that."

"Sorry."

"Actually, we've made a deal."

His stomach sank. "A deal? You and Gracie?"

"That's right," she said, regarding him defiantly.

"You're going to sell her the house?"

"Eventually."

"What does that mean?"

"It means that we'll work something out so the house will be hers, just not right away."

"And in the meantime?"

She smiled happily. "In the meantime, we'll be partners."

"Partners," Kevin repeated slowly. "You and Gracie are going to be partners?"

"Exactly."

"Over my dead body."

Her chin jutted up determinedly. "If that's what it takes."

He stared at her in amazement. Something told him she meant it, too. "What did she do to you?" he asked wearily.

His aunt reached out and patted his hand consolingly. "Darling, please don't be upset. You should be thanking her. She gave me back my dream."

Kevin forced himself to wait before confronting Gracie. He wanted to mull over this latest turn of events, consider the wistful expression on his aunt's face when she'd talked about her lost dream.

He waited, he mulled until after dinner, then he mulled some more. By midnight, he'd worked up a pretty good head of steam. In fact, as he drove to Gracie's, he was mad enough to tear that old Victorian down all by himself, board by board, to prevent this idiotic scheme from ever happening.

To his satisfaction, the lights at Gracie's were out. He figured catching her off guard and half asleep was probably a very good idea. She had a sneaky habit of getting her way when she was operating on all cylinders.

Of course, he hadn't taken into account the effect of her opening the door, looking all sleepy and tousled and sexy as the dickens. It took a little of the edge off his anger and did dangerous things to his body. Lust slammed through him like a freight train.

The oversize T-shirt she was wearing could have covered a tackle for the Washington Redskins, but in his mind's eye every curve was revealed. The blasted thing ended above her knees . . . way above her knees. She was barefooted and at some point she'd painted bright red, kick-ass polish on her toenails. His gaze locked on those feet, and the desire to sweep her into his arms and haul her right back to her bedroom was almost uncontrollable. Almost.

"Kevin?"

Her sleepy, sexy, confused voice snapped him back to reality. He wasn't here to take her to bed. He was here to get a few things straight. He pushed past her and went inside. He aimed straight for a chair, since sitting next to her on the room's only other furniture—a cozy little sofa—seemed like a very risky idea.

"We have to talk."

She eyed him cautiously. "Is this going to be a long talk or do you intend to yell, then leave once you've had your say?"

"It's hard to say. Why?"

"I could use some coffee, if you actually want to have a conversation."

"Fine. Make the coffee," he said, and trailed after her into the kitchen.

He sat at the kitchen table and watched her efficient movements. Whenever a little bolt of lust slammed through him, he worked at controlling it. He was getting pretty good with so much practice, he concluded. By the same token, he was crankier than ever by the time she finally sat down with a mug of coffee in hand.

"What's up?" she inquired, regarding him with bright eyes and a fully alert expression.

Obviously he'd given her way too long to gather her composure. They should have had this out when she was half asleep. It might have gone more smoothly.

"What the hell kind of arm-twisting did you use on my aunt?" he demanded bluntly.

"I take it you've heard about her idea that she and I go into business together."

"Damn right I've heard," he said, shoving his chair back and starting to pace. He paused beside her and scowled down into her upturned face. "Of all the sneaky, underhanded things to do, waiting until I was out of town and then taking advantage of an old lady."

"I didn't take advantage of anyone," she said quietly. "She invited me over. She told me the house was hers, something which you might have mentioned, by the way. As for the rest, it was her idea. Ask her."

"Well, of course she would say that. She probably thinks it was her idea. You're the one who planted it, though. She'd certainly never have come up with it on her own."

She regarded him calmly. "Actually, I told her it was a bad idea."

His gaze narrowed. Aunt Delia certainly hadn't mentioned that. "Why?"

"Because I knew you wouldn't approve."

"Well, I don't." He regarded her warily. "So we're agreed that nothing will come of this lame-brained idea?"

Perversely, Gracie shrugged. "I don't know about that. I've been thinking it over. She really seems to want to be involved.

She knows people around here. She could probably get things done faster than I could, pull the necessary permits, stuff like that. It could work."

"It will not work!" he shouted. "It will be a disaster. She's eighty-seven years old, for heaven's sake. It will kill her."

"Her choice," Gracie reminded him.

"No, by God, it's my choice, and I say that this will not happen." He slammed his fist into the wall for emphasis, then ruefully rubbed his knuckles.

"Did that help?" Gracie inquired.

"Yes."

"Good."

His gaze narrowed. "Gracie, you're not taking me seriously. I will not allow my aunt to get involved in this."

"Admittedly I don't know your aunt very well, but she has all her faculties, doesn't she?"

"Yes," he conceded grudgingly. This was the second time today someone had reminded him that his aunt could outwit the armed forces of any three nations combined.

"And she still has energy to spare?"

"Yes."

"Then I don't see the problem."

"The problem, is . . .." His voice trailed off. "I don't know what the problem is exactly. It's just a bad idea."

"Your opinion."

"Whose money is going into this?"

"Mine."

"Who's going to arrange for all the work?"

"She can point me in the right direction, but I will."

"Then what exactly is my aunt contributing to this arrangement?"

"The house, moral support, whatever she feels like contributing, I suppose. We didn't discuss that."

"What happens the first time you disagree over the color of the paint or the wallpaper?"

"We'll discuss it like rational adults."

"I'll bet. Have you ever tried to argue with an old woman with the grit of General Patton?"

"Not really," Gracie said, then grinned. "This will be the first time, though, that she's met her match."

He stared at her and sighed. "I really hate this idea."

"It will work," she promised.

"And if it doesn't?"

"It will."

He threw up his hands in a gesture of surrender. Two against one wouldn't be bad odds under normal circumstances, but the two were Gracie and his aunt. He might as well have been up against Atilla the Hun and his troops. "Okay, fine. Go for it," he muttered. "Just don't expect me to climb ladders, hang wallpaper, or fix leaky pipes."

"Wouldn't dream of it," Gracie assured him. "You'd probably just mess it up anyway."

He opened his mouth, clearly ready to snap out a retort, but then he backed down. "You're not getting me to fall into that trap," he said.

"Too bad. I guess I'll just have to be sneakier about it next time."

"You're a menace. You know that, don't you? First you trick a sweet old lady into going along with your crazy scheme and now you've almost got me snookered into it, too."

She regarded him innocently. "Do I really?"

He cupped her chin, forced her to meet his gaze. "Gracie, I don't want my aunt's heart broken."

"How on earth would that happen?"

"For some crazy reason, she's viewing this as the fulfillment of a dream. I don't want it to turn into a nightmare."

"It won't," Gracie assured him. "You should have seen her yesterday. She was so excited she could barely sit still. Her ideas were tumbling out almost as fast as mine. I think we'll make a great team."

"Why is it then that when I think of the two of you working

on this together, the first thing that comes to mind is Lucy and Ethel?"

Gracie grinned. "They might have been wacky and unorthodox, but in every *I Love Lucy* episode I ever saw they got the job done."

Kevin only recalled the chaos.

Eighteen

The sound of hammers echoed through the house. Dust was swirling in the air and it was hotter than a sauna, but Gracie stared around at the mess with satisfaction. It was happening. It was actually happening. A few weeks from now she would have her bed-and-breakfast inn.

For the past two weeks she and Delia had engaged in a whirlwind of activity. She'd tried as much as possible to steer clear of Kevin, who continued to regard the whole scheme as a personal betrayal. Still, he hadn't tried to interfere, and for that she was grateful.

She'd left hammering out the legal details to Delia. The woman was amazing. She had the grit and determination of someone a quarter of her age. Besides, she wasn't the least bit cowed by Kevin's disapproval. Gracie, for all of her staunch defense of the plan, hated that she was going against his wishes. It would have been much more fun if he'd been an enthusiastic participant.

"Gracie, you're wool-gathering again," Delia chided. Her expression turned sympathetic. "Is it Kevin? Hasn't he come around yet?"

"No. He's still furious about this. Haven't you been able to tell from his attitude at home?"

"I haven't really worried about it. I know him. He'll get over it in his own good time."

"Will he? You said yourself he's a stubborn man."

"I exaggerated. He can be won over if you put your mind to it."

"I don't have time to put my mind to it. This place is taking up every waking second. When you start a project, you set a grueling schedule."

"I'm old. I don't have time to spare," Delia retorted. "Now, stop worrying about Kevin. He'll come around. In the meantime, we have to decide on the wallpaper."

There were enough samples to paper a dozen houses, with some left over for the entire city of Richmond.

"Where'd you get all of this?" Gracie asked, daunted by the task.

"I put Abby on it. She made a few calls."

Gracie glanced up as the girl came in from the kitchen where she'd had her head poked under the sink so she could see exactly how the plumber was repairing the pipes. There were smudges of dirt on her face and her pigtails were askew, but she looked ecstatic. She had turned up the first day of the renovations and every day since. Since no one else seemed to object to her presence, including Kevin, Gracie had welcomed her help. Still, she worried that this wasn't the best place for Abby to be spending her time.

"Abby, are you sure this is how you want to spend your summer vacation? Wouldn't you rather be playing with your friends?" Gracie asked.

"No way. You should have seen the gunk in the pipes. It was totally gross."

"And you liked that?" Gracie asked doubtfully.

"Sure." She peered at the wallpaper samples. "Have you picked any yet?"

"None," Delia said with a feigned note of disgust. "I can't get Gracie to concentrate."

Abby shot a knowing look at Gracie. "You're thinking about Uncle Kevin again, aren't you?"

"Yes, that's exactly what she's doing," Delia replied before Gracie could open her mouth.

"I'll bet he'd come over if we asked him," Abby said. "I just know he's dying of curiosity."

"I'm not asking him to come over here," Gracie said adamantly. "I told him he wouldn't have to get involved."

"Maybe he wants to get involved," Abby suggested. "Maybe he just doesn't know how, now that he's made such a fuss about it."

"My thoughts exactly," Delia said.

"I am not calling him," Gracie repeated.

"I will," Abby volunteered.

"You're not calling him, either," Gracie told her. She caught the look Delia and Abby exchanged. "You're not to call, either, Delia."

The pair sighed. "If you say so, dear," Delia said. "Then let's get to these samples."

They had narrowed them down to twenty by lunchtime. Delia had insisted that they stop every day and have a decent meal.

"To keep our strength up," she insisted.

Gracie suspected the truth was she liked going out to restaurants so she could catch a glimpse of her friends and update them on the progress being made on the bed and breakfast. The whole town was buzzing about it. Delia had reported with glee that half of them seemed to be taking sides on whether Delia had lost her mind.

"I'll show 'em," she vowed. "Wait until they want to book rooms for their relatives and we don't have a single one available."

"You're getting a little ahead of yourself," Gracie warned as they slid into a booth at the Beachside Cafe, Delia's favorite choice for lunch. "We haven't gotten the first reservation yet."

"We will. Just wait until that advertising kicks in."

"What advertising?" Gracie grumbled. "Who's had time to sit down and think up a halfway decent ad campaign?"

"Not to worry," Delia reassured her. "I put Helen to work on that. She'll be by this afternoon with some ideas."

Gracie regarded her in amazement. "Is there anything you haven't thought of?"

"Not so far," Delia replied with satisfaction.

Jessie finally made her way to their table to take their order. "How's the work going?"

"Moving right along," Delia told her. "Start telling your out-of-town customers that next time they visit, they'll have to try the new bed and breakfast."

"Does this place have a name yet?" the waitress asked.

Delia and Gracie exchanged a look.

"Oh, dear," Delia murmured.

"I know," Abby chimed in. "What about Riverview?"

"Not bad," Gracie conceded. "How about something a little more historical? Wakefield Inn, for instance, named after Washington's birthplace."

"If you have to explain what it's named after, what's the point?" Abby asked.

"What about Southern Comfort?" Delia asked.

Gracie regarded her wryly. "I think that's taken. Besides, I don't want to start a court battle with an alcoholic beverage over trademark infringement."

"Maybe you all should have lunch. Seems to me like you could use a little brain food before you tackle this name business," Jessie said.

"I think she has a point," Gracie said. "I'll have a chef's salad."

"A cheeseburger for me," Abby said. "And a chocolate shake."

Delia groaned. "Oh, to be young again. Bring me a tuna sandwich and a glass of iced tea." She glanced at the door and smiled. "And set another place, while you're at it."

Gracie followed the direction of her gaze and saw Kevin heading their way.

"Ladies," he said politely, his gaze skimming over the three of them.

"Well, don't just stand there," Delia said. "Sit. Scoot over, Gracie, and make room for him."

Gracie didn't scoot. Kevin remained standing, his expression growing more amused by the second. Finally she sighed and moved over.

"Join us," she said.

He grinned at her weary tone. "If you insist, especially since you're being so gracious about it."

He slid in next to her, deliberately crowding her. Gracie felt the shockwaves from the brush of his thigh all the way down to her toes. It made her realize just how much she'd been missing his kisses.

"You should come see the house, Uncle Kevin. It's totally awesome," Abby reported. "Dad came by twice. Mama's been by, too."

"Is that so?"

"Oh, don't be such a sourpuss," Delia chided him. "You might as well get used to the idea. It's a done deal."

Kevin sighed. "I know. I've seen the bills."

Gracie's gaze shot to his. "What do you mean you've seen the bills? They're supposed to be coming to me."

"You see, darlin'. That's the problem. You're a stranger and you're a woman. Now that's never bothered me, but to some contractors that's two strikes against you. They've hedged their bets by sending everything to me."

"Well, you can just pass them right on to me," she said. "And I'll speak to the contractors. Believe me, it won't happen again."

"Oh, I suspect it will," he said, retrieving the bundle of envelopes from his pocket and handing them over. "By the way, you're being overcharged for the electrical work. I could speak to Eddie, straighten it out."

Gracie gritted her teeth. "I'll speak to Eddie."

"Just trying to help."

"Thanks all the same."

"You might want to reconsider that bid on the wallpapering, too. I know it's the lowest, but I've seen the work in a couple of other places. It's shoddy. They save on paper by not bothering to match the print."

"I appreciate your opinion," she said tightly.

"Anytime."

Fortunately, their food came just then so Gracie could concentrate on cutting all the little strips of ham and turkey and cheese into tiny, bite-size chunks, then pushing them around until they were buried beneath the lettuce.

"Anything wrong, darlin?" Kevin inquired, his expression as innocent as a babe's.

She scowled at him. "What could possibly be wrong?"

"That's what I asked."

"You expected this to happen, didn't you?" she accused. "You knew that I was going to be up against some tight-knit, old boy's network and that every one of these contractors would assume you were footing the bill or, at the very least, in charge of the whole renovation." Her gaze narrowed. "Or did you see to it that they got that impression? Have you been talking to them behind my back?"

"I told you I was steering clear of this project."

"I know what you said. What are you doing?"

That innocent mask returned. "Darlin', you know I never work unless I have to."

"That's a bunch of bull and you know it, Kevin Daniels. I'm on to you."

"Really? I'll bet you haven't figured out what I'm thinking right this second."

With his eyes blazing pure lust, Gracie didn't have any trouble at all guessing exactly what was on his mind. However, with two very fascinated onlookers—more if she counted the rest of the restaurant's patrons—she couldn't spell it out to him.

"Never mind."

Kevin grinned. "Come on. What's wrong? Cat got your tongue?"

Gracie held onto her temper with a very tight rein. "Could you excuse me, please?"

He didn't budge.

"Kevin!"

"Let her out of there this instant, young man," Delia ordered.

Kevin slid out of the booth and allowed Gracie to pass. She aimed straight for the restroom.

"See what you've done," Abby chided. "You made her cry."

Gracie heard the teen's footsteps coming after her. By the time Abby caught up with her, Gracie was already splashing cold water on her face to cover the stupid tears.

"Uncle Kevin can be a jerk sometimes," Abby told her, watching her reflection worriedly. "He just likes to tease. He only does it 'cause he likes you."

"I know," Gracie said. "I can't imagine why I let him get to me."

"It's because all those guys sent their bills and stuff to Uncle Kevin, like you don't have a brain in your head. I'd be ticked, too. Mama says some men just can't cope with a woman who's smart. I used to ask her sometimes if that meant I ought to play dumb, but she said no. She said if they weren't smart enough to love me the way I am, then I'd be sick of them in no time anyway."

Gracie grinned. "Your mother is a very smart woman."

Abby smiled back. "Yeah, she is. Too bad Daddy couldn't cope with it. Instead, he ends up with an airhead like Sara Lynn. He only likes her because she drives him crazy. If he ever had to spend ten consecutive minutes talking to her, he'd realize she's clueless." Her expression turned wistful. "Do you think that's why he's been calling Mama more lately?"

"I suppose," she said carefully. Gracie figured she was

treading on thin ice, poking her nose into family matters, but Abby clearly wanted to talk. "Do you think he'd ever go back to your mom?"

"I used to want that, but now I'm not so sure. I mean if he doesn't get it, if he can't even see what he lost, who wants him, right?"

Gracie had the feeling Abby was talking about her own relationship with her father now. "He'll always be your dad, Abby. You don't stop loving him, just because he doesn't know how to love you back."

Abby sighed. "Yeah, I know, but it's hard sometimes. Uncle Kevin is so cool. Why couldn't my dad have been more like him?"

"Sorry, kiddo. It just doesn't work that way."

"You like Uncle Kevin, though, don't you? I mean, I know he made you mad just now, but deep down you really like him, right?"

This time it was Gracie's turn to sigh. As irritating and annoying as Kevin could be, the truth was that deep down she more than liked him. She couldn't help wondering, though, if her dream of turning his aunt's house into a bed and breakfast wasn't clashing with some dream of his own, maybe one he hadn't even acknowledged to himself.

"Gracie?"

"Yes, sweetie."

"You didn't say. Do you like Uncle Kevin?"

"When he's not being a pest, yes, I like him very much."

"All right!" Abby enthused just as the restroom door opened.

"What on earth is taking so long in here?" Delia demanded. She scanned Gracie's face intently. "Are you okay?"

"I'm fine."

"Well, then, get on back out here and finish your lunch. Time's awasting." Her expression turned innocent. "Oh, and Kevin said maybe he could spare some time this afternoon to help us pick out wallpaper."

"Oh, did he?" Gracie muttered. "How very special of him."

Abby and Delia exchanged another one of their knowing looks.

"I saw that," Gracie said.

"Oh, don't mind us," Delia said. "We're just a couple of fools for love."

Love? Gracie swallowed hard. That was absurd. She didn't love Kevin. Half the time she didn't even like him very much, despite what she'd conceded to Abby.

She squeezed Delia's hand. "Stick to picking out wallpaper, okay? I'll find my own man."

"If you say so," Delia said, not looking the least bit daunted. "Seems to me, though, that you already have."

Helen spread half a dozen rough sketches along the board that spanned two sawhorses in the middle of what would be the parlor of the renovated house. Right now, it looked more like a war zone.

"This was tough to do without a name for the place," she said pointedly.

"I know," Gracie apologized. "That has been brought to my attention more than once today. I'll think about it overnight. I promise."

"I could help," Kevin offered, grinning at her. "Maybe provide a little inspiration."

"More likely a distraction."

"I don't know. You want it to be romantic, don't you? I can definitely put you on that wave length."

"In your dreams," she shot back, still irritated by those bills he'd received and delivered along with a lot of unsolicited advice.

"Children, children," Delia scolded. "This isn't helping."

"I'm sorry," Gracie apologized at once. "You're right. And Helen, these ideas of yours are wonderful. I especially like this pen-and-ink sketch. It looks old-fashioned and romantic and elegant."

Helen seemed startled by the praise. "It's just an idea. It's not as if I'm an artist or anything."

"I like it just the way it is," Gracie insisted. "There's a simplicity and charm to it."

Kevin peered over her shoulder, his hands on her waist. "I like it, too. Helen, I never knew you could draw."

"I dabble, that's all," she said, clearly embarrassed by all the praise. "Max said he liked it, too."

"You've shown this to Max?" Gracie asked, uncertain how she felt about that. It did explain why he'd left half a dozen messages for her over the past forty-eight hours. She hadn't returned his calls. Obviously, though, he'd been shaken by the evidence that she was truly settling in Virginia.

Helen nodded. "I faxed all of them to him just to get his opinion. I didn't want to bring you something that was so far off the mark you'd laugh."

"Why on earth would we laugh?" Delia demanded. "We're all winging it here, except for Gracie. She knows the hotel business. The rest of us are just along for the fun of it."

"What did Max have to say?" Gracie asked, proving once and for all that she cared about Max's professional opinion.

"He was very encouraging. He seemed a little surprised about the B & B, though." She studied Gracie worriedly. "I'm sorry if I let the cat out of the bag."

"Never mind. I suppose he would have found out sooner or later anyway."

"I was sure you'd mentioned it to him while he was here."

"No, I hadn't, but it's okay, Helen. Really."

"He wants what's best for you, you know that, don't you?"

"Only if it doesn't inconvenience him," Gracie said. "I imagine he told you this whole idea was insane."

"He doesn't think that at all," Helen protested. "He thought it was a terrific idea."

Gracie hadn't realized she'd been holding her breath until she felt a sigh of relief shudder through her. "He said that?" She glanced up and caught Kevin's expression. "Okay, so his opinion matters. Sue me."

"Hey, darlin', I never said a word."

"You didn't have to. Your expression said it all."

"Could we get back to the point," Delia coaxed. "Are we going with this ad or not?"

"I vote yes," Abby said. "I think it's the best, Aunt Helen."

"Thank you, sweetie." She looked at Kevin. "Do you have an opinion, too?"

"An opinion, but no vote," he said. "I like it."

"Me, too," Delia chimed in. "Gracie?"

She nodded slowly. "I love it. As soon as we settle on a name to plug in there, you can finalize it. I'll come up with a list of publications we need to put it in."

"When on earth will you have time to do that?" Delia demanded. "You're here practically twenty-four hours a day."

"In the middle of the night would be my guess," Kevin said, his gaze intent. "I'm recommending a break."

"I don't have time for a break. I just got back from lunch. There are a million things left on my list for today."

"Forget the damned list. And I'm not talking about a little break," he retorted. "I'm talking about an entire afternoon and evening off." He held out his hand. "Let's go."

"I can't."

"Of course you can," Delia said.

"The wallpaper samples," Gracie protested.

"Will be here in the morning."

"There are paint chips, too. And I need to go through those catalogues for kitchen appliances."

"They'll all be here," Delia repeated. "Our target date for opening is not until Labor Day weekend."

"That's only six weeks away," Gracie pointed out. "We don't have time to spare."

"Abby and I càn begin sorting through this stuff," Delia said.

"And I can help," Helen added. "I've redecorated my house so many times I can do it blindfolded. I think that ad proves we're on the same wavelength, don't you? Trust me."

Kevin's hand was still outstretched. "Well?" he said.

"You'll get even more done tomorrow if you're well rested," Delia reminded her. "A nice long break will clear the cobwebs."

"Okay, okay," Gracie conceded, and placed her hand in Kevin's.

The minute she did, the instant her skin made contact with his, she knew with absolute certainty that the one thing she wouldn't be getting that night was rest.

Nineteen

The trip back to Gracie's took only a few minutes, but Kevin used the time to remind himself that it made absolutely no sense whatsoever to sleep with a woman who'd practically stolen something right out from under him.

He told himself Gracie couldn't be trusted.

He told himself a whole lot of things, but they didn't add up to a hill of beans when compared to this driving need to make love to her. He'd wanted her for so long now, denied himself for so long that the aching had almost become a part of him.

He parked in front of her house and sat perfectly still, his hands clamped around the steering wheel to prevent himself from reaching for her.

"Gracie, you can say no now."

She peered at him with wide, innocent eyes. "Oh? What's the question?"

He glanced over and caught the amused smile tugging on her lips. "If you don't know that, darlin', then I really should let you out right here and be on my way."

She was the one who reached then. She touched her hand lightly to his forearm and sent a jolt straight through him.

"Don't go," she pleaded softly.

He felt some of the tension ease out of him then only to be replaced by another sort of tension entirely. "Do you have any idea how much I want you?" he murmured, surprised by it himself. He'd been surrounded by neediness for so long now, he'd never had time to indulge in it himself. He'd always pushed his own desires aside to take care of everyone else.

"Maybe I don't," she teased. "You've done an excellent job of controlling it."

"You have no idea."

"I wish you'd stop."

"Stop what?"

"Controlling it."

He grinned at the plaintive note in her voice. He wondered if she even knew it was there. A little anticipation served its purposes apparently. He leaned back against the door and studied her.

She was a mess, with streaks of paint on her clothes and her hair tousled. He thought she looked charming, delectable. She also looked as nervous as a new bride, jittery and excited at the same time. A smoldering sensuality burned in her eyes.

"Now the way I see it," he said, "we could go about this nice and slow."

"Slower than this?" She sounded thoroughly horrified by the suggestion.

Kevin grinned. "Afraid you'll change your mind if I give you too much time?"

"I'm afraid I'll be too old to remember what's happening," she said dryly.

The teasing startled him, challenged him. "Oh, you'll remember," he vowed. "I guarantee that."

"Big talk, mister, but I sure don't see much action. A couple of paltry little kisses hardly amounts to a seduction. I've about given up."

"Paltry little kisses!" Kevin protested, rising to the bait.

"Hardly memorable at all," she insisted.

Even though he recognized that it was exactly what she'd intended, his ego kicked in with a vengeance. "I guess slow isn't the way to go then," he said, reaching for her.

His mouth settled against hers. He could have been satis-

fied with that much alone . . . for a time. The brush of silk
against his lips was erotic enough, but he remembered the
possibility of more. He recalled the taste of her and simply
had to prove that memory served him correctly. That, too,
could have been enough to last . . . for a bit.

But then she slipped her hands into his hair and molded
her body to his, and then the sweet, summery scent of her
surrounded him and nothing they could possibly do in the
front seat of a car was even remotely close to enough. Years
ago he could have managed . . . something, but that wasn't
what he wanted with Gracie. He wanted to savor every second. He wanted to explore and excite and inflame.

And he sure as heck didn't want to do it in public.

"Time out," he murmured, his breath catching as if he'd
sprinted a dozen laps around a ballfield, instead of pacing
himself.

Her reluctance to move away was plain. So was her confusion.

"We're taking this inside," he explained. "I don't want the
entire town to know by sunset that you and I were caught
making love in the front seat of a car."

"And you don't suppose they'll know we went inside in
the nick of time?"

He sighed. "Let 'em use their imaginations all they want.
At least there won't be witnesses."

She shot him an impish look. "I'll race you," she said,
already scrambling out the other side.

Kevin stared after her for a second, then burst out laughing.
Amazing, he thought as he followed. The woman was absolutely amazing.

Gracie had never been more afraid in her life than she was
on that short race for the house. She knew that Kevin had
doubts about her, about them. She knew that he was as com-
mitment-shy as any man she'd ever seen, thanks mostly to

the slew of family commitments he already had. Even the few yards from car to house could give him long enough to think things through, to change his mind.

He was, above all, an honorable man. She knew that as surely as she knew that the sun rose in the east every morning. Would he conclude that sleeping with her under such circumstances defied his moral code?

She waited at the back door, her heart in her throat. When he didn't bolt after her, she was sure that his first words would be a polite and hastily concocted excuse for leaving. Then she saw the look in his eyes, the flaring of heat. His desire hadn't waned at all. The only question was whether his head would win out over his heart.

He came through the back door and shoved it closed with an emphatic crash. All the while, his gaze was locked with hers. Gracie swallowed hard and waited, stomach knotted, pulse skittering wildly.

"I'm not starting over in the kitchen," he warned quietly.

That was just dandy with her, as long as they didn't waste too much time getting to . . . wherever. She nodded.

Honor warred with yearning. She could see that much in his eyes.

"Last chance," he said.

Fearing he was the one who'd take the out, if she let him, she took a step closer and touched a hand to his cheek. His skin was burning hot, as fiery as the glint in his eyes. Her caress, light as it was, was apparently message enough. This time he nodded, his satisfaction and relief apparent.

And then he scooped her into his arms and aimed straight for the stairs, unerringly finding her bedroom and kicking that door shut behind him, as if he feared that the gossips might be lurking outside that, too.

It didn't seem to bother him a bit that she probably had paint on the tip of her nose and splattered on her clothes. Nor did he seem too worried about the tangle her hair was likely in. In fact, he was gazing at her as if she were Cinderella all dressed up in a dazzling gown for the ball. Suddenly that was what she wanted to be. She wanted to come to him after she'd been polished and buffed and scented with something wickedly provocative.

"I think I should take a shower," she murmured, touching her hair and trying ineffectively to rake her fingers through it.

His eyes lit up. "Could be interesting," Kevin said. "I could join you."

"I don't think so. The whole purpose is to clean up so you'll see me at my best."

He chuckled. "Too late, darlin'. Actually, I kind of like this look. It's . . ."

"Messy?"

"Approachable. Until today I'm not sure I've ever seen you when you weren't at your best."

"You seem to have forgotten the first cooking debacle."

His eyes lit with amusement. "Ah, yes, that was a close second."

Gracie stared at him, horrified. "I look worse than that? I really am going to take a shower."

"Not without me."

"Think of it this way," she coaxed. "I'll come out all soft and silky and smelling like something other than sawdust and sweat."

He brushed her hair back from her face and kissed her neck. His tongue touched a spot behind her ear and sent a jolt straight through her.

"No trace of sawdust there," he assessed thoughtfully. "Maybe a hint of roses."

Gracie stared at him in wonder. "You really think I'm beautiful just the way I am, don't you?"

"No doubt about it." He studied her a bit. "Actually, I'm pretty proud of my handiwork."

"Your handiwork? What's that supposed to mean?"

"You've loosened up, darlin'. Another few months and

that tidy, sophisticated facade will be stripped away completely."

"And you think that's a good thing?"

He grinned. "Of course I do. Makes us better suited, don't you think?"

"I suppose," she said doubtfully. Even so, she backed out of his loose embrace. "I still think I'll like me better if I'm all cleaned up. This ought to be an occasion, after all."

He gave a resigned sigh. "It's not the soap and water that will make it an occasion, but if you'll feel more confident, I'll just relax right here on your bed and wait."

She kissed his cheek. "Thank you."

"Gracie?"

"Yes?

"Don't take too long, okay?"

"I'll be back before you can blink."

She stepped into the bathroom and closed the door behind her, then leaned against it. Her heart was pounding so hard, it felt as if she'd just finished an aerobic workout and hadn't cooled down. Of course, the likelihood she'd be cooling down anytime soon was slim to none.

She stripped off her clothes, jumped into the shower and lathered up in record time. She shampooed her hair. When she emerged, she slathered lotion over her body, then ran a brush through her hair. She eyed the dryer, but guessed that Kevin wouldn't wait patiently for her to blow-dry her hair. She fluffed it into damp curls with her fingers instead, added a touch of lipstick and a swish of mascara and left it at that.

Only then did she realize that she hadn't brought a single piece of clothing into the bathroom with her. Nor was there a sexy robe hanging on the back of the door. There was no way in hell she was climbing back into the filthy clothes she'd just removed. She gazed at her reflection in the mirror and smiled. Her entrance was going to be very provocative. She hoped Kevin hadn't had second thoughts while she was gone.

She wrapped herself in the most voluminous towel she owned, but the truth was, it barely made her decent. Nor was there any truly secure way to assure it would stay on for more than a heartbeat. She could only pray the makeshift knot would hold long enough for her to cross the room, otherwise she was going straight from sophisticated to scandalous.

Drawing in a deep breath, she opened the door. Sunlight spilled across the bed, bathing Kevin in gold and shadows. At the sound of the door opening, his gaze shot to her.

"Holy . . . kamoley," he murmured, his voice ragged.

"Worth the wait?"

"Better than any ballgown I've ever seen. Get over here."

Gracie crossed the room very carefully, one hand locked on the knot of terrycloth between her breasts.

Kevin drew a little circle in the air. "Turn around."

Gracie's cheeks flooded with heat, but she dutifully turned.

"If Cannon knew what you did for one of their towels, they'd hire you for an entire ad campaign."

"The towel as fashion statement?"

"Something like that." He reached up and touched the hand securing the knot. "What happens if you let go?"

"I'm afraid to find out."

"Come on. Be daring. Let's check it out." He gently pulled her hand away. The towel stayed where it was. Kevin regarded the knot with a disappointed gaze. Then he slipped a finger into the twist of fabric and gave a little tug. The towel slowly parted and slithered to the floor.

Gracie swallowed hard, but forced herself not to look away. Kevin looked awestruck.

"You are so beautiful," he murmured. "I think I like this look best of all."

"It might not be appropriate for church on Sunday," she pointed out, her voice shaky.

"Darlin, this look's not appropriate for anyone but me to see. Remember that, okay?"

"Agreed." She surveyed him slowly, boldly. "I've noticed something, though."

"What's that?"

"I'm standing here stark naked and you have on way too many clothes."

"I can fix that in a heartbeat," he promised, stripping off shirt and jeans and briefs before she could blink. He beckoned to her. "Now, come on over here, so I can touch you."

He held out his arms and Gracie moved into them. It was odd, she thought, as their naked bodies came together, fit together. It felt as if she'd just come home.

There was only a moment to savor that stunning sensation, though. Kevin knew all sorts of wicked and wonderful things to do to her body. Maybe that's how he spent all those lazy hours in the hammock, dreaming up new and inventive ways to drive a woman crazy. Gracie was relatively certain that no other man on earth was quite as clever or adept with his fingers, that no other man had discovered quite so many erogenous zones. Her senses reached new limits, then topped them, and all the while Kevin took nothing for himself.

To her frustration, he kept her hands pinned idly over her head while he worked his magic. Only when she had come apart once, twice, three times, the incredible tension dissolving into shuddering waves of pleasure, did he finally heed her pleas and slowly enter her, shattering her all over again with his deep, penetrating strokes.

This time, though, he was with her, his body shuddering as forcefully as her own, an exultant cry ripped from deep in his chest.

In the aftermath of that, the feelings that stole over her scared Gracie to death. Contentment, powerful and soul-deep. Wonder. Joy.

And love. That was the most terrifying of all, because when she looked in Kevin's half-shuttered eyes, she wasn't sure she saw anything to match it.

No, what she read in his eyes was satisfaction, delight,

maybe even a touch of masculine smugness. Warmth. A trace of affection, perhaps, but no more than that. He looked like a man who had made love, thoroughly and enjoyably, but not one who was *in* love.

Suddenly overcome with regrets, she slammed the door on her own emotions, hoping that nothing of what she felt was visible on her face or in her eyes. For some idiotic reason, she had leapt to the conclusion that this afternoon was about the future. Now she knew without any doubt at all that it had only been about the here and now.

She felt the sting of tears in her eyes and turned away before Kevin could spot them and see her for the fool she'd been. When the phone beside the bed rang, she was only too eager for the distraction. She grabbed it, even as Kevin protested.

"Yes, hello."

"Is Kevin there?" a man demanded roughly.

"Yes. May I tell him who's calling?"

"Bobby Ray."

She rolled over and handed the phone to Kevin, who was regarding her with a watchful, worried look. "Bobby Ray," she mouthed silently.

He took the phone with obvious reluctance. "This had better be good, Bobby Ray, or I'll have to break every bone in your body."

Bobby Ray was shouting now, cursing Kevin. Gracie could hear just about every bitter word, enough to know that Bobby Ray was blaming him for something.

"If you don't calm down and tell me what the hell is going on, I'm hanging up," Kevin said quietly, sitting on the edge of the bed, his back deliberately toward Gracie.

"Sara Lynn's gone," Bobby Ray said bleakly, but still at full volume, which suggested he'd been drinking for some time now. "She's run off with that son-of-a-bitch jeweler."

"I warned you," Kevin began. "I suppose they made off with all the money, too."

Gracie shut him off with an elbow to the ribs. "This is not the time for a lecture," she whispered fiercely. "Tell him to come over."

"Here?" Kevin asked, whipping around to stare at her incredulously.

She nodded, already scrambling out of bed and searching for clothes to put on. Kevin stared at her for a minute, then sighed heavily.

"Come on over, Bobby Ray. We'll figure out something."

He slowly replaced the receiver on the hook. "Mind telling me why you're so all-fired interested in having my cousin drop by to spill his guts?"

"He's upset, drunk most likely from what I heard. He needs to talk. He needs our help."

"He needs *my* help, you mean. This is my problem, not yours."

She regarded him wryly. "Actually, it's Bobby Ray's problem, don't you think? What he needs from us is moral support. I'm as good at giving that as you are. Better, more than likely, since you seem to think he's an idiot for marrying Sara Lynn in the first place."

Kevin stood up and jerked on his pants. "My opinion of Sara Lynn is no secret. That doesn't mean I'm incapable of being sympathetic."

"We'll see," Gracie responded.

"The minute Bobby Ray gets here, I'm going to take him out to Greystone Manor. There's no reason for you to get mixed up in this," he repeated, his expression grim, his jaw set determinedly.

"Is it that you think I can't offer a shoulder to cry on?" Gracie demanded indignantly. "Is it that you don't want me to know the family secrets? Or do you just like carrying all those burdens around singlehandedly?"

He glowered at her. "What the hell is that supposed to mean?"

"It means I think you enjoy having everyone lean on you. It's the only kind of intimacy you understand."

"Don't be absurd." He turned his back on her and went scrambling for his shirt and shoes.

"I think I'm right," she persisted. "I think you're afraid if they start to solve their own problems, they won't need you anymore and you'll be left all alone."

"I have never in my life heard such worthless psychobabble," he said, and stormed out of the bedroom without a backward glance.

Gracie stayed right on his heels. "Prove me wrong," she said.

He sat on a chair in the darkening kitchen and yanked on socks and shoes. "I don't have to prove anything to you or anybody else," he muttered.

"Maybe not to me," she agreed quietly. "Maybe you just need to prove it to yourself."

Twenty

Bobby Ray was weaving and bleary-eyed when he stumbled his way onto Gracie's front porch twenty minutes later. At least he'd had the good sense to call the area's only cab for the ride over. Kevin watched his arrival with a mixture of disgust and trepidation. He had a feeling this was a very bad idea, in more ways than one.

Gracie had turned his cousin's crisis into some sort of test, and for the life of him he couldn't figure out what she was up to. It was absolutely absurd to think that these incidents gave him some sort of perverse pleasure, which was what she was implying. He wanted Bobby Ray—all of them, for that matter—to stand on their own two feet. It just hadn't happened. In all these years, they'd run to him every time they'd so much as stubbed a toe.

As much as he wanted to haul his cousin as far from Gracie's as he could take him, there was no way to pull it off now. She was waiting inside with a pot of coffee brewing and a plate of cookies warm from the oven. Apparently, she thought they were going to have some sort of blasted tea party.

Bobby Ray made it to the front door under his own steam. He even tried to throw a punch at Kevin, but Kevin anticipated it and Bobby Ray's aim was off anyway.

"Ought to tear you apart," Bobby Ray said.

"Ditto," Kevin said, tucking an arm around his cousin's

waist and guiding him into the kitchen. Bobby Ray leaned heavily against him.

Kevin tried to make himself remember all the good times they'd had as boys. They'd gotten into more mischief than brothers or best friends. In fact, back then, Bobby Ray had been his best friend.

He knew precisely when that had changed. They'd been at college then. Roommates, in fact, though Kevin had been finishing up law school and Bobby Ray was still a senior thanks to his lackadaisical attitude toward his classes and his fervent concentration on partying. That was the year Bobby Ray's daddy had called Kevin and told him he was dying and that he wanted Kevin to be in charge of managing his estate.

"Bobby Ray's not responsible," his uncle had declared from his sickbed. "None of them are."

"And who saw to that?" Kevin had asked him point-blank. "Has there ever been a time when you weren't only too eager to bail them out of a jam?"

"Maybe not. Maybe it is my fault. But truth's truth and it's too late to fix it now," his uncle Steven had lamented. "They'll fritter that money away in a year, if I don't leave somebody sensible in charge."

Kevin hadn't wanted the responsibility, had guessed that it would drive a wedge between him and his cousins, but his uncle had been adamant. It wasn't as if this were the first time. His own father had reminded him of his duty to half a dozen other relatives as he lay dying, too.

What had made it so much worse this time was that his uncle hadn't bothered telling his children about the arrangements, hadn't even told them how ill he was. He'd left all of that to Kevin, as well. It was little wonder there'd been so much resentment.

Bobby Ray had retaliated by going after Marianne. Kevin had been stunned, but not heartbroken when she had chosen his cousin. He'd wished them well, had even stood up for

Bobby Ray at the wedding. Only recently had he come to realize that the expression on Bobby Ray's face that day hadn't been happiness, but a gloating triumph.

There was none of that in his expression now. He was, quite simply, drunk as a skunk. Gracie started clucking over him the minute they entered the kitchen. Naturally Bobby Ray promptly made a halfhearted pass at her, aiming a kiss straight for her lips. Kevin told himself that his cousin was drunk, and besides that, flirting came as naturally to Bobby Ray as breathing. It was the only thing that kept Kevin from decking him. Gracie had ignored the overture anyway, dodging the kiss and steering Bobby Ray toward a chair instead.

"Sit down, Bobby Ray. Let me pour you some coffee. Have a cookie." She studied him worriedly. "Or maybe a sandwich would be better."

"Stop fussing," Kevin grumbled. "He's survived worse."

She scowled at him, then beamed at Bobby Ray. "Why don't you tell us exactly what happened? Maybe we can help."

Bobby Ray seemed stunned by the offer. "You'll help me get Sara Lynn back?"

"If that's what you truly want," Gracie promised in a tone that suggested she didn't believe for a minute that it was what he wanted.

His head bobbed up and down. "It's what I want."

"Tell me about her," Gracie encouraged.

Kevin sighed and resigned himself to a very long evening and one that would be a far cry from what he'd envisioned. He hadn't planned on leaving that bed of Gracie's for hours to come.

Bobby Ray embarked on a long, complicated tale of how he'd met Sara Lynn and fallen head over heels in love with her. "She thought I was a hero, straight out of a storybook. That's what she said." He smiled sadly. "Never been a hero before."

"Marianne thought you were," Kevin reminded him. "Until you disillusioned her."

Bobby Ray's expression turned even more sorrowful. "Made a mistake with Marianne. Married her for all the wrong reasons." He looked at Kevin. "Trying to get even with you. When she figured it out, she left me."

"So you married Ginny on the rebound," Kevin said. "Even though the two of you had about as much in common as an octopus and an elephant."

Bobby Ray nodded. "Another mistake," he conceded. He looked at Gracie. "Ginny left me, too. Took my new Jaguar with her."

"It was the least you owed her," Kevin said. "She could have taken you for a bundle."

"You saw to it she didn't," Bobby Ray said. "I can always count on you. Good old Kevin. Saint Kevin."

To Kevin's astonishment, Gracie waved a finger under Bobby Ray's nose. "Don't you dare talk about your cousin that way. He could let you twist in the wind, you know."

"Not Kevin," Bobby Ray insisted. "Wouldn't do that. It's not his nature."

"Maybe I should," Kevin said. "Maybe just once I should let you work your own way out of trouble. I may be every bit as bad as your father."

The remark was as effective as a slap at snapping Bobby Ray out of his drunken self-pity. "You wouldn't abandon me now, would you, Kev?"

"I don't know what you want from me."

"Help me get Sara Lynn back," Bobby Ray said again.

"Because you love her?" Gracie asked. "Or because you can't stand losing another woman?"

Both Kevin and Bobby Ray stared at her. Bobby Ray looked thoughtful, or as thoughtful as a man drunk on bourbon could look.

"Could be.you're right," he admitted. "Tired of seeing 'em get away."

"Have you ever considered trying to get Marianne back?" Gracie inquired casually.

Kevin almost choked on his coffee. "Gracie!"

"Hush. I want to hear what Bobby Ray has to say to that."

"You don't know what you're suggesting," Kevin protested.

"I think I do," Gracie said stubbornly.

"Marianne wouldn't take me back," Bobby Ray said. "Too much water under the bridge."

"Why'd she throw you out, Bobby Ray?"

"Because I used her to get even with Kevin," he repeated.

Gracie nodded, a satisfied expression on her face. "Not because she didn't love you, right? She chose you over Kevin, didn't she? And she hasn't dated anyone seriously since, according to Abby."

Kevin was dumbfounded. "Where did you hear all this?"

"From Abby."

"She's a kid," Kevin argued. "She's not a very reliable source."

"I'll bet she knows her mother pretty well," Gracie countered.

"She's like every other kid. She daydreams about having her family together again," Kevin protested. "That doesn't mean it's the right thing for Marianne."

"Maybe Marianne and Bobby Ray should be the judge of what's best for them," Gracie argued right back.

"Stop meddling in things you know nothing about."

Bobby Ray had listened silently to the entire exchange, then regarded him wryly. "Still looking out for Marianne, aren't you, cousin? That was always the problem. I thought I'd won, but you were always right there between us."

"Maybe in your mind, not in Marianne's and certainly not in mine," Kevin insisted. "Why couldn't you see that, Bobby Ray? Was it because even after you married her, you were still too busy trying to get even with me?"

"Probably," he conceded. He looked at Gracie, his expression wistful. "Do you think second chances are possible?"

"Always."

"Even after I've made such a mess of things?"

Gracie nodded with certainty. "Even then, if you're sure about what you want."

"Which he's not," Kevin said emphatically. "A half-hour ago he came in here moaning because Sara Lynn had abandoned him. Now you've talked him into rebounding straight into Marianne's arms. It'll be a disaster."

"They're old enough to decide for themselves if it's what they want and to work out whatever obstacles are in the way," Gracie retorted. "All I've done is plant the idea in his head."

"Well, I hope to hell you'll be around to pick up the pieces when it all blows up in our faces."

She stared him down, a stubborn jut to her chin. "I guess that all depends on you now, doesn't it?"

"Me? How?"

"You can kick me out of your life for meddling in family affairs or you can learn to share the problems with me. It's up to you."

"Well, I can't very well kick you out now, can I?" he grumbled. "You've managed to get yourself entwined with me and my relatives so tight, it would take a crowbar to pry us all apart."

Gracie gave him a tight little smile. "You don't have to sound so downright elated about it."

"Believe me, I am not elated."

"Scared, maybe?"

"Of you? Never."

Her grin broadened. "Bet you are."

"Hey, you guys, don't mind me," Bobby Ray said, backing away from the table. "I think I'll just slip on out before the fight picks up steam. Got enough troubles of my own."

"Where are you going?" Kevin asked.

"Home," Bobby Ray said. "The cab's waiting down the

block. Jimmy said he'd stick around till I was finished up here. I've got some thinking to do. I figure it's time I thought first, then acted. Maybe I'll avoid making another mistake that way." He winked at Gracie. "It's about time, wouldn't you say?"

"Something tells me you're going to get it right this time," she told him.

After he'd left, walking considerably more steadily than he had when he'd arrived, Gracie faced Kevin defiantly.

"Are we going to fight about what just happened here?"

"One of these days," Kevin said, reaching for her. "But not just yet."

"Oh, no," she said, backing away. "I'm not going to bed with you now, knowing that you're going to fight with me later. Let's get it out in the open now."

He sighed. "Okay, then, what you did here tonight was risky and ill-conceived and, more than likely, a huge mistake."

"That's your opinion. I think I gave him something to think about."

"Darlin', Bobby Ray never thinks. He acts impulsively. He'll be over there proposing before daybreak. I don't want Marianne and Abby getting caught up in that again."

"It's not your call," Gracie said. "Marianne's capable of telling him to take a hike, if it's not what she wants."

"That's the problem, sweetpea. I'm afraid she might want it too much. She'll grab on, only to find out it's another one of Bobby Ray's impulses with no substance or staying power behind it."

Gracie shrugged off his concern. "Then I guess it'll be up to you and me to see that doesn't happen."

For some reason he couldn't entirely explain, the weight that had settled in his stomach when Bobby Ray first called began to ease. The reaction defied logic, because his head was practically screaming that things were going to get a whole lot worse.

But not until after he'd had one more chance to make very passionate love to Gracie.

Gracie knew she had taken a huge risk by interfering in Daniels family business the night before. Obviously, Kevin hadn't appreciated it, and it remained to be seen if Bobby Ray or Marianne would thank her. Still, she couldn't help thinking that Abby deserved one last shot at having her family back together. From everything she'd heard and observed, there were still sparks amid the ashes of Bobby Ray's relationship with Abby's mom.

By the time Gracie arrived at the Victorian, Delia, Abby, and Helen were all seated around the huge worktable Gracie had moved to the kitchen. Wallpaper samples had been stacked into neat little piles, paint chips had been sorted, and there was a whole new collection of carpet and linoleum samples.

"Abby's been making calls again," Delia said as she ran her fingers over a lush piece of carpet in a soft weeping-willow green. She held it up for Gracie's inspection. "What do you think?"

"It's beautiful, but I though we were going with blues."

Helen winced. "Sorry. When I went through the wallpaper samples, I hated most of the blues." She plucked up a pile. "See for yourself."

Even Gracie had to agree most were either bland and uninspired or too much like every other historic home that used Williamsburg blue for its decor.

"Now look at this," Helen said, and showed her a pattern that had the same soft green as the carpet, along with a tiny touch of blue and a bit of gold.

"Better," Gracie admitted.

Helen's eyes lit up. "And look at it with this," she suggested, tossing a fabric swatch across it.

The fabric had blue-and-gold irises on a light beige background, but the predominant color was the soft green of the leaves.

"It's fabulous," Gracie declared, drawing a collective sigh of relief from the other three. She grinned at them. "Were you all worried?"

"Well, it wasn't what we talked about," Delia said.

"And I didn't want to go against your wishes," Helen said. "It is your bed and breakfast, after all."

"They had a backup in blue, just in case," Abby revealed. "But we all liked this one best."

"Helen, do you have time to do the measuring and then order what we need?" Gracie asked.

Helen looked pleased by the request. "Of course. I was hoping you'd ask. I haven't had this much fun in years."

"Speaking of fun," Delia began, studying Gracie with open curiosity, "why don't you tell us how your evening went."

"As productive as ours?" Helen inquired, a mischievous gleam in her eyes.

"That remains to be seen," Gracie said enigmatically. "By the way, how far along are they upstairs? Has anyone checked?"

"I was up there first thing," Delia said.

"And guess what?" Abby chimed in happily. "Daddy's here."

"Oh, really?" Despite the previous night's activities, Gracie was startled by that particular turn of events. She'd figured Bobby Ray was going to be laid low for days with a monumental hangover. "What's he doing?"

"He and Uncle Kevin are painting."

"And so far they haven't turned the brushes on each other," Helen said. "You have no idea what a triumph that is." She regarded Gracie curiously. "How'd you manage it?"

"Manage what? I had no idea they were going to be here."

"But you were behind their peace treaty," Helen said.

"You must have been. Nobody else has ever had any luck. I actually heard them laughing a while ago."

"It's true that Bobby Ray came by the house last night and we all talked," Gracie conceded. "I wasn't expecting this, though."

"I was thinking, since it's Saturday, maybe I should call Mom and ask her to come over and help," Abby said. "Is that a good idea or not?"

Seeing the longing in the child's eyes, Gracie squeezed her hand. "I think it's a very good idea."

"You do?" Helen and Delia said in unison. They both sounded skeptical and more than a little worried.

Gracie opted not to explain about Sara Lynn's departure. That was Bobby Ray's revelation to make. But she didn't see any harm in throwing him and Marianne into close proximity.

"Call your mom," she repeated to Abby.

"But for heaven's sakes, don't tell her your father's here," Delia warned. "She won't get within twenty miles of the place."

"I know that much," Abby said. Ignoring the phone on the wall, she practically ran from the room to use the phone Gracie had had installed in the foyer.

Delia chuckled. "I guess she figures we're better off not hearing what sneaky scheme she uses to lure her mother over here."

"Well, I for one am glad she left the room," Helen said. She turned to Gracie. "What on earth went on last night when Bobby Ray came by?"

"Don't tell her, Gracie," Bobby Ray said, coming down the back stairs into the kitchen. "She's been snooping in my affairs since the day I was born."

"Somebody had to keep an eye on you, for all the good it did," Helen muttered. "I'm your big sister and I want to know what happened last night. At this very moment, your daughter is trying to lure her mother over here. What's that all about?"

Bobby Ray looked sheepish. "I can't speak for Abby's motivation, but I'll have to admit I'm glad she's taking the initiative in this particular instance."

"Why?" Helen asked suspiciously.

"Because I'm not sure how long it would have taken me to work up the courage to go over there or what Marianne would have done when I showed up."

"Whapped you upside the head with a frying pan, if she had any sense," Delia commented.

"Thank you, Aunt Delia. You never did have much patience with my shenanigans, did you?"

"Not since you got old enough to know better," she agreed. "And that was many a year ago, young man."

"Thanks to Gracie, I'm a reformed man," he announced.

"We'll see," Delia retorted.

"Bobby Ray, stop gabbing with the women and get the hell back up here," Kevin shouted just then from the top of the stairs. "I'm doing more than my fair share."

"That's the way it's supposed to be," Bobby Ray shouted back. "You're the responsible one." He winked at Gracie, grabbed a couple of sodas out of the refrigerator and bounded back up the stairs.

Gracie chuckled, then realized that Helen and Delia were staring at her as if she were some sort of miracle worker.

"Okay," Helen said seriously. "I want to know exactly what went on last night."

"From the beginning," Delia chimed in.

Gracie thought of the beginning, in her bedroom, in her bed, and concluded that neither of them needed to know every detail about that. Nor about the way the evening had ended.

"Well, you see, Bobby Ray called . . ." she began, and told them the basics of the conversation she and Kevin had had with him the night before.

"Marianne won't take him back on a bet," Delia said when she was done. "Not if she has any sense."

"Oh, come on, Delia, she adores him. She always has," Helen said. "Despite everything he did to her, all of it lousy, she still loves him."

"I'm sorry," Delia said. "I'm afraid I'm with Kevin on this one. It's going to be a disaster and Abby's the one who'll pay the price."

Gracie was shaken by the older woman's fierce declaration. Had she been wrong to try to get Bobby Ray and his ex-wife back together? Had she jumped feet-first into something she knew far too little about?

"Stop looking so glum, Gracie. Delia's just worried about Abby," Helen said. "The kid's been to hell and back, thanks to her father's foolishness. That hasn't stopped her from loving him. I don't think it's stopped Marianne, either. And if the changes I've seen in my brother this morning are any indication, it could just work this time around."

"I hope you're right," Gracie said.

For all their sakes.

Twenty-one

Abby came bounding back into the kitchen, beaming.

"Mom said she'd be here in an hour, as soon as she's done with the laundry. I told her we needed her to stop and pick up lunch. She's gonna do ham and cheese and tuna sandwiches from the coffee shop. I called ahead and ordered lots and lots. Is that okay?" She regarded them worriedly. "I know we usually go out, but I couldn't think of anything else to get her over here."

"You could have tried the truth, young lady," Delia chided.

Abby looked shocked. "You mean told her Daddy was here?"

"That's correct."

"No way," Abby said, shaking her head emphatically. "She wouldn't have come. You said so yourself."

"And now I think I was wrong. Sue me. It should have been her choice."

"Come on, Aunt Delia," Helen protested. "Leave Abby alone. We need to eat. What difference does it make if Marianne brings us lunch?"

"That's right," Gracie said. "It'll give us more time to decide whether to sand and polish the floors upstairs or to carpet them."

"You don't carpet over fine oak floors," Delia protested, clearly horrified by the suggestion. "What on earth are you thinking?"

Helen grinned at Gracie. "Oh, I suspect I know exactly what she was thinking."

"Hush," Gracie warned. "It worked, didn't it?"

"What worked?" Delia demanded. "Would the two of you stop talking in riddles?"

Helen stood up and tucked a hand under Delia's elbow. "Come on.Let's go see what kind of shape those floors are in, okay?"

"Can I help Daddy and Uncle Kevin paint?" Abby pleaded. "I'll be careful. I'm bound to be neater than they are."

Gracie nodded. "If your father says it's okay."

"All right! He never says no."

"More's the pity," Delia grumbled.

Despite her complaints, though, Delia beat the rest of them up the stairs and led the survey of the wide-planked floors. "Nothing a little elbow grease and polish won't fix right up," she declared. "The last few years I was here, I couldn't keep up with them the way I should have. And since then, well, no house fares well when it's been untended. I suspect we can rent a buffer and fix these up in no time."

"Perhaps you're right," Gracie agreed, which she had all along. There was no way she would have put carpet over the wood, but Delia never had to know that. Fussing over the floors had gotten her mind off Abby's deception.

"Well, of course, I'm right," Delia huffed "I ought to know my own floors." She sighed, a nostalgic expression on her face. "Oh, my, how they used to gleam. There's nothing quite like the look and scent of good wood, when it's just been waxed."

Just then Kevin stuck his head out of the bedroom door at the end of the hall. "Gracie, could I see you in here a minute?"

"Sure," she said and went to meet him.

"Inside," he insisted.

When she stepped into the room, he closed the door behind her, then backed her against it in a movement so swift it caught her totally off guard. His mouth slanted across hers in a hungry kiss. Several breathless minutes later, he stepped away and smiled.

"Morning, darlin'. Seems like I've been waiting for hours to get the day started right."

Gracie's senses slowly stopped spinning. When she could finally gather her wits, she murmured, "Good morning to you, too. You must be having a good day." Apparently, he was also over his irritation with her.

"Good night, good day," he said. "They're all sort of rolling together lately."

She glanced around. "Where have you stashed Bobby Ray? I thought he was in here with you painting. You haven't locked him in the attic, have you?"

"No. I just sent him on to the next room, so you and I could have a little privacy."

"And Abby?"

"She's with him. Bonding, I hope."

"I don't think you need to worry any more about the two of them bonding, not if it's left up to Abby. She has plans. Big plans."

Kevin's expression turned worried. "Oh?"

"Marianne's on her way over."

His good mood soured at once. "Gracie! I thought we discussed that. I thought we'd decided to stay out of it, now that the idea's been planted in Bobby Ray's head."

"I don't recall agreeing to any such thing. Besides, I didn't have anything to do with it, I swear. It was Abby's idea."

"But obviously you didn't try to stop her."

"No," she said with a touch of defiance.

"I'm amazed Marianne agreed to come."

"Actually, she thinks she's coming to bring lunch. I don't think she's aware that Bobby Ray is here, unless she happened to wonder at the number of sandwiches she's picking up. Abby said she called ahead to the restaurant and ordered enough for an army."

Kevin sighed. "I see."

He didn't sound convinced. "Marianne can leave right away if that's what she wants to do," Gracie pointed out, trying to sway him.

"I suppose."

She stood on tiptoe and gave him another smoldering kiss. "Stop worrying."

"I can't. It's what I do."

"And you're very good at it. Everyone appreciates the fact that you care so deeply about them."

"You must not have been around all those times I was told to mind my own damn business."

"True. I missed that."

"Taking care of this crowd is not terribly rewarding."

"You're looking for the wrong sort of rewards then. Take Helen. Have you noticed the sparkle in her eyes?"

"No."

"Well, I have. I suspect we can thank Max for that."

"Is that supposed to thrill me?"

"It should if what you're really interested in is her happiness. And then there's Bobby Ray."

"What about him?"

"Just look how he's pitching in today. Last night was a turning point for him."

"If it was, it's because of you."

She waved off the comment. "It doesn't matter why. All that's important is that he's obviously trying to change. Then there's Delia. She has a whole new lease on life. I'm thinking of asking if she wants to come over for a few hours every afternoon and have tea with the guests, shower them with a little of her southern charm."

Kevin groaned. "Which means I'll have to drive her over. I'll never get in any good rest time in my hammock again."

Gracie winked at him. "Oh, I think I can come up with an incentive for you to do that, something a whole lot more interesting than lounging around in that old hammock of yours."

He looked fascinated. "Oh, really? I do love my hammock, you know."

"Believe me, I've noticed. Not to worry, though," she said. "Pretty soon there won't be anyone left for you to worry about anyway. You won't need to do all that mulling and pondering you do out there."

"Obviously you haven't heard about Bo and the others."

"Actually, I have. You'll get them straightened out one by one."

"You mean that you will. You're sneakier than I am. My guess is they won't even know what hit them."

She grinned at him. "Is that a bad thing?"

"Not necessarily," he said, gathering her close once again. "I certainly haven't figured out what hit me, but you don't hear me complaining."

"What do you think? Is it working?" Helen whispered.

"I can't see anything," Delia protested. "Stop hogging the window."

"Hey, they're my mom and dad. I should get to look," Abby grumbled from behind them. "Has he kissed her yet? I don't want to miss that."

Kevin stood back and watched the three of them jockeying for position at the attic window. It was the only one that had a decent view of the shady spot in the backyard where Bobby Ray and Marianne were engrossed in conversation.

"You all are pitiful," he declared, drawing three guilty looks. "Why can't you give them some privacy?"

"We are," Aunt Delia insisted. "That's why we're up here instead of down there with them."

"I thought you didn't approve of this any more than I do?" he said.

"I didn't." She shrugged. "Could be I was wrong. Marianne seemed surprisingly pleased to find Bobby Ray here. Maybe the others are right and there is hope for the two of them."

"I'm amazed Gracie isn't up here with you since this is her pet project," Kevin said.

Actually, Gracie was the reason he'd come up to the attic. He'd been relatively certain that she was the one scuffling around up here and he'd hoped to steal a few more minutes alone with her. Those kisses he'd managed before lunch hadn't been nearly enough to tide him over until dinnertime. That neediness inside him was getting worse by the day.

"Over there," Abby said, gesturing across the hall. "She's going to make that her office. She's in there measuring."

Actually, she was in there daydreaming as near as Kevin could tell. She was seated by one of the floor-to-ceiling windows, staring out to sea.

He stood in the doorway and observed her for several minutes, undetected. The room was oddly shaped and small, but filled with glass on all three sides. It had a clear view of the river in any direction, which made it seem bigger than it was. The branches of a huge oak tree were close enough to touch. Gracie looked as serene as he'd ever seen her. He wondered how she'd feel if she knew this particular room's history. It had been closed off for decades, though naturally he'd broken into it every chance he got as a child.

"Hiding out in your tree house?" he asked eventually.

She glanced up at him and smiled. "It does feel like that, doesn't it?"

"I hear you're going to turn this into your office. Won't the climb to the third floor be a nuisance?"

"It'll be worth it."

"It's awfully small."

"I won't need much more than a desk and a filing cabinet."

"I'll bet it's a far cry from what you had at Worldwide."

She regarded him with a quizzical expression. "Is there

some reason you're trying to discourage me from using this room?"

Kevin hesitated, uncertain whether to tell her the room's sad history. Naturally, she caught on to the implication of his hesitation.

"Kevin, did something happen in this room?"

He nodded slowly, then settled on the floor behind her, drawing her back against his chest and wrapping his arms around her.

"Tell me," she pleaded.

Kevin was reluctant to get into it and spoil the room for her, but now that her curiosity was aroused he doubted he could get out of it.

"According to family legend, Great-great Aunt Anne—that would be Delia's aunt—spent all her time locked away in here around the turn of the century," he began.

"Locked away?" Gracie asked, clearly horrified. "Who did that to her?"

"It wasn't like that. She chose to be here. She was watching for her husband to come home from the sea. Even after she was told his ship had been lost, she stayed here. She wouldn't eat or sleep. Nobody could get through to her. She just waited, wasting away until finally she died of a broken heart."

Tears spilled down Gracie's cheeks. "Oh, my, that is sad. How awful for her."

"They say her ghost still lives here and that sometimes at night you can hear her crying."

She turned to face him, eyes suddenly shining, the sad mood banished. "A ghost? I thought you said there wasn't one?"

"Because I don't believe it."

"I want to stay here tonight and see for myself."

He stared at her. "Gracie, I don't think she appears on command, if she appears at all. Never once, in all the times I was over here, did I hear a thing."

"You're a man, for one thing," she said dismissively, as if that were a logical explanation. "Oh, please. Stay here with me. We can have dinner right up here. There's plenty left over from lunch. I think there might even be a bottle of wine in the refrigerator. Helen brought it so we could have a toast when we're finally finished. Given how long the repairs are taking, I have plenty of time to replace it."

Kevin tried one more time to dissuade her. "Do you really want to sit around on a bare floor and wait for a ghost to turn up?"

"Yes. Just think what it'll do for business if I can claim a real, live ghost." She winced. "Well, not live, actually, but you know what I mean."

"Something tells me Great-great Aunt Anne wouldn't be thrilled with all the attention. She shooed away everyone who tried to come up here while she was alive."

Gracie's chin jutted up. "Well, she's just going to have to get used to me."

"Like all the rest of us, I suppose," he murmured. "I'll go kick everyone else out and bring up dinner."

She reached over and rested a hand against his cheek. "Thanks, Kevin."

Given his reluctance to deny her anything, it was probably a very good thing that this was all she'd asked for. Besides, an evening alone with Gracie in a room with an incredible view definitely wouldn't be all bad.

He walked back across the hall, where Helen, Delia, and Abby were still spying on Bobby Ray. "Okay, everybody out," he ordered.

"Not yet," Helen insisted, waving him off. "I think he's about to kiss her."

Abby elbowed her aunt aside. "Let me see."

Kevin snatched his niece up and tossed her over his shoulder. "That's enough." He glowered at the two women. "You, too. Let's go."

"What makes you think you get to boss us around?" Delia demanded.

"History," Kevin retorted. "Now, move it. I'm in a hurry."

"Why?" Helen asked, studying him curiously. "Does this have something to do with that little tête-à-tête you just had with Gracie?"

"You bet."

Delia's eyes brightened. "Oh, well, then, in that case we'll leave right away. Never let it be said that I stood in the way of romance. Helen, can you give me a ride home?"

"Certainly."

"Abby, you can come with us," Delia said. "Spend the night, too."

"Can I really?"

"Much to my surprise, something tells me your mother and father won't mind a bit," Delia said with a touch of irony. "I doubt they'll even notice we're gone."

"They're going, too," Kevin said determinedly.

Ten minutes later, he'd completed the first stage of evacuating the premises. He stuck his head out the back door. "Bobby Ray, I'm locking up. Is there anything you need from inside?"

"Nothing," Bobby Ray said, barely sparing him a glance.

Marianne regarded Kevin with a bemused expression. "What about Abby?"

"She's gone home with Delia. She's going to spend the night, if you don't mind."

Still looking dazed, Marianne shook her head. "No, that's fine."

"Can we go to dinner then?" Bobby Ray asked her, brushing back a stray curl and tucking it gently behind her ear.

To his amazement, Kevin saw her nod, then he closed the door and locked it. Bobby Ray could handle his own romance, Kevin had plans of his own. Still, it astonished him that Gracie's instincts about those two had apparently been right. The woman had good instincts. Amazing instincts, in fact. She'd managed to set up a cozy, intimate dinner for the two of them without him even realizing what she was up to, hadn't she?

He snagged the leftover sandwiches from the refrigerator along with the bottle of wine and a couple of glasses. At the last minute he tucked the portable radio under his arm, then climbed the stairs to the third floor.

He found Gracie exactly where he'd left her. She'd opened the front window and a soft, salt-air breeze was stirring, scented with roses. There was a nostalgic expression on her face he found troubling.

Lowering himself to sit beside her, he put the food and wine aside. "Everything okay?"

"Sure."

He debated with himself, then finally broached the subject that had been nagging at him lately. "You're not getting homesick for Cannes, are you?"

She seemed surprised by the question. "Cannes wasn't my home. It was where I worked."

"You lived there, didn't you?" he pointed out dryly.

"That's not the same as it being home." She looked up at him, her expression filled with sadness. "That's what I realized when I decided to leave. I didn't have a home to go to."

"So you ended up here?"

"Funny, isn't it? I'd only been here once before in my life for less than a week and yet I was drawn back. I wonder why that was?"

"Instinct?" he suggested. "Maybe even all those years ago it felt like what home should feel like."

"Maybe."

"Or fate," he suggested.

Her gaze flew to his, lingered, while the atmosphere around them seemed charged with electricity. "Could be," she agreed quietly.

"Does it feel like home now?" he asked, his heart in his

throat as he waited for her answer. Despite the evidence of her enthusiasm for this restoration, what if it was no more than a passing fancy. What if she'd concluded that this was all wrong for her, after all? What if she decided that she needed to travel the globe to be happy? Was there anything he could say that would make her stay? Or would he have to let her go?

Instead of answering him, she slipped into his lap and rested her head on his shoulder. "Now it does," she told him. "Now it feels like home."

Kevin agreed. This house, far more than Greystone, had always felt like home. Once he had attributed that to Aunt Delia's warmth, but he felt it now, too. Perhaps it was the house itself that drew him with its history and family secrets. There were some, he knew. Secrets that people once spoke of in whispers. It was the hidden truths—not Great-great Aunt Anne—that haunted the place.

And yet something told him if he ever discovered what those secrets were, he wouldn't find them half as troubling as the silence.

Twenty-two

"They were over there dancing until two in the morning," Bessie Johnson told Delia. "You should have seen them. First they had something fast on the radio and they were laughing like a couple of fools. I'm telling you, Delia, Fred Astaire never did moves like those two did. Then the music turned all soft and dreamy. It was all I could do not to cry, they looked so much in love."

"Good," Delia said with satisfaction. "Things are coming along nicely. Are they still over there?"

"Kevin's car is still out in front of the house, so I imagine they are."

Delia chuckled. "Perfect. Not that I much approve of such shenanigans outside of marriage," she said, perfectly aware of the irony, "but something has to jump start those two if we're going to manage a fall wedding."

"Maybe you'll just have to settle for a Christmas wedding," her longtime neighbor suggested. "You can't have everything your own way."

"I don't see why not. Somebody's got to take charge. Who better than the boy's own grandmother?"

"Delia! I thought you'd vowed never to tell him," her friend protested. "You kept it from his mother that she was your very own daughter. Why go blabbing old secrets now?"

"Because it's time," Delia said. "There were so many times when I wanted to tell Mary Louise the truth. I could see she was so unhappy at home, that her mother deliberately made her life miserable, but I kept silent, like I'd promised. Now I want Kevin to know before I die. I don't want that secret to die with me."

"You always said it should, that if you didn't have the gumption to acknowledge your child, then you'd have to live with the consequences."

"Well, I changed my mind. Sue me."

"Oh, Delia, think this through," Bessie pleaded. "Are you sure you're not just being selfish?"

"I've had more than fifty years to think it through. I should never have allowed my child to be raised as theirs by my sister and her husband. Back then, though, it would have been such a scandal and I didn't want Mary Louise to bear the burden of my shame. Kevin will understand that. He will see it for the sacrifice it was. I know he will."

"You hope he will," Bessie corrected fiercely. "What if he resents all the years you cost him of having a grandmother?"

"He had a grandmother," Delia argued.

"One who paid as little attention to him as possible and treated his mama like dirt," Bessie said with disgust. "You were the one he ran to, especially after his mama died. At least you've had Kevin in your life all these years. His mother wasn't adopted by strangers and taken away from you. Isn't that bond enough?"

"Not anymore."

"He could hate you, you know. He knew how miserable his mother was. What if he blames you for not stepping in and making things right?"

Delia sighed. "That's just a chance I'm going to have to take."

His aunt was as nervous as a Junebug. She had been for most of the past week, Kevin noted. Every time he came

into a room, she scurried out. Or, if they were at the renovation site, she made sure that someone else was in the room
with them. Something was up with her, but for the life of
him he couldn't figure out what.

More than once she opened her mouth as if she was about
to say something, then clamped it shut again. He might not
have Gracie's intuition, but even he could tell that Aunt Delia
was torn over telling—or not telling—him something. Was
she desperately ill? Sorry that she'd gotten into this bed-and-
breakfast business? What?

He finally caught her by herself in the kitchen at home.
She jumped when he walked in, and her gaze darted around
nervously as if she were looking for a quick escape route or
else Molly's protection. Fortunately for him, Molly had already left for the market. There was no one around to save
his aunt or interrupt them.

"Everything okay?" he inquired lightly.

"Of course. Why wouldn't it be okay?" she asked, already
edging toward the door.

"You tell me. And don't try sneaking out of here."

She paused where she was. Her hands fluttered nervously
before she finally seized the back of a chair to steady them.
She fixed him with a steady gaze, bold as you please, but
the grip she had on the chair gave her away.

"I can't imagine what you mean," she said, though her
voice hitched when she said it.

Kevin resigned himself to guesswork. "You aren't having
second thoughts about what's going on over at your house,
are you? It's not too late to back out. Gracie would be disappointed, especially after all the work that's gone into it,
but she'd adjust. We'd find another house for her. Maybe you
and I could spend a few days every week in town so you
could get together with your old friends. I know uprooting
yourself after so many years to move out here with me hasn't
been easy."

"No," she said adamantly. "I want Gracie to have that house."

"Okay, if it's not the house, what is it? You aren't sick, are you?"

"No, of course not."

"You'd tell me if you were?"

"Yes, darling, I'd tell you."

"Then what's going on? I can see you're upset. Don't even bother denying it."

She sighed and a tear trailed down her cheek. "Oh, Kevin."

Horrified by the sight of his indomitable aunt in tears, he whispered, "Aunt Delia?"

She brushed at the tear with a hankie, then sat down heavily. "I suppose now's as good a time as any."

"Time for what?"

"Sit down," she said. "I can't talk with you hovering over me."

Kevin pulled out a chair and straddled it, facing her. "Okay, I'm sitting. Now what on earth is so terrible that you're scared to tell me? Haven't we weathered a lot of storms together?"

"Of course we have. It's just that there's never been anything quite like this."

"Like what?"

"Hush," she said. "I'm getting to it. Give me time."

Kevin had the feeling if he gave her all the time she wanted, they'd still be sitting here at Christmas. "Come on, Aunt Delia," he coaxed. "It can't be as bad as all that. Did you wreck the car?"

She frowned at him. "You know perfectly well I haven't been behind the wheel of a car in over a year. We made an agreement. Besides, you hide the keys."

"Which you'd only know if you'd looked for them," he pointed out, fighting a grin. Another tear slid down her cheek sobering him once more. He was still worried about her health. "You're not ill, are you?" he asked one more time.

"Heavens no," she insisted, brushing at the tears. "I'm fit as a fiddle."

"Then tell me. Don't make me pry it out of you."

"As if you could," she said with a haughty sniff. "Not unless I was willing."

He grinned. "Okay, okay. We're agreed you're one tough cookie."

"Not so tough," she corrected with a sad look. "If I had been, maybe things would have been different."

"What things?"

"You and me. Our relationship."

He was totally lost. "What's wrong with our relationship? I thought you and I always got along great."

"We did. We do." And with that she began to cry in earnest. Her hands covered her face and sobs shook her shoulders.

Kevin was out of his chair in a heartbeat, hunkering down in front of her and folding her hands into his. "Aunt Delia, don't cry," he pleaded, his heart aching for her misery. "Please, just tell me what's wrong."

"I should have told you years ago. I just pray when I tell you now that you'll be able to forgive me."

She was talking in circles and he was losing patience, but she was so obviously shattered by whatever she was trying to say, he couldn't shout at her to get on with it. For once he held his impatience in check.

He grabbed a handful of tissues from the box on the kitchen counter and handed them to her. "It's okay. Take your time."

"I've taken too many years as it is," she said, as she blotted up her tears. "It all started years ago, before your mother was born."

Kevin felt his heart slow. So, he thought with a sense of dread, the secrets were finally coming to light, for better or worse. He sat quietly, waiting.

Her eyes took on a faraway gleam, still glistening with

tears. "I met someone, a nice man, or so I thought. From a good family. They were here for the summer. He was going back to finish college that fall and, then, well, I thought we'd be getting married."

"He seduced you," Kevin guessed.

"Not the way you mean," she said fiercely. "Believe me, I was all too eager to be with him. I was in love. I had never been happier."

She closed her eyes, but before she did, Kevin could see the anguish of old hurts.

"After he'd gone, I found out I was pregnant," she confessed, her voice so low he had to strain to hear it.

"You had a child?" Kevin asked, shocked.

"I had a child," she confirmed. "A beautiful baby girl. As I'm sure you've guessed by now, the father didn't want her or me. I never heard from him again after I told him about her. He simply vanished, dropped out of that fancy Ivy League school and went off to who-knows-where so I couldn't pester him, I suppose."

Kevin couldn't begin to imagine what that had done to her, the dent it had put in that staunch pride of hers. Since she had never married, he could only assume the bastard had been the love of her life. He had ruined her, then left without a backward glance.

"What happened to the baby? Did you give her up for adoption?"

"Yes." Fresh tears were tracking down her cheeks.

"I'm so sorry. You must have been devastated. Did you ever see her again? Or find out what happened to her?"

"I saw her often," she admitted. "I didn't have to go far."

Kevin's heart began to thud. "Who?"

"The baby was your mother."

Kevin rocked back on his heels and concentrated very hard to make the room stop spinning. "My mother?" he repeated.

"That's right."

"That means you're my . . ." He couldn't even bring himself to say the word. He thought of the bitter old woman he'd always thought of his grandmother, the woman who'd made life hell for his mother, always resenting her for reasons he'd never understood. Now he knew. She had blamed his mother for her own failure to give birth to a child. His sweet, fragile mother had been a constant reminder of her inability to conceive.

He stared at Delia, thinking of all the times he'd run to her, counted on her, wished so very hard that she were the one, that she were his grandmother. And now, to discover that she had been all along . . .

"Kevin, say something. Please."

"I don't know what to say." On the one hand, he loved Delia with all his heart, always had. On the other, to discover that she had robbed him and his mother of knowing exactly how she fit into their lives was too painful to cope with. He thought of the times he'd seen his mother's anguished tears when his supposed grandmother had chastised her yet again for some imagined sin. Delia had stood by and watched that happen.

"Why didn't you tell her?" he demanded roughly.

"I couldn't. That was the deal I made with my sister, that she would be Mary Louise's mother, that the truth would never be spoken. I went away to have the baby and she went with me. She came back with my daughter and I stayed on in Maine for another six months so no one here would be suspicious. I thought it was for the best, Kevin. I didn't want my girl to live with the shame of me being an unwed mother."

"So instead you left her with a woman who resented her from the day she took her in."

"Not always," Delia protested. "When Mary Louise was a baby, Hettie loved her. She did. It was only later, when Mary Louise instinctively seemed to form a bond with me, that the resentment started. I never broke faith with my sister, but there was no mistaking the bond that Mary Louise and I shared. You felt it, too. I know you did."

Kevin couldn't deny it. Nor could he deny that Delia had always been there for his mother, a safe haven, just as she had been for him. He sighed heavily.

"I have to think about this."

"You don't hate me, though. Please, Kevin, tell me you don't hate me."

He bent down and pressed a kiss to her cheek. "I could never hate you," he said fiercely. "Never."

She patted his hand. "Then we'll be okay."

He started to leave, then paused in the doorway. "Why now? Why tell me now?"

"Because of you and Gracie. Bessie says I'm being selfish after all these years, but I wanted to share in your happiness. I wanted everything out in the open so you'd know who you are. It's not just Daniels blood that runs in you. It's mine, too."

"So my genes aren't all bad, is that it?" he said, unable to prevent a smile.

"Something like that," she said with a brief flash of a smile. "I thought maybe you'd look at me and see just what kind of strength and staying power you truly have."

"I've known that all along," he told her. "Because you've always been there to make me believe it. It never had anything to do with blood."

She shrugged that off. "My mistake. Sue me."

"How could I?" he asked wryly. "How could I possibly sue my own grandmother?"

Kevin had vanished, simply disappeared. Gracie had watched for him each day, had expected him to drop off Delia at the very least, but there'd been no sign of him. Helen brought Delia with her every morning and took her home every evening.

As for Delia, she was looking more distraught with each day that passed. She evaded all of Gracie's questions with pat, tight-lipped answers that revealed nothing. She had just done it again, then left the house to go next door to visit Mrs. Johnson, leaving Gracie staring after her. She turned to Helen.

"Do you know what's going on?"

"I have no idea."

"Have you seen Kevin?"

"Not a sign of him."

"Have you asked?"

"Well, of course I have," Helen snapped impatiently. "Don't you think I'm as worried about this as you are."

"I'm sorry. I didn't mean to imply you weren't," Gracie apologized. "I just don't get it, though. One minute everything was fine, the next Kevin's gone and Delia's walking around looking miserable. Has there been some crisis with one of the cousins?"

"None that I know of," Helen said. "For once, no one's pestering Kevin. Bobby Ray's too busy trying to convince Marianne to give him another chance. It's summertime and Uncle Bo's out on his fishing boat every day. That pretty much keeps him out of trouble until fall. As far as I know, all of his boys are out of jail and gainfully employed for once."

"Could Kevin have gone to Richmond on business? Is there a court case involving some estate he's handling?"

Helen shrugged. "Your guess is as good as mine." She eyed Gracie knowingly. "You seem awfully worked up over his absence. Does this mean what I think it means?"

"It means I'm worried about him. Don't go trying to make anything out of that."

"You're in love with him, aren't you?"

"Don't be ridiculous. I'm no more in love with Kevin than you are with Max," she said, and watched the color bloom in Helen's cheeks. "Ah, I see I struck a nerve. Could it be that I'm wrong about you and Max?"

"Don't you dare try to change the subject by turning the

tables on me. We are not discussing my relationship with Max Devereaux."

"We are now," Gracie said. "After all, I introduced the two of you. I think I have a right to know what's going on."

"And I'm Kevin's cousin. I think I have a right to know how you really feel about him."

Gracie sighed. "Either we both talk or we both remain in the dark. Is that the way it's going to be?"

"I suppose so," Helen said with a touch of defiance. "Besides, I already know how you feel. It's plain as day."

"No plainer than your feelings for Max," Gracie countered. "I couldn't be happier about that."

Helen grinned. "And I couldn't be happier about you and Kevin."

"Things are not serious between Kevin and me," Gracie repeated, knowing as she spoke that the denial was futile. Helen's opinion wasn't going to be swayed. For that matter, neither was her own regarding Helen and Max.

From what she'd gathered the two of them had raised the use of e-mail, faxes, and international calling rates to new heights. She'd tried to get through to Max herself on several occasions lately, only to be told by the hotel staff that Monsieur Devereaux was not to be disturbed, that he was on an important call to the States.

"We assumed he was talking to you," André had revealed only the day before. "It is not?"

"No, it is definitely not me," Gracie had told him. "How is everything there?"

"Running smoothly enough," Andre conceded.

"No trouble in the kitchen?"

"Not recently."

"Or with the vendors?"

"None."

"The asparagus is being delivered on schedule?"

"Every day."

Even though she'd been relieved by the news, she hadn't

been able to help feeling a little tug of dismay. Max no longer needed her, not for the hotel, not in his personal life. The tie appeared to be severed . . . just as she'd wanted.

Maybe that was why she'd been so anxious to see Kevin the past few days. Even with all the renovation work, she was feeling emotionally adrift. When she was with him, she felt grounded, centered.

Of course, the very last thing Kevin needed in his life was somebody else leaning on him. She would never in a million years want to add to the burden he already carried.

"Gracie, is everything okay with you?" Helen asked.

"Fine," she said, forcing a smile. "Everything is fine."

"Are you sure?"

"Positive. Now let's get busy on these floors while Delia's not around to criticize everything we do."

"Maybe we should take the day off, do something outrageous."

Gracie paused and stared. "Outrageous? Such as?"

"I don't know. Go shopping."

"I suppose I could look at fabric for curtains."

"No, no, I meant for clothes, lingerie, perfume, whatever."

"Clothes are the last thing on my mind these days."

"But a shopping spree can be every bit as good for stress as a session with a shrink. I ought to know. I've tried both."

"Chocolate works better for me," Gracie said.

"Then we can wind up the shopping spree with hot fudge sundaes." She grinned at Gracie. "You're tempted, aren't you?"

"A little," Gracie admitted.

"Come on, then. Let's do it. We'll work ten times as hard when we get back."

"Okay. Shall we take Delia along? She may need cheering up more than either one of us."

"Why not? The more the merrier."

"Where are we going?"

"Leave all that to me. Give me an hour to make the arrangements. I'll pick you up at your place. Bring an overnight bag."

"Helen, I can barely shop for an hour without getting bored silly. I don't need two days."

"You will for this shopping spree. Stop arguing and go home and pack."

"You're a very bossy woman. Does Max know that?"

"Of course he does. He finds it stimulating trying to thwart me when I take charge."

"And that's a good thing?" Gracie inquired doubtfully.

"Trust me, that is a very good thing. We will never grow bored. Now, get moving. I have plans to make."

Gracie paused at the back door. "I'm not going to regret this, am I?"

"Not if I can help it," Helen vowed. "You're going to remember this for years to come."

Twenty-three

Kevin had spent close to a week holed up in his apartment in Richmond, trying to accept what Delia had told him. In the end, he'd concluded that he'd made more of the deception than he should have. The lie had cost his mother far more than it had cost him.

The truth was, in everything but name, Delia had been a grandmother to him all these years. She'd been his most stalwart champion and, in many ways, his best friend. He doubted he could have loved her any more if he'd learned the facts years ago.

Unfortunately, by the time he got back to Seagull Point to explain all of that to her and put her mind at ease, she was gone, and Helen and Gracie were missing as well. He'd checked his house, where Molly, too, had been given a few days off and had run off to spend them with her family in Washington. He'd checked in town, only to find that Gracie's house was locked up tight and all work on the Victorian had been halted.

A knot of dread formed in the pit of his stomach at the sight of the house sitting empty and silent and no more than half complete. With only a month to go before the scheduled opening, it should have been a beehive of activity.

What the devil was going on? Where had everyone gone and when? He was sitting on the front steps of the Victorian pondering the possibilities when Abby exited Bobby Ray's car in front of him.

"Hi, Uncle Kevin. How come you're here?"

"I thought I'd stop by and help, but no one's around to tell me what to do." He glanced up to see Bobby Ray regarding him with smug amusement. "Okay, what do you know that I don't? Where's Gracie?"

"Gone," Abby said.

Kevin felt as if he'd been sucker-punched right in the gut. All the air seemed to whoosh right out of him. "Gone? Gone where?" He barely managed to get the panicked words out around the tightness in his throat.

"France," Abby said as if it were no more than a trip to the supermarket.

"Gracie went to France?" he repeated. Back to Max? Back to Worldwide?

"Sorry, pal," Bobby Ray said with more satisfaction than sympathy as he lowered himself to the step beside Kevin. "Guess you weren't paying enough attention to her."

"That's absurd. I was only gone a few days."

His cousin chuckled at his immediate defensiveness. "You're pitiful, you know that don't you?"

"Oh, go to blazes," Kevin muttered, aware that he'd given away way too much about his emotional state.

"That's a switch, you telling me where to go."

"Daddy, stop teasing him," Abby protested. "Can't you see he's miserable?"

"Of course I can," Bobby Ray said. "I thought I'd let him wallow in his misery for a few minutes."

"But he thinks Gracie's run off to be with Max."

Bobby Ray's eyes gleamed. "I know," he said happily.

"Daddy!"

"Okay, okay," his cousin said. "It's not what you're thinking."

"Then what the hell is it?"

"It's true that Gracie has gone to France, but Helen and Delia are with her," Bobby Ray explained. "So's Marianne."

Kevin stared at him. "They've all gone? What the hell went on around here while I was out of town?"

"As near as I can tell—and don't forget I'm a mere man, so the workings of the female mind often elude me—Delia was moping around for some reason and Gracie was stressing out about her and about your absence, so the next thing I knew Helen had gotten the notion to take them all shopping."

"In France?" Kevin repeated, dazed.

"Paris, to be precise. As far as I know, they'll be back tomorrow, unless, of course, there's some sale they can't resist in Rome or Milan or London. You know Helen once she gets her credit card in gear."

"You're sure about Paris being the destination, though. They weren't taking a side trip to Cannes, were they?"

Bobby Ray chuckled again. "No need. Max was meeting them in them in Paris to show them around."

Kevin groaned. "I don't believe this."

"Obviously, this is not a group of women you can turn your back on," his cousin suggested.

"How the devil did Marianne get involved?"

"Helen called to fill her in on where they'd be," he explained, then stopped.

"Tell him the rest, Daddy," Abby insisted. "Tell him about you and Mom."

To Kevin's astonishment, a sheepish grin spread across Bobby Ray's face. "Marianne and I, we're thinking about getting married again. We're looking at Labor Day weekend. The minute they found out about that, Helen invited her along to buy some fancy stuff for the honeymoon."

Things were moving way too fast for the comfort of a man who liked to keep his life slow-paced and relaxed. Uncomplicated. Kevin regarded Bobby Ray intently. "May I point out that you're still married to Sara Lynn, or is that just considered a minor inconvenience?"

"She's agreed to a quickie divorce," Bobby Ray explained. "Of course, it will cost me, but so what? It's only money."

"Which you don't have." Kevin reminded him.

"Well, actually, I was counting on you to come through for me again. I figured you might want me back with Marianne and Abby enough to bail me out."

Kevin studied his cousin closely. Bobby Ray looked vaguely uneasy, but he supposed that could be attributed to his fear that Kevin would refuse to give him the money for Sara Lynn. When it came to marrying Marianne again, he seemed totally confident. Just to be sure, though, he asked, "This is what you really want? You're not just playing some sort of emotional game because you can't bear to be alone and uninvolved for more than a second? You're certain? Forever and ever, amen?"

"Till death do us part," Bobby Ray assured him. "I never should have let Marianne get away in the first place. My pride got in the way."

"He's learned his lesson, Uncle Kevin. I swear it," Abby told him solemnly. "Please give Sara Lynn whatever she wants, okay? Maybe she'll move far, far away, like Alaska."

Alaska would almost certainly chill Sara Lynn's overly active libido, Kevin thought, but kept that particular opinion to himself.

"And once all of this business with Sara Lynn is straightened out, you'll never have to worry about me bugging you for money again," Bobby Ray promised.

Kevin regarded him skeptically. "Oh?"

"I've gotten a job with Ray Mason."

"The contractor?" Kevin asked, astounded. "Doing what, for heaven's sakes? Have you realized that you'll actually sweat, if you do this, that you won't be wearing those fancy suits you love to work?"

"Yes, I've realized all that," Bobby Ray responded.

"Then what on earth brought this on?"

"Working on this place with you guys, I realized how much I enjoy working with my hands, building things, painting. Maybe it has something to do with me getting a second chance, but I kind of like seeing a house get a new lease on life, too. Best of all, I'm pretty good at it."

"You know he is, Uncle Kevin," Abby said. "He never messed up the painting the way you did."

Bobby Ray grinned at the loyal backing of his daughter. "Thanks, kiddo. Anyway, Ray says he'll train me and, if I do okay, I can start taking on renovation projects of my own once I'm licensed."

"Well, I'll be," Kevin mumbled.

"Isn't it great, Uncle Kevin?" Abby said, slipping her hand into her father's and gazing at him with adoration rather than the justifiable cynicism she'd displayed far too often.

Kevin leveled a look straight into Bobby Ray's eyes and saw no signs of deception or wavering enthusiasm. He seemed to be throwing himself wholeheartedly into this new plan for his life. For once, the concept of hard work didn't seem to faze him. He wasn't looking for a quick buck or an easy way out. It was the first time in years that Bobby Ray seemed to have found a purpose.

"You've got it all figured out, haven't you?" he asked at last.

"Took me long enough, don't you think?"

"The point is, it didn't take you too long. Marianne and Abby were still waiting."

"We would have waited a hundred million years," Abby insisted.

Bobby Ray dragged her into his arms and began tickling her. "You can't even count that high, kid."

"Well, I could have, if we'd had to wait that long," she said with her unerring logic. She peered at Kevin. "Are you going to wait that long before you marry Gracie?"

Kevin reached over and ruffled her hair. "You meddle in your father's life," he instructed her. "Stay out of mine."

"But—"

"No buts, short stuff."

"You know you like her," Abby argued, undaunted by Kevin's scowl. "You looked awful when you thought she'd gone back to France to be with Max."

"Of course, I like her, but—"

"Then marry her, Uncle Kevin."

Bobby Ray chimed in with his two cents. "Yeah, Kev, for once in your life, stop worrying about the rest of us and do something that's right for you."

Kevin regarded his cousin with a touch of irony. "Do you honestly think you're the one to be giving me advice when it comes to romance?"

"Why not?" Bobby Ray retorted. "I've made more mistakes than you'll ever think about making, but I've finally got it right. Listen to the voice of experience. When the good one comes along, grab on and hang on tight."

Kevin considered Bobby Ray's advice as he lounged in his hammock that afternoon. For once, though, peace seemed to be eluding him. He was restless and uneasy. For all of Bobby Ray's reassurances that the women—all of them—would be coming home tomorrow, he knew for a fact that Gracie could be unpredictable.

What if Max finally came up with a convincing argument to lure her back to Worldwide? What if he threw buckets of money at her, as she'd once worried he would? What if she just realized that she missed France and couldn't bear to leave the country again? What if Seagull Point's quaint charm just didn't hold up against the lights of Paris?

Well, he supposed he'd just have to brush up on his French and find someplace over there to live. He wasn't letting her slip away. That much was certain.

As for marrying her, though, that was a whole other kettle of fish. Gracie was as independent as anyone he'd ever met. She hadn't relied on him for a single thing since he'd known her, hadn't asked for much, either. He didn't know what to make of a relationship that wasn't based on neediness of one kind or another.

If he'd known precisely where Gracie was, he would have gone traipsing after her to get a few answers. But based on Bobby Ray's information, it was more than likely that the whole bunch of them was getting ready to fly home. In fact, they might be in the air at this very minute.

Irritated that he couldn't get Gracie off his mind and relax, he finally muttered a curse and abandoned the hammock. He got in his car and headed back to town, straight for the Victorian. If he wasn't going to get any peace anyway, he might as well be doing something productive. When he'd been in that tower room with Gracie the other night, he'd gotten a few ideas. Well, more than a few actually, but some of them he'd acted on at the time, he recalled with a smile.

He climbed the stairs to that cramped little room where they'd waited for the ghost of Great-great-Aunt Anne to make her presence known. Once up there, he surveyed it again. It seemed to him it might be possible to knock out the narrow wall between that room and the one next door to create an office and sitting-room arrangement. The wall at that point wasn't much broader than a wide doorway, but it would do. He knew enough to be sure it wasn't a bearing wall before he took a sledgehammer to the old plaster.

Amazing, he thought as dust flew and settled all over his bare shoulders and filled his nose until he had a minute-long sneezing fit. Physical labor, which he'd always avoided like the plague, did provide a certain amount of distraction. Maybe it would keep Bobby Ray on the straight and narrow.

As he worked, Kevin thanked heaven for the summer he'd worked for Ray Mason during college. He had a basic knowledge of the rudiments. With any luck, he wouldn't send the whole house crashing to the ground.

He was barely aware of the passage of time as he cut the doorway into the next room, framed it and installed wallboard from the supply the contractor had left downstairs.

The second room was larger, better for an office, he concluded, envisioning where Gracie could put her desk and still have a view of the river and room enough for file cabinets. She was going to love it.

As for the tower room itself, he imagined a couple of comfortable chairs in front of the tall windows, with a table in between for a pitcher of lemonade and some sandwiches. He also envisioned a narrow daybed along the back wall, something Gracie could use to catch a few winks when she was tired.

Something they could share for a few stolen moments of steamy sex, if he had his way. The floor was damned uncomfortable, and it wouldn't get any less so as the years passed by and their bones grew creaky.

He sat down against the wall and sipped at the cold beer he'd brought up with him and let his imagination run wild. His flesh heated with the combination of memories and vivid expectations. More years of expectations than he'd ever considered with any other woman.

He wasn't sure at first whether Gracie was real, when he heard the rustling beside him and the low, sweet murmur of his name. It was the perfume that convinced him, something fancy and sexy. French, no doubt. Meant to drive a man crazy.

"So," he said without opening his eyes. "You're back."

He felt the swish of something silky settling down next to him, then another teasing hint of that perfume.

"I'm back," she agreed. "I'm surprised to find you here in the middle of the night."

"What time is it?"

"After two A.M. The plane got in at midnight. I spotted

the light on up here when I was driving home and stopped to check on the place. I see you've been busy while we were gone."

"I had an idea."

"Apparently."

"I figured if you were determined to hang out up here in the attic, you needed more room to move around." He opened one eye then and glanced at her. She looked sleepy, but there was no mistaking the fact that she'd been buffed and polished and fancied up by experts. She even had a sassy new haircut that emphasized her eyes. It made her seem more mysterious, more out of reach than ever.

"Gracie?"

"Yes?"

"I'm curious about something."

"What?"

"Why don't you ever ask me for anything?"

"I don't need anything."

He sighed heavily. "That's what I figured."

"Kevin?"

"Yes?"

"Need isn't what makes a relationship work."

He forced a half-smile. "Couldn't prove that by me."

"Just wait," she said with a confidence he didn't fully understand. "You'll see."

"You gonna stick around that long?"

She seemed surprised by the question. "Of course. Where else would I go?"

He voiced his worry, tried to keep his tone casual. "I thought maybe you'd be having second thoughts about Cannes about now, since you've had a taste of France again."

"Heavens, no," she said emphatically, reassuring him. "The trip was fun. I've never shopped so much or so fast and furiously in my life. Helen is astonishing. The rest of us just hung on for the ride."

"Did you get Marianne outfitted for the wedding?"

"Oh, my, yes. You should see all the sexy lingerie." She grinned. "Not Marianne's, of course. That's for Bobby Ray's eyes only. But I got a few things, too. Interested?"

His spirits perked up ever so slightly. "Now? Here?"

"Not in the middle of this dust and debris. No way. You'll have to rouse yourself enough to walk over to my place."

He glanced sideways at her. "But you're going to make it worth my while."

"I'll do my best," she assured him.

"Couldn't ask for anything more," he said. He stood up and held a hand out to her, drawing her to her feet and straight into his arms. "I missed you, Gracie."

"I missed you. Maybe one of these days you'll tell me where you disappeared to."

"Not far. Just to Richmond."

"On business?"

He touched a finger to her lips. "Enough. We'll talk about all of that another time. Right now I have a very important fashion show to attend."

As it turned out, it was the very first time in his adult life that he'd enjoyed watching a woman slip into clothes as much as he'd thrilled to watching her strip out of them.

And when she'd shown him everything and his body was aching with wanting her, he swept off the last little lacy number and replaced the scraps of silk with his hands and tongue, until Gracie was every bit as hot and bothered as he was.

Only later, after she'd fallen asleep with her head resting against his shoulder and her arm flung across his chest, did he finally find the peace that had been eluding him all day long.

Twenty-four

The lightning-quick restoration of the Daniels house and the equally fast reconciliation of Bobby Ray and Marianne were the talk of Seagull Point, topped only by the gossip about the unorthodox romance going on between laid-back Kevin Patrick Daniels and that uptight Yankee, Gracie Mac-Dougal.

Who ever heard of kissing up on a rooftop for all the world to see? Henrietta Jenkins had seen it with her own eyes during her morning walk.

"Have you ever in all your life heard of such goings-on?" Henrietta demanded with a sniff.

"Well, that's nothing. I heard Delia walked in on them going at it in the attic," Laura Lee Taylor said while she sipped coffee after her regular morning walk along the riverfront with the girls, not one of whom was a day under seventy.

"Did not," Henrietta said. "Delia couldn't make it up all those stairs, for one thing."

"Well, she did," Laura Lee countered, clearly miffed at the skepticism.

"Is it true that Delia's changed her will to leave the house to Gracie?" Florence Major wanted to know.

"Not with Kevin as her lawyer she hasn't," Henrietta declared. "That boy wouldn't allow it. He's been watching out for Delia all these years. I doubt he's going to change now.

He's not going to let some stranger sashay into town and take her for everything she's got."

"Maybe he would," Laura Lee said thoughtfully. "Long as he gets Gracie for himself in the bargain."

Kevin heard all of this—an astonishing mix of fact and speculation—as he hesitated in the doorway of the Beachside coffee shop. He hadn't heard so much speculating about his love life since he broke his very brief engagement to Linda Sue Grainger in the middle of the boardwalk at high noon. Linda Sue hadn't taken kindly to the humiliation. She had stuffed a just-out-of-the-grease corn dog in his face. He still had a scar from the burn it had left on his cheek. He'd been twelve at the time and hadn't yet realized that even women that age didn't like being scorned.

"Mornin', ladies," he said, bringing an abrupt halt to the conversation. If he'd expected a one of them to look the least bit guilty, he'd have been disappointed. They seemed delighted by his timely arrival.

"You going to marry that girl?" Henrietta inquired. She always had been direct and she definitely believed in going straight to the source whenever possible.

"Hadn't thought about it," Kevin said, though he'd thought about little else since Gracie's return from France the night before. Besides, he figured if he decided to plunge off an emotional cliff and marry Gracie MacDougal, she ought to be the first person he told about it.

"Then don't you think you ought to stop this shameful behavior before she winds up with a tarnished reputation?" Laura Lee demanded. "This is a small town. Word gets around, you know."

"And just what shameful behavior would that be?" he inquired. "And who might be spreading it besides the three of you?"

They acted as if he hadn't just accused them of being a bunch of old gossips.

"The kissing in plain sight, for one thing," Laura Lee said with a touch of indignation.

"And the dancing on the rooftop," Henrietta added.

"And whatever the two of you've been up to in the attic," Laura Lee offered.

"And whatever else has been going on," Florence said to cover anything they might have missed.

Kevin grinned at them. "Ladies, if I stopped all that, what would you do with your morning?"

Henrietta shrugged off the sarcasm. "I suppose we'd just have to discuss Bobby Ray and Marianne. Maybe you can tell us when they're planning to get married. Last I heard they hadn't booked the church yet. I was over there talking to the preacher just yesterday."

"Maybe they're just going to run off to a justice of the peace someplace," Laura Lee suggested.

"Or fly to Vegas and get married in one of those tacky chapels," Florence countered with surprising enthusiasm. "After the service, they could go to one of those glitzy shows. It's good enough for some of them fancy Hollywood celebrities, don't you know."

"I know that you've been reading those tabloids again," Henrietta charged. "That's what I know."

Kevin concluded that the smartest thing he could do was head for a secluded booth in the back, out of their line of fire. He only prayed they'd leave before Gracie showed up. He wasn't sure she was ready to have her privacy so thoroughly and enthusiastically invaded.

Naturally this was one of those prayers that was incidental to heavenly powers. Gracie walked in two minutes later and was subjected to an interrogation that any detective would have admired.

Looking shellshocked, she finally made her way back to his table.

"Any secrets left?" Kevin inquired as she slipped into the booth.

"Quite a few, to their obvious disappointment," she said dryly. "I don't think that will slow them down for long, though. They seem to have pretty active imaginations."

"That they do," he agreed.

Jessie whisked by, set two cups of coffee in front of them and promised to be back any minute to take their order. Gracie took her first swallow of coffee as if it held the promise of eternal youth.

"Jet-lagged?" Kevin inquired.

"That," she agreed, giving him a long, mischievous look, "plus staying up half the night pretty much turned my brain to mush."

"And here I just thought I was welcoming you home properly."

"There was nothing proper about it," she retorted, smiling at the memory. "If those three over there knew how you say hello—"

"They'd be green with jealousy," Kevin finished.

"Or stunned into silence."

"I don't think a bomb going off under their noses would stun them for very long," he observed. "They'd be too anxious to spread the news."

Gracie took another long, deep swallow of coffee, then looked him squarely in the eye. "Okay, Kevin, let's hear it."

"Hear what?"

"What drove you to Richmond to hide out."

He sighed. He'd figured they were going to get back to this sooner or later, but the wound was still too raw for him to want to start picking at it again. Besides, he ought to get into it with Delia first. He'd been by the house briefly this morning to clean up, but she'd been sound asleep.

"Can't this wait?" he asked.

"From my perspective, yes," she said. "But something tells me it has something to do with why Delia's so upset. I won't ignore that."

"Since when did you get so protective of Delia? She's my

aunt," he said, not yet ready to acknowledge the real relationship.

"She's my friend."

"And I'm your what?"

She regarded him archly. "That remains to be seen." Her
expression sobered. "Come on, Kevin. Spill it. How can I
help Delia if I don't know what's going on?"

"Maybe Delia's not the one who needs help. Maybe she's
the one who threw a curve at me."

"Now you're talking in riddles."

Thankfully, before he had to explain what he meant, Jessie
came back to take their order. He chose the biggest breakfast
on the menu—eggs, bacon, home fries, and toast. He
couldn't answer questions if his mouth was full. He noticed,
however, that Gracie ordered an English muffin. Obviously,
he concluded grimly, she didn't intend to let food hamper
her cross-examination.

He sat back stoically and waited for the onslaught of questions to begin.

It didn't take long. Jessie had no sooner left for the kitchen
than Gracie was studying him intently.

"Okay, Kevin. Let's hear it."

"You realize, of course, that this is none of your business."

If he'd thought—or hoped—she would take offense at that,
he was very much mistaken. She merely smiled and regarded
him patiently.

"Have you ever found out something about yourself that
changes everything?" he asked.

"As a matter of fact, yes," she said.

"What?"

"We were supposed to be talking about you."

"Humor me."

"Okay, I found out after years of roaming around the globe
that what I was really looking for all along was a home."

"You had a home in Pennsylvania. You sold it."

"I meant one that fit my image of what a home ought to be, complete with a whole community of people who cared."

The response took him aback. "And you found that out here?"

"Here with you," she amended with total sincerity.

All that advice to ask her to marry him came flooding back. He pretended it hadn't.

She studied him worriedly. "Is that what happened to you? You found out something about yourself?"

"Yes."

"From Delia?"

"Yes." He regarded her ruefully. "You're not going to give up on this, are you?"

"Nope."

Resignation sighed through him. He might as well blurt it out and get it over with. Maybe Gracie could offer some perspective he'd missed, solidify his own conclusions. "She told me that she's my grandmother."

Gracie's eyes lit up. "She is? Oh, Kevin, that's wonderful." Her expression turned worried. "It is, isn't it? You adore her, don't you?"

"Of course I do."

"Then I don't see the problem. I'd give anything to suddenly discover I had a grandmother and it turned out to be somebody I love."

"You're missing the point," he groused.

"Which point is that?"

"Aunt Delia was the one person on earth I thought I could trust. Now I find out she lied to me and to my mother. All these years, she lied to us. Isn't that important?" he asked, even though he'd already concluded it didn't really matter in the larger scheme of things.

"I might not have known your aunt very long, but one thing I know about her is that she worships you. If she kept this a secret, there must have been a very good reason for it."

"I suppose." He repeated the whole, sad story. "She thought she was protecting my mother."

"Well, then, that explains it."

"Gracie, it's not that easy. Okay, maybe for me it wasn't a tragedy, even it did shake the trust I thought we shared. I had my dad and, for a while anyway, my mom. But my mother lived her whole life with a bitter old woman, thinking that she never did anything right, not understanding that there was a reason for that resentment."

Gracie reached for his hand. "I know that must have been awful for her and for you, but did you ever consider that it might have been worse if Delia had kept her."

"How so? What could possibly have been worse?"

"You just sat here and listened to the gossip about us and about Bobby Ray and Marianne. At least none of that was vicious. Can you imagine what it would have been like fifty or sixty years ago to be a pregnant teenager with no father in sight? Can you imagine what your mother would have had to endure being called a bastard back then? She might never have married a man like your father because of the stigma. Wouldn't that have been a hundred times worse than the problems she had with the woman she thought of as her mother? At least she had Delia in her life. You said yourself that your aunt provided a safe haven for both of you."

"I see what you're saying. It's just . . ."

"A shock," she supplied.

He nodded.

"Do you love Delia any less?"

"Of course not. I just don't know if I can ever trust her again."

"Kevin, there's never been anything else she lied about, has there?"

"No, not as far as I know."

"Just this one thing and you know she had her reasons. Maybe you should concentrate on understanding her side and tell her that you haven't stopped loving her."

"I thought I had."

"But then you left town, probably after making some enigmatic remark about needing time to think," she suggested, making him wince. "It obviously terrified her. I'm sure she's scared to death of losing you."

"It'll never happen. That old lady is too much a part of me."

"Tell her," Gracie repeated. "Don't let something that should be fabulous news end up splitting you apart."

"Has anyone ever told you you drive a hard bargain?"

"All the time. One of these days I'll take you to France and you can talk to the asparagus farmer," she teased. "Will you go to Delia?"

"Okay, okay. Right after we finish breakfast," he promised.

She grinned. "I'm finished now," she said, gesturing to her empty plate.

Kevin's eggs and bacon and potatoes were beginning to congeal into a greasy mess. He eyed them with disgust. "I suppose I am, too."

Outside the cafe, Gracie stood on tiptoe and brushed a kiss across his cheek. "Good luck."

His gaze settled on her "When I've taken care of this, you and I need to talk."

"Isn't that what we just did?"

"You talked. I listened. Now I have a few things I'd like to say. Where are you going to be?"

She regarded him with apparent uneasiness. "At the Victorian."

He wondered just how uneasy she would be if she realized what he intended to talk about was marriage. He pressed a hard kiss against her lips. "See you soon."

Her wariness clearly escalated. "Take your time."

Kevin chuckled at her obvious attempt to put off whatever he had on his mind. "Gracie, you can dish it out, but you sure can't take it."

Her chin immediately tilted up a defiant notch. "I certainly can take whatever you intend to dish out, Kevin Patrick Daniels."

"We'll see, darlin'. We'll see."

Gracie hadn't even had a full ten seconds to be relieved that things between Delia and Kevin were going to be smoothed over. Now, with this enigmatic promise of his to have a talk with her, all she could do was worry. She hadn't liked the gleam in his eyes one little bit. There'd been an awful lot of speculation about marriage going on at the Beachside this morning. She certainly hoped Kevin hadn't had anything to do with sparking the gossip or that he hadn't been taking it to heart.

"Well, it's about time you got here," Helen announced, pouncing on her the instant Gracie climbed the steps to the Victorian a few minutes later. "We've got a lot to do."

"There's no need to panic. Ray Mason and his crew are back on the job this morning. I hear them hammering away. We can take a breather."

"Forget the house," Helen declared. "We have a wedding to plan."

Gracie broke out in a cold sweat. "A wedding?" she repeated cautiously. "Whose?"

"Bobby Ray's and Marianne's, of course. Whose did you think?" Helen asked, then chuckled. "Were you afraid we were going to do a surprise event for you and Kevin?"

"Of course not," she said defensively, then hastily improvised. "I was thinking of you and Max."

That drew a frown. "Oh, when the time comes, if it ever does, I suspect we'll just elope," Helen said lightly. "Max probably won't want to leave the hotel for more than a day or two."

Something in her tone alerted Gracie that something had

happened in Paris that she'd missed. "Trouble brewing?" she asked.

"Between Max and me? Heavens, no," Helen said, a little too brightly.

She was obviously lying through her teeth.

"Into the kitchen," Gracie ordered.

Helen actually did as she'd been told, another clue that something was seriously wrong.

"Sit."

Helen sat.

Gracie poured them both cups of coffee from the pot that Helen had brewed. "Okay, what happened?"

"Nothing, really." Helen grinned ruefully. "I'm being silly, I'm sure."

"Helen, just tell me."

"Okay, okay. It's just that he seemed so distracted the whole time we were in Paris, like he couldn't wait to get back to Cannes."

Gracie chuckled. She couldn't help it, even though it drew a scowl from Helen. "I'm sorry. It's just that the trip to Paris was probably the most spontaneous thing Max Devereaux has ever done in his entire life. He had, what, maybe twenty-four hours notice that we were coming?"

"Less than that, actually."

"Yet he put everything aside and raced to Paris."

"Well, yes."

"Helen, Max does not drop things and take a holiday. He plans every little detail. Even when he came here, he spent a whole week working out the logistics, making sure he had staff to cover for him while he was gone. You actually got him to do something totally impetuous."

"Which he obviously regretted."

"I don't think he regretted being with you for a second," Gracie reassured her. "I do think he worried about all the work he'd left on his desk. Old habits are hard to break. Give it time."

Helen's expression brightened. "Do you think so?"

"Yes. I think so. I can't think of another person on earth who could have gotten him away from Cannes on a moment's notice like that. Most women couldn't even get Max to take an unscheduled coffee break."

"Really?"

"Really."

Helen preened. "I guess I'll just have to practice my technique on him more often."

"The more often, the better," Gracie agreed.

"Good," Helen said, obviously relieved and reenergized. "That's settled then. Let's get busy on the wedding. We don't have much time. Bobby Ray insists he won't wait a minute longer than Labor Day weekend."

"That's the weekend this place is supposed to open," Gracie protested. "How can I manage both?"

"Think of it this way. You'll be guaranteed a full house with all the wedding guests coming from out of town."

"Ah, yes, the silver lining," Gracie said. "I knew there had to be one."

"There always is," Helen agreed.

Twenty-five

Kevin found Aunt Delia in the garden. Not that she was doing much weeding, though. She was kneeling by the bed of pink-and-purple petunias, her gloved hands idle, her gaze focused on some point in the distance. Her strawberry-blond hair, which still astounded him, was smushed by a wide-brimmed straw hat.

"Aunt Delia?" he said softly.

Her head snapped around. A tentative smile formed. "Kevin? I didn't hear you come up. I wasn't even sure you'd come back home from wherever you were."

"I got back yesterday. Just now, though, you were lost in thought. Everything okay?"

She searched his face. "I'm not sure. Is it?"

He reached down and squeezed her shoulder. "Everything is fine," he reassured her. "I'm sorry if I've worried you. I just needed some time to think. Your news took me completely by surprise. I couldn't help thinking of how much my mother missed by never knowing the truth, how different things would have been for her if she had. Bottom line, though? I love you. I'm very glad that you're my grandmother."

She struggled to her feet then and hugged him, tears trembling on her lashes. "Oh, you darling boy, I've been so worried you'd never forgive me."

"It was never a matter of forgiveness. I just needed to

understand what you did. Gracie helped me put things into perspective," he admitted.

"She's very smart, our Gracie is."

"That she is."

She eyed him speculatively. "So when are you going to stop wasting time and marry her? I think it's way past time you two set a date."

"Aren't you getting a little a-head of yourself, asking about the date. She hasn't even said yes yet."

"Have you asked her?"

"No."

"Well, why on earth not? You've thought about it, haven't you?"

"Yes."

"Then what's the problem?"

"I've been working that out in my mind."

"Trying to believe she could love you and not be dependent on you," Aunt Delia guessed.

As always, he was startled by his aunt's—his *grand-mother's*—insight into his thoughts. "How'd you know?" he asked.

"Because I'm a grandmother and I'm smart and nobody on earth knows you any better than I do," she said confidently. "Kevin, Gracie may not rely on you for money or career advice or to handle this crisis or that, but she loves you. That's what really matters and I'd stake my life on that. Besides, there are lots of other ways to need someone."

"Such as?"

"In Gracie's case, I think she very much needed you to show her how to take things one day at a time, to bring some balance into her life. And, more than that, she needed you to give her a home, people to care about. Even a strong person like Gracie could use a little support every now and again, even if she never needs to be rescued."

He thought about that. Gracie had said much the same thing herself. Maybe he did have things to offer her that didn't involve money. Maybe he could share the most important things of all with her, his heart and soul.

And maybe she could give him back his faith in human beings again. After all, she'd seen the potential in Helen and Bobby Ray and gotten their lives back on track, when all he'd seen was Bobby Ray's frustrating inability to handle responsibility and Helen's spending excesses. Maybe he was more like his father and his uncle Steven than he'd realized. Maybe he'd encouraged them to lean on him to satisfy some need in himself.

"Thanks, Aunt Delia."

"No thanks necessary," she assured him. She regarded him wistfully. "But maybe one of these days you'll get around to calling me Grandmother."

"Grandmother." He tried it out and found he liked it. It had never had much meaning to him before, nothing that wasn't negative anyway. He grinned at her. "You're amazing, Grandmother."

"Well, of course I am," she said briskly. "Now get along with you. I have weeding to do. The gardener never gets it quite right. Besides, Gracie's waiting. A smart man doesn't keep a woman like that waiting too long. Somebody else might sneak in and snap her up."

Kevin decided that the matter of proposing required a bit of planning and ingenuity if he was going to pull it off successfully. He might have resolved the last of his uncertainties, but he doubted Gracie had. He anticipated a fight.

For all of her talk about finding a home in Seagull Point, he wasn't sure she genuinely believed herself capable of settling down. Nor was he sure if she saw that owning a small town bed and breakfast could compensate for the glamour of running elegant intercontinental hotels. He suspected she still saw this as a project to tide her over a rough patch in her life and viewed him as an intriguing distraction. He would just have to convince her otherwise.

He bought the fanciest bottle of champagne he could find, scrounged up some caviar from Helen's well-stocked pantry and made a quick trip to the finest jeweler in Richmond. He waited until dusk, when the air was soft and still with only the twinkle of fireflies lighting it. Then he went looking for Gracie in her brand-new third-floor office, where she had taken to ending the day.

She took one look at him with his tuxedo pants and fancy pleated shirt and her mouth dropped open. Instantly, wariness darkened her eyes.

"Going to a party?"

"Bringing one," he corrected, holding up the tray laden with champagne, glasses, and caviar.

"What's the occasion?"

"I told you this morning that I wanted to talk to you."

"It must be something pretty important if you've gone to all this trouble to butter me up."

"Just trying to point out the benefits of having a man around to see to your every whim."

"And you think my whims include champagne and caviar?"

"Don't they?"

"Sometimes, I suppose."

He grinned. "Name another one then. I'm flexible. I can improvise."

"Kevin, what's really going on?" she demanded, her expression more guarded than ever.

"I'm trying to set a mood, darlin'."

"Why?"

"So you'll hear me out."

"Kevin, you don't have to go to all this trouble just to get my attention."

"Too much?" he inquired. "What put me over the top? The caviar?"

The tight line of her lips eased into a slow curve. "I'd have to say the tuxedo. It made me feel underdressed."

"That's why I left off the jacket and the tie."

"My shorts and T-shirt are no match even for what's left." She wiggled her bare toes. "I don't even have shoes on."

"I think you're beautiful just the way you are. And that red polish on your toenails is sexier than shoes."

"And I think you're full of it. Would you just get to the point. You're making me nervous."

He moved to the window and beckoned to her. "Come over here by me."

Barefooted and clearly reluctant, she slipped up beside him. He tucked an arm around her waist. "Look out there. What do you see?"

"The river."

He nodded. "That river will take you anywhere you want to go if you follow it far enough. It'll carry you into the Chesapeake Bay, into the Atlantic, all the way to Europe." He gazed down into her eyes. "If you want to go."

"I've told you before, this is where I want to be."

"Forever?"

She hesitated for the space of a heartbeat, long enough to make his pulse thud dully.

"I think so," she said eventually.

"Then marry me," he said. "Commit to me, to staying here. If the lure of the river ever gets to be too much, it'll always be there, ready to take you wherever you want to go. We can always go together."

She sighed and turned to rest her head against his chest. He felt the dampness of tears soaking his shirt, touching his skin. A cold, wrenching fear swept through him then. He was going to lose her.

"I can't," she said, confirming his fear. "I can't make that kind of commitment."

"Tell me five good reasons why we shouldn't get married," he demanded, angered not so much by her words—he'd anticipated them—but by the aching emptiness left in their wake. He hadn't expected to feel so panicked by her refusal.

"I could give you a thousand," she countered.

"I'll settle for one."

"Ambition," she said readily. "I have it. You don't."

Ambition? That was it? It might have amused him if she hadn't been taking it so seriously. "I thought you'd stopped worrying about climbing the corporate ladder," he said.

"What made you think a thing like that?"

"Have I missed something? Are you planning on running this little bed and breakfast of yours long distance? Maybe from France? Were you planning on having Aunt Delia cooking and straightening up after everybody while you raced back to be at Max's side?"

"Of course not." She hesitated. "I guess the truth is, though, I haven't really thought much beyond getting the doors open the first weekend in September. I just assumed, well, that I'd take things as they come. One day at a time."

She seemed totally bemused by how little thought she'd given to tomorrow, and the day after, and the day after that. Nothing she might have said could have given him more hope. He regarded her with approval. She was coming along very well, after all. He only needed to give her a little more time and she would see how well suited they were. His day-by-day philosophy was taking hold nicely.

"Seems to me that's evidence you're getting to be almost as laid back as I am," he told her.

She seemed shocked by the assessment. "That can't be." She regarded him worriedly. "Can it?"

"Looks that way to me."

"Then why are you asking me to plan a whole future? You never think that far ahead."

"Because it's time, Gracie. For both of us. I love you. I think you love me. Marriage is what people in love do."

"But I still haven't figured out when you work," she said a little plaintively.

"I get most of it done when I can't sleep for thinking about you."

"I keep you awake nights?" She seemed very pleased by that.

"Darlin', it's a wonder I've caught a wink of sleep since the day we met. I figure the only way I'll ever catch up is for you and me to get married."

She laughed at that. "Now there's a romantic proposal if ever I've heard one."

He grinned unrepentantly. "I suppose we could go on sleeping together instead. That would probably solve the problem every bit as well. In fact, we could get up to speed right now in that fancy new honeymoon bedroom you just decorated downstairs. Somebody ought to test it before you take in your first paying guests."

"Nice try," she said, but her heart wasn't in it. In fact, she seemed distracted.

He studied her worriedly. "Gracie? What's really going on? Talk to me."

"Nothing," she said, and wandered off without giving him a chance to ask her any more uncomfortable questions.

Fighting disappointment, Kevin let her go. He'd been thinking about marrying Gracie for a long time now, ever since Aunt Delia and half the town had begun planting the idea in his head. He supposed Gracie deserved a little time to get used to the idea.

There wasn't a doubt in his mind that she hated the idea at the moment. Hated it almost as much, in fact, as he'd disliked this scheme of hers to go into business with Aunt Delia. Not that that was working out too badly, something she liked to point out to him on a regular basis. Those two were like two peas in a pod, a couple of born conspirators. No wonder Delia had been so taken with Gracie from the moment they'd met.

Living with Aunt Delia had never been dull. Marrying

Gracie promised to be equally rewarding. More so even, if you threw in the way she aroused him without half trying.

Besides, Gracie was the only woman—the only *person*— he knew who didn't need anything from him. Her independence was her best—and scariest—trait. Until he'd spoken with his grandmother, he hadn't had a clue about where he'd fit into her life if she didn't have to rely on him the way everybody else in his family did. Now it all made sense to him.

Even when she'd been scurrying away, anxious to escape the pressure of having to say yes or no to his proposal, he'd seen a hint of longing in her eyes. Gracie wanted what he was offering. He knew it. It just terrified her, the same way it did him. Committing to forever was a risky business.

So he'd give her the time she needed to think it over and evaluate it, do a damned cost-benefit analysis if that's what she needed to do. If she came up with any more rational objections, he'd counter them. After all, he had love on his side, and rumor had it, especially among a certain group of Seagull Point gossips, that love conquered all.

Twenty-six

There wasn't a single moment all through August when Gracie wasn't a hundred percent aware of Kevin watching her, and waiting for an answer to his proposal. Not even the thousand last-minute details for opening the bed and breakfast and planning Bobby Ray and Marianne's wedding served as much of a distraction.

To his credit, though, he didn't push. Whether it was a tactical decision or just more evidence of his take-life-as-it-comes way of living, she was grateful for it.

She wanted to say yes. Oh, did she ever. But Seagull Point was such a far cry from the life she'd envisioned for herself, the life she'd worked so hard to attain. She felt as if she were betraying her dream, drifting into something because it was comfortable and easy, when she'd always, *always* wanted a challenge.

Was that the real problem? she wondered. Did she want to have to battle for Kevin's love, the way Marianne had had to wait and fight for Bobby Ray's? Was Kevin making it all too easy for her, the same way he smoothed over rough patches for everyone else?

"That's absurd," she muttered. Perverse, in fact.

"Talking to yourself?" Helen inquired, sneaking up behind her. "That's definitely a bad sign."

"Sorry. I didn't realize anyone else was around."

"Which must be why you had only yourself left to talk

to," Helen retorted. "Now that I'm here, want to talk to me? For all of my chatter, I can also be a pretty good listener."

"It's nothing."

"It's Kevin."

"No," Gracie insisted sharply. "It's the reservations and the wedding and the fact that the rest of the beds were due this morning and still aren't here."

"Quick excuses," Helen praised. "You're good at avoiding the real problems, aren't you? Is that what you've always done? Filled your life with so many details and crises, you didn't have time left over to deal with your own life?"

Hearing the truth startled her. It also stung more than Gracie would ever have admitted. She busied herself with the stack of reservation slips that Delia had filled in over the past week. That Helen had seen through her so easily was a shock. No one had ever taken the time to look beyond her surface calm and competence before.

"I'm not judging you, you know," Helen persisted. "I can relate to exactly what you're doing, because it's what I've always done. It's been worse since Henry died. I was in so much pain I couldn't stand it, so I filled my days with shopping and charity events and parties. I was so busy I thought I must be happy. It was only after I met Max that I realized what had been missing."

"Love?" Gracie asked.

"Love," Helen agreed. "And, every bit as important, someone to share things with. What fun is it to buy a gorgeous dress if there's no one around to appreciate it? How rewarding is it to hand over a few thousand dollars to charity or even raise a few hundred thousand if there's no one at home to remind you that it's the people, not the dollars, that count? And who wants to go to a party if there's not going to be someone to laugh with you afterward about the drunken guests' tasteless jokes?"

Helen met Gracie's gaze directly, then sighed. "I don't know about you, but I miss the companionship as much as

I miss the sex. I miss having someone sleeping beside me at night and looking at me across the breakfast table. I miss the tenderness, the quick, heated glance across a crowded room, the shared confidences, the stolen kisses when you think no one's looking."

"You'll have all that again," Gracie told her, praying that she hadn't misjudged Max's intentions the last time they'd spoken. He'd sounded as if he'd reached a decision about Helen.

"Yes, you will," a masculine voice assured them both in one of the best bits of timing ever.

Both turned startled gazes on the sight of Max standing in the doorway. Gracie thought the always self-assured Max looked a bit uncertain of his welcome. She could have told him he needn't have worried.

"Darling, I had no idea you were coming," Helen said, rushing over to brush a kiss across his cheek.

Max shot an apologetic look toward Gracie, then swept Helen into his arms and kissed her soundly. When Gracie started to slip past them, Max snagged her hand.

"Stay for this, please. It's important and I want a witness."

"Witness to what?" Helen demanded, not leaving his embrace.

"I want someone around to see if you will put your money where your mouth is. Marry me, Helen. Let me give you back all those things you were telling Gracie you missed."

"You were eavesdropping?" Helen demanded, ignoring the proposal.

"It's the only way to find out what's going on in that head of yours," he said. "You've been amazingly reticent with me on the phone lately. So, darling, what's it going to be? Will you marry me?"

Helen searched his face. "You're serious? This isn't just an impulsive gesture."

Max smiled ruefully. "I don't make impulsive gestures," he assured her. "Ask Gracie."

Helen grinned. "I believe she has mentioned that once or twice."

"Well, then. Will you marry me?"

Eyes shining with tears, Helen didn't hesitate. "Yes. Oh, Max, yes."

This time when Gracie tried to leave the room, no one tried to stop her.

All around her people were saying yes and preparing to walk down the aisle. So what was wrong with her? Why couldn't she take that same leap of faith when her love for Kevin was so powerful she ached with it? She was sure of it, sure of the kind of man he was. Maybe her reluctance was because, like Max, she was not inclined to impetuous decisions.

Yet everything she had done since coming to Seagull Point had been impulsive. She wandered into the almost completed kitchen, where the new appliances gleamed and the glass-fronted cabinets were filled with elegant china and sassy everyday plates covered with bright, bold flowers. The contradiction wasn't lost on her. It was as if the dishes matched the two sides of her personality—one cautious and old-fashioned, the other daring. She was just discovering the joy of being daring once in a while.

"Something troubling you?" Delia asked, coming in the back door and peering at her worriedly.

"No. I'm fine. I just have a million little details on my mind."

"A million details and one man," Delia countered, busying herself at the stove. "I came in to make some tea. Sit down and have some with me."

"I really should get back upstairs."

"And interrupt Max and Helen?"

Gracie managed a smile. "You saw him arrive?"

"Arrive and dash up the steps two at a time. Unless I miss my guess, he's asked her to marry him by now."

"He has," Gracie confirmed. "I was a witness."

"Perfect. That just leaves you and Kevin."

"Please, don't start."

"You know I love you both. I just want to see you happy. Maybe if you told me what's worrying you, I could help." She gestured toward the table again. "Please. I'll pour the tea."

She brought two cups to the table, taking Gracie's acquiescence for granted. Gracie noted she chose the bright ones with the daring red and sunny yellow design. Maybe that was an omen.

"Talk to me, Gracie," Delia encouraged, her voice soft and coaxing.

It took her a while to gather her thoughts and work up her courage, but she finally forced herself to begin.

"I don't know what I was thinking," Gracie told Delia. "I saw this house. The idea of a bed and breakfast just came to me and, *wham,* I was all caught up in it. I never meant to stay here, not when I came. I just needed some time to think."

"Maybe what you really needed were some roots, a real home," Delia responded. "Traveling all over the world's bound to be exciting for a time, but settling down has its rewards. Obviously some part of you knew that."

Maybe so, but Gracie couldn't think of any rewards. Both of her parents had had a bad case of wanderlust and no money to act on it. She'd spent her whole life listening to them complain about being stuck in a one-horse town, though neither of them had had the ambition to leave. She'd vowed not to get caught in that trap. She'd had ambition and drive to spare.

"Name one reward," she said. It would have to be a dandy one, too, if it was going to counter a childhood of terrible memories of an economically depressed town where no one, least of all her own parents, had seemed happy.

"I can list three off the top of my head. A good man, children, growing old together," Delia said, her expression suddenly far away. "That was always what I wanted. Never seemed to find a man that suited me, though. Not after Kevin's grandfather abandoned me. Probably my own fault. I never quite trusted another man's feelings. I suppose I turned cynical."

She regarded Gracie intently. "Don't you do that. Don't turn your back on love and family when a man like Kevin is just waiting for you to say yes. He'll be a good husband and a wonderful father. You've seen for yourself how deep his kind of caring can run. He loves you, too. That can be more exciting than traveling the whole danged world, if you ask me."

Gracie wasn't so sure. In her experience—which was not so dissimilar to Delia's except for the pregnancy—men took off when the excitement of the chase wore off. They married someone else. She had the track record to prove it. It hadn't made her bitter, but it had made her cautious.

Besides, she hadn't left France looking for love. She hadn't come back to the States seeking permanence. She had come . . . well, just because being away no longer satisfied her the way it once had.

To her astonishment she had found challenges right in her own backyard, so to speak. She had found a man who turned her knees to jelly and her insides to mush. So what if he lacked drive and she lacked the ability to sit still for more than two consecutive minutes. There was a lot to be said for unhurried, lingering caresses, just as there was for explosive, passionate, right-here, right-now climaxes. In fact, sometimes the two came together spectacularly well.

Suddenly she could see a little girl with Kevin's sunstreaked hair lounging in a hammock with a book. She could see a little boy with her eyes bounding up the stairs and onto the roof in the blink of an eye. Keeping them safe, encouraging them to grow up with their father's sense of family and commitment would be challenge enough for any woman. And Kevin had promised to take her anywhere, anytime, if wanderlust set in again.

"Where's Kevin?" she asked abruptly.

"Repairing the widow's walk last time I saw him. He was scared to death you were going to be tempted out there and wind up going straight through those rotting railings."

Sure of herself at last, Gracie bolted to the top of the house. Inside her office, she paused for a moment, long enough to observe a shirtless Kevin leaning against the just repaired railing of the widow's walk, sipping an icy glass of lemonade. He had the portable radio tuned to an oldies station at top volume. He was at ease with himself and life, as near as she could tell, two traits she wouldn't mind learning.

"Kevin?"

At the sound of her voice, she saw him go still. He lowered the sound on the radio. Blinded by the brilliant sun, his gaze sought her in the room's shadows. "Yo, darlin'. What's up?"

"Maybe you ought to come inside for this," she suggested.

"Am I likely to be so shocked I'll jump?"

"I don't think I'm capable of stunning you that badly."

"Don't be so sure. Now if you were to stroll out here buck naked, for example, I might lose my concentration."

She laughed. "Don't hold your breath."

He heaved an exaggerated sigh. "Too bad. I was kinda looking forward to that."

"I'll bet you were."

"Well, since just about anything else you could do pales in comparison, I think it's safe enough for you to come on out."

Gracie stepped out onto the narrow widow's walk which was barely big enough for one, much less two, when one of them was Kevin's size. The heat and scent of him was all around her.

"What's on your mind?" he asked, offering her a sip of his drink.

Getting it out wasn't half as easy as she'd hoped. She stumbled over the words, tried to gather her thoughts and tried again. After half a dozen tries, Kevin grinned.

"Are you by any chance trying to tell me that you've changed your mind about marrying me?" he asked.

Gracie beamed at him. "Yes. That's it exactly."

Kevin whooped, then scooped her into his arms and twirled her around. "You won't regret it. We're going to have an amazing life, Gracie."

The DJ on the radio chose that precise moment to play something slow and sexy and romantic, a counterpoint to the fast-paced rock 'n roll that had been playing.

Which was why, when Laura Lee and Henrietta and Florence got together the next morning, all they could talk about was the rumor that Kevin Patrick Daniels had been seen dancing—swaying, more likely—with Gracie MacDougal on the widow's walk of Delia's old house, while Delia herself applauded from her perch on the rocks across the street, where she had a clear view of everything going on and a view of the river so she could pretend that's what had her attention.

"Guess those two are getting married after all," Henrietta said.

"More than likely," Laura Lee agreed.

"Ought to be interesting, don't you think?" Florence said.

"What I think is, we'd better change our walking route to go past there," Henrietta said. "We don't want to miss any more of the really good stuff going on in this town and it seems to me those two are bound to be at the center of it."

Epilogue

In the past the prospect of planning her own wedding would have sent Gracie into a tailspin, filling entire notebooks with lists, but Kevin's influence was rubbing off after all. She actually managed to put the whole thing out of her mind while she concentrated on getting the bed and breakfast open on the same weekend Bobby Ray and Marianne remarried.

Then a week after that, she and Kevin and Delia and Abby flew to Cannes to see Helen marry Max. Bobby Ray and Marianne interrupted their honeymoon in Italy to join them for the ceremony in an ancient stone church in a nearby village.

"Is that the kind of wedding you'd like, Gracie?" Delia asked as they were flying home.

She gazed at Kevin. Couldn't take her eyes off of him, in fact. It struck her that staring at Kevin could become a fascinating lifetime occupation. "Whatever," she murmured.

"Well, someone has to plan this wedding," Delia grumbled. "I suppose it'll just have to be me."

"Whatever you'd like, Grandmother," Kevin murmured, never taking his eyes from Gracie.

"This laid-back nonsense has gotten entirely out of hand," Delia muttered, but even as she said it, she was pulling a stack of bridal magazines out of her tote bag. She slipped across the aisle to the seat next to Abby. "I suppose it's up to you and me."

"Do we have a budget?" Abby asked.

Delia glanced over and gave Gracie and Kevin a challenging look. "The sky's the limit."

"I heard that," Kevin said.

"Me, too," Gracie chimed in.

"Well, I'm not hearing any arguments now, am I?" Delia demanded.

Gracie grinned at Kevin. "Not from me," she said.

"Just don't book the National Cathedral," he said. "I want to get married at home."

"At Greystone Manor?" Delia asked, clearly startled.

"No, at your house," he said, then placed his hand against Gracie's cheek. "Our house," he corrected. "Okay with you, darlin'?"

"Whatever."

Delia gave a nod of approval. "Perfect. We'll hold the ceremony indoors and the reception in the garden. The weather's lovely this time of year."

Gracie thought back to what seemed a thousand lifetimes ago, when she'd uttered much the same comment to Max as she'd prepared to depart for Virginia. She'd lived through spring and summer and a touch of fall so far. As near as she could tell, with Kevin in her life, all the seasons were bound to be spectacular.